THE SECRET OF THE LEADER'S STAFF

WRAK-WAVARA: THE AGE OF DARKNESS
BOOK THREE

LEIGH ROBERTS

DRAGON WINGS PRESS

CONTENTS

Dedication   v

Chapter 1   1
Chapter 2   9
Chapter 3   21
Chapter 4   33
Chapter 5   59
Chapter 6   73
Chapter 7   87
Chapter 8   127
Chapter 9   153
Chapter 10   173
Chapter 11   185
Chapter 12   201
Chapter 13   217
Chapter 14   251
Chapter 15   267
Chapter 16   289
Chapter 17   307

Please Read   319
Acknowledgments   321

Editing by Joy Sephton http://www.justemagine.biz
Cover design by Cherie Fox http://www.cheriefox.com

Sexual activities or events in this book are intended for adults.

ISBN: 978-1-951528-28-7 (ebook)
ISBN: 978-1-951528-29-4 (paperback)

Dedication

For those to whom a starlit sky still whispers—

What If?

CHAPTER 1

Under Tyria's careful eye, Pan continued her recovery, her mother's warning about the possibility of losing the offling never leaving her mind. The occasional sharp pains that pierced her abdomen reaffirmed her commitment to bedrest.

Pan reminded herself as often as possible of her mother's statement that there was a way for her father someday to be freed from the Order of Functions. Every sunrise and every sunset, and many times in between, she vowed she would not fail him, that she fully accepted the mantle of Guardianship and that the path to his freedom would not be forfeited.

While Pan was unavailable to lead Kthama, more and more Mothoc had turned to Rohm'Mok for guidance. He did his best to make the decisions he believed his mate would have made.

But each time Rohm'Mok was called away from Pan's bedside, he was filled with unease. At evening's end, he would hurry back to the Healer's Quarters to relish the time they had together before sleep overtook them.

This evening, he came in bearing Pan a serving of longfish, one of her favorites.

"Tell me about your day," Pan said, sitting up to eat what he had brought her. "I am restless and bored having to be so removed from the workings of the High Rocks."

"Nothing out of the ordinary. Hunting parties going out, coming back. Switching the watchers' rotations. Some have been stationed quite far away, but they do seem to prefer working in solitude. It certainly is not a life for everyone, but those who choose it seem to be able to handle the isolation, at least for a while." He handed her a piece of fish and waited to offer another as he looked down at her belly.

Pan saw his gaze and anticipated his question. "Tyria said it will not be that much longer, my love. But I am glad of this time for our people to get to know you. I am afraid that being the mate of a Guardian is a burden."

"It is no burden. You could never be a burden to anyone, Saraste'. Listen, I have been meeting with Dochrohan and Bakru regarding what you said about preparing Takthan'Tor to take over leadership here."

Takthan'Tor was of direct 'Tor descent, from Ny'on's bloodline. Ny'on had been Moc'Tor's Second Choice. Out of support for Moc'Tor's direction, Ny'on's daughters and subsequent family females chose to be seeded by the Others. Despite the heavy influence of the Others' blood, the male offling in her line had the largest and most robust build of any of the Akassa.

"Takthan'Tor's silver hair reminds me of my brother's coloring," said Pan, "though of course, it is not anywhere as prominent as Dak'Tor's."

"I do not know if I will ever totally get used to their lack of a thick coat like ours. Though they do have a fine coat, and it keeps most of the males comfortable during the cold weather, it is barely noticeable."

Pan shifted to a more comfortable position. "How do you find Takthan'Tor's temperament?"

"Strong, yet not highly strung. I believe he will be a successful Leader."

"He is not paired—" Pan started to say. "Ooh."

"What is wrong?" Rohm'Mok asked, quickly taking her hand. "More pain?"

Pan grimaced again and placed her hands on her swollen belly until the spasm passed. "I think you should fetch Tyria, please."

Tyria examined Pan and declared that it was nearly time. The birthing stone, absorbent grasses, and wrappings were brought in. Jhotin, the Helper, was there to assist, though as a male Healer, was to wait outside unless called for. Tensil, the Akassa Healer, and Vel and Inrion were waiting outside with him and Rohm'Mok.

Rohm'Mok was unable to stop pacing, but before long, he heard a healthy cry, and Tyria called him in to see his daughter.

He hurried to Pan's side and peered down at his mate and their offling. "I am so glad you are okay. You are both okay. She is beautiful. But—I do not understand. Her coloring—is she a Guardian?"

"No, she is not a Guardian. Peculiar that we were just talking about Dak'Tor's coloring, and here she looks to have almost the same markings." Pan unwrapped the little bundle to show him the rest of her coat.

"What are you naming her?" asked Rohm'Mok.

"Tala."

"She will be a true beauty, with those silver highlights," Tyria said.

Rohm'Mok looked at the Healer with something like alarm.

"Oh, do not worry, it will be a long time before you have to think about the young males, but I am sure she will have their attention," Tyria laughed.

"Pan," she added, "your sisters are outside waiting to see you."

"Send them in, please."

In the midst of her own happiness, as Pan waited for Vel and Inrion to enter, she suddenly remembered that nothing had come of Vel's request to be paired.

Several days later, Hatos'Mok arrived at Kthama. Rohm'Mok greeted his father, pleased to see him. On the way to see Pan, they talked of the Deep Valley and Bahr'Mok.

After introducing Hatos'Mok to little Tala and placing her in the nest for a nap, Pan listened as he relayed what his two sentries had discovered—the rich meadows, the powerful vortex below, and the benefits of the cooler weather in the northern setting. He then told her about the abandoned Mothoc camp the sentries had come across on their way home.

"B'Hit and Asolp scouted the area thoroughly before leaving. It had a plentiful water source and thick surrounding woods, so it looked to be a suitable living space aside from the obvious structural flaws. In addition, the vortex below was fairly strong.

"As far as the inhabitants are concerned, we believe they were the rebels whom Straf'Tor exiled from Kthama. If not, another explanation is that they were followers of Straf'Tor who did not go with him to Kayerm for some reason. We know that several

Sassen groups set out on their own, even though they were strongly advised against it."

"I remember that Straf'Tor told my father about the rebels and how he banished them after their Leader murdered Ushca," Pan put in. "Still, they are Mothoc, and I hope that wherever they ended up, they made it safely to another location."

Then she asked if he had been meeting with the Akassa from the 'Mok House line back at the Deep Valley.

"Yes, both Bahr'Mok and I have been doing so. But it seems a bit premature. Bahr'Mok has only recently taken over leadership of the Deep Valley. He has his entire life ahead of him yet to serve, and I am sure the other Leaders are having the same thoughts. So the obvious question is, when are we leaving the Akassa?"

So he had figured out her intent in sending Asolp and B'Hit to find another location for the Mothoc to live in so they could leave the Akassa to lead themselves.

"Sooner than any of us would like, I am afraid. I know this is asking you and the others to have tremendous faith in me, and I pray it is not too much to ask. I will be attending the upcoming High Council meeting, and we shall discuss it then."

"I knew your father well," said Hatos'Mok. "We confided in each other. I know that, from the start, I created the problems between you and me. And I brought trouble to my own house over your relationship with Rohm'Mok." He looked over at his son and then back to Pan. "I hope that whatever rift there may still be between us can be ended."

"I need your support," Pan reassured him. "You are strong, confident. Others listen to you, and I see why my father trusted you so. Let us work toward a strong alliance."

Rohm'Mok showed his father to temporary quarters that had been readied. They stood outside and spoke for a while.

"I am glad you are staying for a few days, Father."

"It is because things are going smoothly back home. Bahr'Mok has taken to leadership the way you took to arguing with me. The people have accepted him. I have to say I do not know how it could go better."

Hatos'Mok let out a long sigh. "Your daughter is quite striking. I wish Deparia had lived to see her, but I have to believe that our loved ones who have returned to the Great Spirit have some knowledge of our lives here."

"I trust they do, Father. That the bonds of love cannot be broken by death."

"When Pan is well enough to travel, please come and stay for a short while. Your brother would be happy to see you and a visit from your mate is always a special occasion. I think it does our people good to see the Guardian."

"Even if she is a female," Rohm'Mok added with a wry smile.

"You know me too well. Some prejudices take a long time to unseat, son. And I have made it clear that I now accept Pan."

"I know you did not mean any disrespect by it, Father."

"Such folly, I realize. A female can lead as well as a male. I really have no excuse for having said—or thought—such things."

CHAPTER 2

In the quiet halls of Kayerm, many awaited the news of Lorgil's delivery, hoping that her offling had survived Nox'Tor's attack. Small groups of females talked among themselves, occasionally stopping to say a prayer for both mother and offling. Tonis, Pagara, and Kyana were in attendance at Lorgil's side.

Lorgil was in the final stages of her labor and was being supported by Tonis and Kyana. Though none were saying the words, they were all aware that it was taking longer than usual for the offling to come. The water cradle had broken some time ago, and Lorgil was tiring.

Another contraction came, and Pagara told her it was time to bear down. Lorgil grimaced and moaned, squeezing her eyes shut. "I cannot, I cannot," she cried out.

"You must, Lorgil. The offling is almost free. Please, try again," Pagara encouraged her.

Lorgil steeled herself, and when the next wave came, pushed as hard as she could. The females outside Kayerm heard her cry out and turned to each other in concern.

"You did it!" Pagara caught the offling and wrapped him immediately in a soft hide packed with absorbent material. She quickly wiped his face off. "It is a male, as you said," and she gently handed Lorgil's son to her.

"Another male of the House of 'Tor has joined us on Etera," Lorgil said as she took the offling in her arms.

She slowly examined her son from head to toe, and finding him whole, admitted she had no idea what to name him.

"Many other mothers also wait to think of names for their offling," Pagara assured her.

"I know. But I was too busy worrying about whether he would even be born. I was afraid if I chose names, my overconfidence might harm his chances," Lorgil answered, still staring at her tiny offling.

"I did not know you held such beliefs," Pagara answered.

"I suppose I do. Perhaps it is just my way of trying to have some control when I feel I have none."

Everyone was pleased to hear the news. Many of the females sent gifts of food to Lorgil, meant to comfort her but also to ease the burden of the first few days with a new offling. Moods were elevated over the good news.

Wosot watched Kyana as she stood in a small circle speaking with the other females. She glanced up and caught him watching her.

Kyana excused herself and went over to him. "So, Lorgil has a son."

"I am happy for her and relieved the offling is healthy," he said. "Who does he favor?" Wosot wanted to keep the conversation going.

"I think Lorgil. He is lighter-colored than Nox'Tor was."

"The birth of an offling is a time of great joy," Wosot said. "Tell me—"

Kyana looked up into the handsome face of the towering male who had repeatedly professed his love and his desire to protect and care for her and her family.

"You have many years of fertility left. I am interested in knowing if you desire more offling?" he asked.

"Oh," she let escape and looked down. "Yes, I suppose I would, but I sometimes forget how much older you are than me, Wosot."

The instant the words were out of her mouth, she regretted saying them."

Wosot broke into a huge smile and chuckled in

his deep rich voice. "My age is not a problem, trust me."

Then he leaned down and whispered into her ear, his warm breath on her neck sending chills throughout her body. "Do not let my age mislead you, female. I have no doubt that I am more than male enough to fully satisfy you every time you invite me into your bed, and to give you plenty of offling."

Kyana could feel her face burning. Wosot gently removed her hand and pressed his lips to hers. Then he put his arms behind her and pulled her close up tight to him. Kyana held onto his biceps to avoid losing her balance, her knees buckling at his kiss, and the hard feel of him pressed against her.

When he pulled back, her eyes were wide, her lips still parted.

"Please give Lorgil my congratulations. When she is ready to receive male visitors, I look forward to meeting her son."

Wosot gently released her. Kyana's eyes followed him as he left, and she swayed, a little light-headed from his embrace. She knew that others in the area had noticed what had taken place, and the minute Wosot was far enough away not to overhear, a few of her friends came rushing over.

"Wosot wants you!" one exclaimed, grabbing her arm.

"You are blessed," another added.

Kyana looked at her and frowned. "Blessed?"

"Surely you know, Kyana, half the females here would give their canines to be pursued by Wosot," the first female said. "He is always polite to those who have tried to entice him, but most do not even bother any longer."

"His age does not worry them?" Kyana asked.

"Why should it? He is one of the best hunters," said Faeya, speaking for the first time. "He is kind and gentle. He is skilled in tool making. He is wise, and the other males look up to him. Physically, he is one of the strongest males here. I would take him any day over these youngsters who do not know the first thing about stirring a female's passion.

"Consider how he took Lorgil into his protection," she continued. "How many other males would have done that? Oh, they may have taken her in, but they would have expected to mount her. Wosot is one of a kind."

Kyana looked over at Wosot standing a distance away, speaking with some others. The breadth of his shoulders, his strong back. The kindness and strength of character that always shone through his eyes. How the other males were respectfully listening to him.

While she was staring at him, he turned and caught her watching. He locked his gaze on her, and Kyana's insides clenched. She felt she had to get away immediately lest she lose all decorum.

"I have to get back to Lorgil," she stammered before leaving hastily. She glanced back at him one more time before disappearing into the welcome privacy of Kayerm.

In their shared room, Lorgil was sleeping peacefully; having nursed, her offling was now tucked up next to her, safe and warm. Unsure where else to go, Kyana tiptoed back out. She feared Wosot would still be just outside the entrance, and she did not want him to see how flustered she was.

Finally, she turned and oh-so-quietly crept back into the room and eased herself onto her sleeping mat. It was full daylight outside, and she was hiding there like a young maiden unraveled by her first kiss. Of course, he had been with a female before, but how she hated hearing it. Probably more than one, because before Moc'Tor's order, the males had mated indiscriminately.

Kyana tried to stifle her train of thought. She did not want to think about that.

A while later, and not wanting to disturb Lorgil, Kyana was too restless to stay.

She padded down the tunnel and ran into Pagara. "Lorgil and her offling are asleep."

"Good. I am glad to hear it. I also heard that

Wosot kissed you in front of quite a few of your friends."

Kyana closed her eyes and let out a huff.

"I hear it was quite a kiss too," Pagara continued, smiling at her friend.

"As a matter of fact, it was. I am not sure how much longer I can resist him," Kyana said.

"What is stopping you? It is because it is so soon after Nox'Tor's death?" the Healer asked.

"Yes. I know it does not make any sense to feel I must be respectful to the passing of someone who valued me so little, but it is how I feel, and until I can free myself from it, I cannot move forward."

When Pan was able to return to her quarters, she found that some of the other females had prepared a beautiful, cozy nest for tiny Tala. It was made of woven thick vines and cushioned with soft leaves and shredded bark fiber.

While Tala was sleeping, Pan's thoughts turned again to her conversation in the Corridor with her mother, when E'ranale had told her of the crystal concealed in the top end of the 'Tor Leader's Staff.

Pan removed the staff from its place propped against the wall, and sat down with it. Peering at it closely, she inspected the top end, trying to see where a seam might be. It was a while before she found it.

She carefully pried it open. The top piece, an expertly crafted cap, slowly eased up. Had she not been told it did, she would never have noticed it could be taken off.

Pan carefully removed the wooden cap, again marveling at how the grain between the cap and the shaft had been precisely matched. She set the cap aside and peered into the staff.

At the top was a cavity with a large beautiful clear crystal embedded at the bottom of it. She tried to move it, but it was tightly fitted. If she wanted to remove it, she would have to brace the staff somehow and use both hands to take it out. Not wanting to dislodge the crystal, she simply studied it.

So beautiful. The structure was natural, and she had seen smaller versions of that type elsewhere. What made this one so special?

"What are you looking at?"

Pan startled and looked up, almost dropping the staff. "Dak'Tor! You enter my quarters without announcing yourself?"

She heard Tala stir, but the offling quickly settled back down.

Dak'Tor ignored Pan's remark and walked toward her. "I am sorry if I came at an inconvenient time. I came to see your new daughter. What are you doing with the Leader's Staff? You took it apart! Is that a crystal inside?"

"You cannot touch the staff. It is sacrilege for anyone but the Leader to handle it. You know that," Pan said.

Dak'Tor took another step forward. "I just want to look at it; I will give it right back."

Pan stood up, blocking his path.

"Why are you over-reacting?" Dak'Tor took yet another step toward her.

Pan growled menacingly, baring her white canines. "Stop where you are. Turn around and be on your way. If you do not leave now, I will remove you myself."

"You misunderstand me again, sister. I only want to look at it. I know the staff belongs to you," Dak'Tor said, his voice low and soothing.

Now very angry, Pan was also confused at her brother's stubbornness. "I am not trying to keep anything from you, Dak'Tor. I am not depriving you; I am protecting you. You know the punishment for even touching the Leader's Staff would be banishment."

"You so often misunderstand me," Dak'Tor said. "You seem to think I am always up to something. Besides, no one would know. But since you are making such a fuss, I will leave now.

Pan waited to make sure he was gone before reassembling the heavy staff, taking care to align the two pieces so the grain matched and hid any signs of the seam. She placed it back in its corner and tried to compose herself. Dak'Tor had seen the crystal. No one but the 'Tor Leaders were to know it existed. What would this portend for the future? The crystal was the secret to freeing their father.

Had Dak'Tor's seeing it put Moc'Tor's freedom at risk?

A moment later, she heard her mate's voice, and Rohm'Mok entered with a huge selection of nuts, berries, and greenery. "I did not think you would be coming for the evening meal," and he set it down in front of her. "Did I just see Dak'Tor leaving?"

"Yes," she said. "Thank you, I am famished."

Rohm'Mok went over to peer into Tala's nest. "She is so precious. Just like her mother," and he turned and smiled.

"Dak'Tor came to see Tala. But we ended up having a disagreement," Pan said, picking through the food. "He does not seem to understand boundaries. He wanted to handle the Leader's Staff."

"Does he *want* to be banished? I am glad you have accepted the mantle of leadership, as he clearly was not the better choice."

Then Rohm'Mok changed the subject. "It has been a while since we spoke of your experience in the Order of Functions. Now that Tala is born, I want to know if it is still wearing on you terribly."

Pan sighed. Oh, how she wanted to tell him of her visit in the Corridor with her mother. But would he question her sanity? She so needed someone to confide in, but would only another Guardian truly understand?

"I am doing better. My challenge now is to trust the Great Spirit and accept that events are unfolding for our greatest benefit. I do accept that I am the correct choice to be Leader. That argument with my brother only reinforced it."

"I am sorry to hear that you argued again. Siblings are important. At least you are close to Vel and Inrion."

Rohm'Mok's mention of her sister reminded Pan again that Vel had asked to be paired. She felt terrible that she had forgotten about it for so long.

Dak'Tor returned to his quarters. His mate, Ei'Tol, whom he had brought back from the Little River, was there preparing something to eat.

"You look upset," she said, seeing the deep scowl on his face.

"Another argument with Pan. This time over the Leader's Staff," Dak'Tor said. "I think all the strain is wearing on her."

Ei'Tol looked up again from her work, "Why would you argue over the Leader's Staff?"

"I just wanted to look at it. It is not like I never—" Dak'Tor stopped himself.

"Never what?" she asked, frowning.

"—Never saw it before. We just do not seem to get along. I do not want the leadership of the High Rocks. I never did. The last thing I wanted was to compete with her for that. Anyway, even if I was Leader, they would defer to her as Guardian, and I did not want to fight that all my life. It is better this way."

"And yet you seem so unhappy so often," Ei'Tol said, putting down the food and coming over to comfort him.

She placed a hand on his arm. "I have some good news. Perhaps it will cheer you up to know that I am seeded!"

Dak'Tor squinted down at her belly. "Are you sure?"

Ei'Tol stepped back a bit, frowning. "I thought you would be happy. Yes, I am sure," she said.

"Sometimes females think they are seeded, and then they are not. Perhaps we should wait before making any announcement," he said moodily.

Ei'Tol looked away. "I am going to take a walk. Eat what you want; I will eat when I get back," and she left.

Dak'Tor watched his mate walk away, waiting for her to look back at him as she usually did, only this time she did not.

He did not want her to be seeded. It had been fine the way it was. Now her attention would be focused on an offling, and there would be females around all the time chattering about their female things. Nothing seemed to be going as he wanted it to. And Pan, she could have let him see the crystal. No one would have known.

CHAPTER 3

Pan once more convened the High Council in a special session of the Mothoc only. The absence of the Akassa Leaders went largely unnoticed. The Akassa were content under the watchful care and protective rule of the Mothoc.

But while Pan was opening the meeting, Dak'Tor was making his way to her quarters. Just as he was about to move the stone door to enter, he heard voices inside. He listened long enough to figure out that there was a female talking inside. Someone was sitting with his sister's offling. He quietly backed away.

Pan felt a moment of unease but pushed it aside and turned her attention back to the gathering of dark-haired bodies.

She caught Hatos'Mok's eye, and he nodded ever so slightly at her. It was good to know she had another ally there besides her mate.

Taking a deep breath, she implored, *Great Spirit, give me the words.*

"My father, his brother, Straf'Tor, and my mother, E'ranale, lived their lives in service to Etera," she began. "And they sacrificed their lives for the people and the future of Etera. If the difficult decisions of the Wrak-Wavara had not been made, we would be on our way to the end of all life here. Instead, we are faced with a new, terrible dilemma.

"The Akassa are the future. We know that. We accepted it as fact long ago. Whether those before us saw what the path they chose would come to, I can only guess. I believe they knew it would come to this, and I believe they knew a time would come when certain additional choices would become necessary."

Pan swallowed hard. "It is apparent by now that the Akassa will never lead themselves as long as we are around. Their submission to us is too ingrained now. Perhaps it is in anyone's nature. In their position, living side by side with giants of superior size and strength, we would perhaps defer to them just as the Akassa do. And they have never known a time without our presence.

"The course I believe we must follow is going to be a long one. I am sure some of you realize what I am about to say. Know that I did not come to this lightly. I would never present it if I were not absolutely convinced that this is the path forward that we must take.

"In order for the Akassa to rule themselves, we are going to have to disappear. We are going to have to leave our communities."

Some in the crowd exchanged knowing glances. From the last High Council meeting, they had suspected where Pan's thinking was headed. Others seemed to be caught completely off-guard.

The Healer from the Great Pines spoke up. "You are suggesting every one of us leaves? Where would we go? And what good would leaving do? They will not simply forget about us."

"I know I am asking a great sacrifice of you," Pan said. "All of us have Akassa family members, friends, established relationships. But without this last piece being put in place, my father's plan will not come to bear fruit. Many of you stood with him when Kthama Minor was closed. You have direct knowledge of the strife and struggle that brought us to where we are today. Are we now going to quit, with the battle half won? We are not being asked to make the sacrifice that Moc'Tor, E'ranale, and Straf'Tor made. We are only being asked to make another home for ourselves and leave the Akassa to discover the future of their making. You are right; perhaps they will not soon forget about us, but they will be forced to lead themselves, and in time we and the stories they will tell of us will just become part of history."

"Where would we go?" asked Aceo, mate of Tres'Sar of the Far High Hills.

Pan looked to Hatos'Mok, who picked up her cue. He joined Pan, his dark coat in stark contrast to her light one.

"At the Guardian's request, I sent out some sentries to look for a new home. They have returned, having found a suitable place. It is quite a distance away and to the north. The good news is that the weather is cooler there, which would be a relief to us in the summer and hardly an inconvenience in the winter. It sits on a vortex nearly as strong as the one here at the High Rocks," he explained.

"When would we leave? And what of the Akassa?" asked Aceo again.

"This is not an imminent change," Pan said. "It may take a century to do this. I hope not, but I do not know. It is not only about the Mothoc leaving. There are cultural shifts that must first take place. For example, just to start with, the seating boulders we use. They must be taken away. There is no way the Akassa themselves can use them, and nor could they easily remove them. They would only raise questions for future generations. Of what use would there be for them to be inside Kthama? The heavy granite doors in all the living quarters we use must be replaced with the thinner rock slabs we have for the Akassa.

"And to your question, Aceo, yes, what of the Akassa? Their Leaders are not yet independent enough to lead on their own. So they and especially the Healers and Helpers, those who came forward after the Rah-hora, must be prepared for our disappearance. The Healers must learn a new means of establishing succession other than our heavy reliance on the seventh sense. Methods and practices will take center stage, with the seventh sense no longer the main driver of healing practices. And the Akassa must follow the structure of leadership that we have—they must choose a High Protector. And as it is now, the Healer will be Second Rank, and the Leader's mate will be Third Rank.

"All these things, and many I have not even thought of, will have to be phased in. And not only here. I must go to Kayerm and speak to the Mothoc there. It is not enough that only we who are part of the Akassa communities disappear. Those at Kayerm must, too."

Pan paused before adding, "I think we should take a break. You need to talk about this among yourselves. Then when we come together again, we can discuss it further."

She watched them turn to each other, forming small clusters. At the back, Rohm'Mok stood talking to his brother, and behind them, Dak'Tor came into the room. Pan walked back to meet him.

"I came to see how it is going," he said.

"We are taking a break."

Dak'Tor looked around at all the small groups. "They seem agitated," he said. "I hope everything is alright."

"Nothing for you to worry about; it is just High Council business."

"Are you going to be meeting regularly like this?" he asked.

"Yes, it is necessary, even though some have to come long distances. Why do you ask?"

"Just curious." He looked past her to the raised platform at the back of the huge room.

"If you are looking for the Leader's Staff, it is not here," she said.

"Why would I care where the staff is?" Dak'Tor frowned.

"Brother, I will say it as clearly as I can; do not touch the Leader's Staff. Do not try to get to the crystal. Put it from your mind. That idea will only bring disaster down on your head. You need to make peace with your life and find happiness with your mate."

"I do not know what you are talking about," he answered. "I do not care about the staff or anything to do with it. I was just curious, that is all. I told you I would not ask about it again. And as I can see I am bothering you, I will leave you to your meeting." He abruptly walked off.

When Pan called the High Council members back, she asked first for questions.

Tres'Sar, Leader of the Far High Hills, stood. "If the Mothoc from Kayerm also have to leave, where will they go? Do they know this is what you have decided must happen?"

"No, unless they have figured it out for themselves, it will fall to me to explain it to them and make them understand. As to where they will go, they will come with us."

At that, the crowd erupted.

Pan waited, and the uproar finally subsided.

"If we could not live together before, how do you believe we are going to live together now?" asked Pnatl'Rar of the Little River.

"You intend to reunite us?" asked someone else disbelievingly. "The followers of Straf'Tor living with those of us who followed your father? Have you forgotten the bitter split that resulted in their leaving for Kayerm?"

"Just as we are not the same people we were when Kthama Minor was closed," Pan said, "neither are they. Surely as much has happened in their lives as has happened in ours. It is my belief that they, as well as you, will see the wisdom in this course of action, as I have based it on the simple fact that we are all connected to and receive guidance from the same Divine Mind. And if they have not received this guidance, I do not believe it will take much to convince them."

Hatos'Mok spoke up again, "Despite our differences, they love Etera as we do. That cannot have changed and should never change. They are as committed to serving her as we are. Yes, we may still have differences, but those are no longer of any importance. The decisions were made long ago, and the Sassen and the Akassa are the result. What is done is done, and our mutual service to the Great Spirit will be what unites us."

"What if we leave the Akassa and they do not survive?" asked another.

"We will not leave them until we know they will survive. That is our responsibility. We must make sure they can govern themselves. Provide for themselves. They are already adept at planting, hunting, making tools. The resistance will be that they see us as superior to them and allow us to take the lead. In a way, I believe our strength comforts them, while at the same time it also blinds them to their own strengths and their own ability to take care of themselves."

"They will still talk about us, even if we are not here," said Tres'Sar.

"It is true," said Pan, "but in time, we will just become a memory. And to future generations, just a story. And then eventually, we will become a myth when the following generations are incredulous and deem it just a tale some people made up long ago, a story to entertain offling around an evening fire."

The group was silent for some time. Pan could feel their surrender, their acceptance setting in.

"This new place, can we go to it? Can we see it?" asked Pnatl'Rar.

"In small groups, yes. But the journey there and back will take you away for a while. When you return, I ask that you come prepared to give a report on your viewpoint of the new location, and then the next group can go. But we cannot all go in large numbers. I will find someone to coordinate the visits."

"Perhaps it is for the best for us too," said Bahr'Mok. "We will create new memories; we will create a new future of our own making. We all carry wounds from the past. This will be a fresh start. And our offling will grow up in a new home, untainted by past sins and regrets."

"These communities are our homes," said Aceo, mate of Tres'Sar.

Pagara joined in. "Yes. But in time, you will adjust. We all will. I know it is hard, but remember that others have given up more than their homes for this."

"The Guardian is right," said Bahr'Mok. "We know it in our hearts. The Akassa will never come into their own while living in our shadow."

There were nods among the audience, and the room quieted.

"It seems we are finished with this topic, so it is

time to discuss pairings," said Pan. "Have there been any requests besides my sister, Vel?"

There had not been, so she closed the meeting for the evening. "After you have eaten, spend some time in the privacy of your minds thinking about what we have discussed. No one of us is as smart as all of us. We will succeed together or not at all, and there are no doubt details I have missed. Let us meet again in the morning and together lay out the next steps we will follow."

Rohm'Mok went back with Pan to their quarters.

"Tala needs to nurse, and I am missing her already," she said as they walked.

"I think that went well," said Rohm'Mok. "At least they were discussing it. It is when there is nothing but silence that there is a problem. Anything can be solved once it is out in the open.

"Well, nearly anything," he added. "What did your brother want?"

"Honestly, I think he came to see if I had the Leader's Staff with me. I know him; once he becomes obsessed with something, he does not easily let it go."

"He knows the punishment for touching the Leader's Staff."

"Yes. I was protecting him by blocking him from it, but he does not seem to see it that way. Maybe this move will be good for him, in the way I think it will be for all of us. Let the past go. Make a new start. Look to the future—"

"—of our own making." Rohm'Mok finished it with her, and they both laughed.

"That is what we should name our new home," Pan said. "Bak'tah-Awhidi, because that is exactly what this is for us; the passing of something that was known and the laying before us of the path toward something that is yet to be discovered. I will propose it to the High Council."

The next morning, Pan stood once again before the Mothoc Leaders. "Now that you have had time to reflect, is there anything you would like to share with the rest of us?"

Aceo, who had been struggling with starting over again, was the first to speak. "Last night, I went over this time and time again. I am afraid I kept Tres'Sar up most of the night discussing it. But I understand now. You have my full support."

Others spoke, the overwhelming majority agreeing with Aceo. Pan was relieved that most seemed to have made peace with the idea, and no one was vehemently opposed.

At the end of the meeting, as she dismissed them, she said, "Return to your homes. Prepare your Akassa Leaders, Healers, and Helpers. You must also prepare those Mothoc who were not present to hear this—your Mothoc friends and family. You are their Leaders. They will look to you for reassurance and guidance."

After the crowd had dispersed, Pan spoke to Rohm'Mok. "There is something I must do, and I need your support while I am away."

CHAPTER 4

Under Norland's leadership, some level of normalcy had returned to Kayerm. The tragic story of Nox'Tor's life and lost potential ceased to be the center of conversations. A routine had settled in, and slowly more and more females took a mate. Lorgil's son by Nox'Tor thrived under her watchful eye and loving nurture.

Norland grew in strength as a Leader. He was not arrogant enough to think that he had all the answers. He frequently took counsel from some of the older Mothoc, such as his mother, Kyana, along with Toniss and Trak, as well as Wosot and the Healer, Pagara.

Sitting with them one morning, he said, "You remember the laws that Straf'Tor and the others devised? I have been thinking about them."

"There was supposed to be a scroll with the laws recorded," said Pagara. "I imagine it is at Kthama."

"I remember them, though," said Wosot. "The needs of the community come before the needs of one individual. Females are to be honored and not subjugated. In humility, show forbearance for the failings of others. Raise no hand to another except in defense. In conflict, use the least amount of force necessary. Protect, heal, shelter the sick, helpless, and those in need. Remember that offling are the future and are sacred. Never take more than you need. No contact with outsiders, and never without consent."

Pagara raised her eyebrows at his perfect recital. "Yes, those are our laws."

"Please hear me out before you speak," said Norland. "You know the charge given to the Sassen, the Rah-hora that stated they are to have no contact with the Akassa. It was made very clear that the Akassa and the Sassen must be kept apart. That was the point of it. I need not say that the Akassa are no match for the Sassen. They would be annihilated quickly in any altercation. I suspect that is why the memory of Kthama's location, and those of the other communities, have been removed from the memories of the Sassen. The split between the two communities was bitter in some respects. Even the name, Akassa, which can be used to mean the feeble ones, reflects the Sassen's disdain for their cousins. Straf'Tor himself thought of the Akassa as an abomination. Considering this, my proposal is that the law forbidding contact with outsiders be modified to specify the Akassa. That was the intent of the Rah-hora. I do not see that it violates the meaning to modify the law in order to clarify it."

The group remained silent for a moment.

"*This is Rah-hora. Sassen, make no contact with Akassa lest you yourselves be destroyed. Leave the Others to them,*" Toniss said, quoting the Rah-hora.

"*Leave the Others to them* is clear," said Trak. "The Sassen are not to try to heal the damage done to the Others. The burden of reparation falls to the Akassa. I do not know why the Fathers decreed this. Perhaps because the Akassa are physically more similar to the Others. We do not even know if the Others realize their seed was taken without their consent. We may never know."

"Is that what you call them? The Fathers?" Toniss asked.

"Yes. That is how I think of them. Not as those who caused this great division among us, but as those who did what needed to be done for our blood to continue on Etera."

"The strict prohibition was for the Sassen to avoid the Akassa," Pagara said. "I believe what you are proposing makes sense and is in keeping with the intent of the Rah-hora, and I have no objection to the change. It will leave no room for misunderstanding."

"We must all be in agreement," said Norland. "I do not want to create a problem."

"Then let us mull it over for a while, Adik'Tar," said Wosot. "It is not something that must be decided immediately."

"I agree. What else do we need to discuss?"

The discussion moved on to tasks that needed to be done, the positive new pairings, and general conversation.

"And what of you, Wosot?" asked Norland. "No pairing in your future?"

"In order to pair, Adik'Tar, the female must offer herself to the male. You know that," Wosot answered. "I have made my feelings clear. There is nothing I can do but wait. And I am prepared to do that for as long as it takes."

When the meeting adjourned, Toniss went to find Kyana.

Toniss joined Kyana beside the river, where she was cleaning the longfish she had speared.

"Watch out; you are about to sit on my pile of scales."

Toniss took a place on the other side of her.

"I have more than enough; would you like some?" Kyana asked.

"No, thank you; Trak caught quite a few several days ago. I think it will be a while before I am ready to eat longfish again—or any other kind of fish," she chuckled.

"How are you feeling?" Toniss added.

Kyana kept working. "About what?"

Toniss sighed. "I will be blunt then. It has been long enough."

Kyana put the fish she was working on to the side and wiped her hands on the nearby leaves.

"You are talking about Wosot and me."

"Yes. And so is everyone else. You clearly want him, and he clearly wants you. Before, you said you wanted to wait to make sure Lorgil and her offling would both be well. So what is it now?"

"To tell you the truth, I do not know. Not trusting myself, perhaps. Not sure of my offling and how they would feel," she looked off across the river.

"That is nonsense. Your offling would be thrilled. It was Norland himself who brought it up at our meeting just now. Everyone is waiting for you to come to your senses. What is it you are really afraid of?"

Kyana let out a long sigh and thought for a moment. "Alright. I do not know if I want to love anyone again. I do not know that I want to be that vulnerable."

Since Nox'Tor's death, Toniss had realized that she was sometimes emotionally distant and had vowed to lower her walls. In a rare show of sentiment, she scooted closer and put her arm around Kyana's shoulder, pulling her close. She tucked Kyana's head under her chin as a mother would comfort an offling.

"Oh, Kyana. Do you not know? It is already too late

for that. You already love Wosot; you have admitted it, so you are already vulnerable. That is what love does. It joins our souls to another. I realize now that there can be no deep love without vulnerability. If that is what you are trying to avoid by not joining with Wosot, it is too late. The only thing you are accomplishing is denying you both what is left of a lifetime of companionship, joy, and pleasure. You could no longer stop loving him than I could stop loving Trak."

Kyana hugged Toniss back, suddenly deeply missing her mother. "If my mother were here, that is what she would tell me too, I know."

Then she moved away to look at Toniss. "Thank you. I know you are right. I will not make him wait much longer; I promise."

Kyana looked for Wosot everywhere, but he was nowhere to be found.

She found Pagara sorting her roots and herbs.

"I was looking for Wosot. Do you know where he is?"

"Actually, yes, he and Ras'Or just went out with a group of males in a hunting party. They will be gone for a few days."

Kyana's face fell. "What are they hunting?"

"Buffalo," Pagara answered. "A large herd was spotted moving through."

Kyana cringed. "The most dangerous hunt. I wish I had known they were leaving."

"You know he will be fine; they have hunted Buffalo many times. And though older, Ras'Or is one of our most experienced hunters. Why, he was even one of those who supported Straf'Tor back at the beginning of all this. It hurts my heart to have such magnificent creatures killed, but we are grateful for the Great Spirit's provision of meat for the winter."

Days and more days passed before there was any word of the hunting party's return. Finally, one of the younger offling came running toward Kayerm, shouting that the males were returning.

Kyana was helping Lorgil with her son when they heard the noise. It took a few moments to get outside, so they ended up behind the other onlookers.

Cheers slowly quieted when the crowd realized that one of the hunting party had been hurt and was being carried back. Kyana could not see through the crowd of heavy bodies, and her heart skipped a beat in fear that it was Wosot.

Cries for the Healer broke out, and Pagara pushed her way forward, rushing immediately to the wounded male.

"Set him down gently, gently," she ordered.

The male was covered in blood with an angry

wound in his side. Pagara examined it gingerly, concern worrying her face.

Kyana still could not see who it was, and thinking it must be Wosot, she broke out into sobs. Suddenly, a pair of strong hands were on her shoulders, turning her around.

"Why are you crying?" a strong male voice asked.

Kyana looked up to see Wosot. She threw her arms around his neck. "Oh, oh! I was so afraid it was you who was hurt. Oh, Wosot. You are safe," she cried.

He held her tight and let her calm down in his protective embrace.

Finally, she disengaged herself and looked up into his eyes, "I have been stupid and silly." She placed a hand on the side of his face. "Oh, Wosot. I do love you. It is you I want, now and forever. I choose you! Please, pair with me."

Wosot smiled and smoothed the hair from her face, "I will pair with you. Happily."

Kyana then remembered the fallen hunter, "Who is it? Who was hurt?"

"Ras'Or" he said.

"Ras'Or? Oh no, we cannot lose him."

"I know. Let us go and see what the Healer says."

By then, several of the largest males were moving Ras'Or into Pagara's living area.

Everyone remained outside to give the Healer time and space to work on the older male, and waiting for word, most did not leave the area.

Finally, Pagara emerged. "I believe Ras'Or will recover, but I cannot guarantee it; he has lost a lot of blood. He is resting now, and I have given him what I can to ease his pain."

Ras'Or's mate and his daughter stepped forward.

"May we please see him now?" the daughter asked.

Pagara took them in to see him and the crowd slowly dispersed.

Out of respect for Ras'Or, Kyana and Wosot did not announce that they were to be paired. A cloud had fallen over all of them, and now was not the time for a happy announcement. But waiting for Ras'Or to recover would prove even more excruciating than might be expected, now that they had declared their love for each other.

Finally, Ras'Or did recover. Word came that he would be able to rejoin the community at the evening fire. Everyone was in high spirits, so Kyana gathered her offling to tell them her good news.

Norland, Dotrat, Lai, and Somnil waited patiently for their mother to speak. Wosot was standing next to her, so Norland and Dotrat, who were older, guessed what was coming.

"I wanted to tell you before we announce it tonight. I have chosen Wosot, and we are to be paired." Kyana carefully searched the faces of her offling, looking for any sign of unhappiness.

"That is excellent news," exclaimed Norland, and the others grinned and nodded their agreement.

"I will do right by your mother and by you," declared Wosot. "I pledge my life to your protection, support, and wellbeing."

"Mother, we are all truly happy about this," Dotrat said. "We have talked about it among ourselves. We have no concerns, other than that it took you too long."

Kyana smiled, and a wave of relief swept through her.

The offling gathered around them as Wosot turned to Norland. "I know I will not replace your father. That is not my intention."

Norland shook his head, "Wosot, you helped guide my brother and me during our younger years, and for that, I will always be grateful." Then he reached up and placed his hand on Wosot's shoulder.

"When do you want the ritual to take place?" he asked.

Kyana tilted her head and smiled. "You are Leader. You will do the pairing, so you should decide that."

"As soon as possible; we have waited too long already. How about tonight? At the evening fire?" he asked. Kyana looked at Wosot, who nodded.

"Wonderful," said Kyana. "But we must first tell

Pagara, Lorgil, Toniss, and Trak." And off they went together to tell their friends and family.

That evening, after everyone had expressed their relief at Ras'Or's recovery, Norland stood and announced that he had joyful news, that a couple was to be paired.

Heads turned as everyone tried to figure out who it was. Usually, community gossip carried news well ahead of any event. Finally, smiles crept onto faces as, one by one, they worked it out.

After Kyana of the House of Nul and Wosot of the House of 'Tar were paired, everyone offered their congratulations, with much chiding again about how long it had taken them to finally come to a decision.

"I am not to blame for that," Wosot laughed. "Kyana has always been the only female in my heart."

"I have been the reason for the wait," Kyana confessed. "But you all know that. I am honored to become Wosot's First Choice."

Wosot turned and said to her very seriously, "You are not just my First Choice. You are my only choice. And always will be."

Kyana leaned into him and rested her head on his chest. Thoughts of what the night would bring flooded her with desire. She looked up at him, and he read the longing in her eyes.

"Thank you, everyone, but my mind is no longer on the celebration," Wosot said, still looking at Kyana.

Then he lifted her up and cradled her in his arms.

As he carried her away, he called back to the others, "See you in a few days," to which they and Kyana all laughed.

Knowing that the two were to be paired, Norland and his siblings had prepared Kyana's quarters with the help of Lorgil and Pagara. Then Lorgil and her offling had relocated to Wosot's space, and Kyana's daughters would move in with Toniss and Trak for a few nights.

Wosot carried Kyana through the tunnels of Kayerm. His hard muscles held her securely, and she nestled in closer, enjoying his rich, warm male scent. She felt safe, protected, loved.

As he got to her living space, he parted the hide curtain and carried her inside. Kyana took in the beautifully decorated room, now filled with flowers and luminescent fluorite. A fresh, very thick sleeping mat was where her old one had once lain.

Wosot set her down, and they both looked around.

"Beautiful," she said. "I must remember to thank them."

Wosot looked into her eyes, "Are you nervous?"

Kyana lowered her head, "A little."

"I dreamed of being with you for many years, then for many years after, when you and Nox'Tor were paired, I mourned the loss of that dream. I found a way to live with waiting for something that would never come, so if you wish, I can wait a while longer."

"I do not want to wait," she said, turning back to him. "I want to be yours, in every way," and she stood as tall as she could and offered him a kiss.

Wosot leaned down and pressed his lips to hers. He snaked his arm around her waist and pulled her hard against him. Kyana could feel his desire for her, and it fanned the fire already within her even higher.

"Make me yours," she whispered. Wosot scooped her up and carried her over to the sleeping mat. He gently set her down there, then knelt next to her.

He gently ran his hand down the side of her face, running his thumb over her lips. She playfully captured it with her teeth, to which he smiled. Then she lay back and opened her arms to him. He leaned over her and kissed her again, this time more urgently. She met his passion with her own and pulled him closer to her. More than anything, Kyana wanted to feel his hard strength satisfying them both, fulfilling the longing they shared for each other.

When Wosot finally took her, something uncoiled inside Kyana, and for the first time, she felt that the difficult times were behind her. No matter what challenges were to come, they would all be surmountable with this giant yet tender male at her side.

Finally, exhausted, their passion sated for the moment, they lay together in the faint glow from the fluorite.

"I am so very happy," she said, looking up at him. "I will do everything in my power to deserve you."

"Hush," he answered. "That is my pledge to you." Kyana curled up against him, flinging one leg up over him and settling in for some cuddling.

They both reveled in their happiness until their passion returned. It was a night of celebration, satisfaction, and joy for them both.

The next morning, still in each other's arms, Kyana and Wosot awoke to a great commotion. Kyana threw off the bed covers and waited for Wosot, and they both went outside.

Standing up on the ridge, backlit by the rising sun, stood a large figure. Even the rays of light from behind could not disguise the silver-white coat. Everyone looked at each other in surprise and concern. The Guardian. The Guardian of Etera had come to Kayerm.

Pan waited for the Leaders of Kayerm to approach. Slowly, six Mothoc figures walked toward her, leaving a large crowd waiting behind them at the cave system's entrance.

As they approached, one of them raised a hand in greeting.

"Welcome, Guardian of Etera. We are honored by your visit," said the male in front.

Pan looked at the others with him. A female who looked enough like him to be his mother, a large male of considerable build standing with her, another female whom she could feel was their Healer, and an older male with a younger female, who she sensed were newly paired.

"I am Pan, daughter of Moc'Tor. Guardian of Etera. Leader of the High Rocks. I come to you in peace."

"I am Norland, Leader of Kayerm, son of the son of Straf'Tor."

"The blood of Straf'Tor is strong in you," Pan said. "You have come into leadership early in your life."

"My father, Nox'Tor, son of Straf'Tor, was Leader. But he is dead. The mantle has passed to me," Norland explained.

Pan turned to the Healer. "You are the Healer here."

"Yes, Guardian, I am Pagara."

"Tyria now lives at the High Rocks," Pan said.

"She has made a life for herself with us and is now our Healer."

"Thank you, Guardian; she was my apprentice. I miss her and am glad to hear she is alright. She was very promising, and I am sure she makes a fine Healer."

Norland introduced the older male and female, who nodded respectfully. Pan knew Toniss's story. She was one of the females Straf'Tor had favored, but she was later paired to Trak and Straf'Tor to Ushca.

"Guardian, my name is Kyana, and this is my mate, Wosot. May we offer you something to eat? A drink of fresh water? How may we serve you?" asked the third female.

"I have come to serve you. I serve all of Etera; it is not your duty to serve me," Pan smiled.

"I need to speak with you, Adik'Tar Norland, and your Healer," she continued. "It is about the future of your people. If you wish these others to hear what I have to say, that is up to you. But it is your place as Leader to decide if you would both prefer to meet with me alone."

Then Pan looked at the others. "There is no slight to you if he chooses to do that."

"Whatever it is that you are here to tell me, I want everyone to hear," Norland answered.

"Walk with me then to the riverside. I have much to tell you," Pan said. "But it falls to you, Norland, and your Healer, to decide what to share with the Sassen and the rest of the Mothoc and when."

As they walked, Pan asked that one of them tell her about Kayerm, how they were fairing, and the collective mind of the community as far as the events of the past were concerned.

Toniss told Pan how the rebels who had been banished by Moc'Tor were already living at Kayerm when Straf'Tor's group had arrived there and of the friction that resulted between the two communities. She also told her about Ushca's death by poisoning at the hand of the rebel Ridg'Sor. Then she shared how Straf'Tor had killed Ridg'Sor and banished his followers, sending them off into the wilderness. How Nox'Tor, son of Straf'Tor, became embittered over his father's abandonment of him and lost his way, making rampant changes that caused disruption and strife within the group.

Pan asked a few questions but mostly listened attentively, not only to the words but to the feelings and currents underlying what Toniss was saying. Finally, when Toniss was finished, Pan said to her, "Kayerm is blessed to have your wisdom and guidance."

Norland spoke next. "We have had much tragedy here. There have been too many deaths. We, those of us who seek to guide our people here, pray for peace and an end to the turmoil and heartache. So it is with some concern that I await your message."

"I understand your feelings, but before I say what I have come to say, what happened to the son of Straf'Tor, that now his son leads Kayerm?"

"I came with Straf'Tor from Kthama and served at his side," said Wosot. "Nox'Tor died at my hand, in defense of Kyana here, and another female now under my protection."

Perfectly matched in height to him, Pan stepped over to Wosot. She looked him squarely in the eye and then, after a moment, said, "You did what had to be done. Loosen and release any guilt you have over his death and the taking of this, his mate, for your own."

"Guilt is a hard master, Wosot," she continued. "Step out from under its weight and enjoy your life. You are no good to Etera if you are weighed down by unnecessary and unfounded regret."

"Thank you, Guardian." He met her eyes again, and indeed, a great burden fell from his heart.

"I have come to you because, despite the differences that separated us, we are all Mothoc. We live to serve Etera. It falls to us to do our best to protect her, even if it requires sacrifice. You experienced the Rahhora. Some of you perhaps were involved in the Ror'Eckrah called forth by my father. The division between the Akassa and the Sassen had to be created, but it was never intended for the Mothoc to be divided."

Norland never took his eyes off Pan and listened intently to every word as she continued.

"What is done is done; time has passed, and we must now reunite and move forward as one people again."

Then Norland spoke. "You are talking of reuniting all the Mothoc? Are you talking about us returning to live among your people at Kthama?"

"The Mothoc who live at Kthama are my people, but not any more so than you are," said Pan. "We are all Mothoc. And no, I am not talking about living with the Akassa—or living with the Sassen, either. It is time for us to come out from among them and move on together to a future of our own making."

Everyone stopped talking. Silence.

"What will happen to the Sassen if we leave them?" asked Toniss, finally.

Pan turned to Norland, "Answer her, Leader; what will happen to the Sassen if the Mothoc no longer live among them?"

Norland let out a long breath before speaking. "They will adapt. They will survive. It will be tough at first. But in time, they will learn to trust themselves, to lead themselves." He paused. "And in a way in which they will never do as long as we are here."

"Exactly," Pan said. "It is the same with the Akassa. We overshadow them even more so than you do the Sassen because you are more like the Sassen in build than we are like the Akassa. They all defer to us. They look to us to make the decisions. As long as we walk among them, the Sassen and the Akassa will never become who they are meant to be."

"If we leave Kayerm, where are we to go? And when?" asked Pagara.

"There is another location, well suited to our needs," Pan said. "Sentries who were sent out to look for such a place have found one. It is quite a way north of here, so it is cooler, which will be a relief in the summer months. The vortex is strong, and there are enough resources for us to build a new life there. Together," she added.

"You are the Guardian," said Wosot. "I do not doubt your wisdom or question your guidance. It will be another big adjustment for us and for the Sassen. When do you propose that this should take place?"

"There must be a transition. You must first prepare the Sassen to live without your help and to accept leadership of themselves. The Sassen Leader must be someone of the House of 'Tor. He must be sworn to abide by the laws which were agreed on by the Leaders before Straf'Tor traveled through the communities, collecting his followers and leading them here to Kayerm."

"There was a scroll. It was recorded by the Healer, Lor Onida. Is it at the High Rocks?" asked Toniss.

"There is a story of this scroll, as you say," Pan answered. "But it has never been found. It seems to be lost to us."

"We were just speaking of the Sacred Laws. We have them memorized," said Kyana.

"They must be honored by the Sassen," said Pan. "The laws and the words of the Rah-hora. Whatever will happen, what is meant to happen, will be built on that foundation."

"What of the rebel Mothoc?" asked Trak. "Those whom Straf'Tor exiled? Will they be joining us in this new home?"

Pan shook her head. "Of that, I cannot say. Ideally, yes. It is the Great Spirit's will that all Mothoc be united and live in harmony. Whether it is possible to heal what divides this splintered group from the greater community, I do not know. As the sentries were returning from finding a suitable new home, they came across an abandoned location. There was evidence of a disaster, a cave-in. I suspect now that this was where the rebel group you spoke of first stopped after leaving Kayerm."

"Was no one there?" Trak asked. "Did they all perish?"

"Though the place was heavy with tragedy, I believe some live still, and if so, I must find them. Thank you for meeting with me. I will leave you now. While I am gone, prepare yourselves. Prepare the other Mothoc for what is to come. Prepare the Sassen. Teach them to be mindful of their pairings, the crossing of their bloodlines. Select a Sassen

Leader. Pagara, select a Sassen Healer and teach him or her all you know about the collecting and preparation of medicinals. Let not one of you tarry in your duty. You must lay the foundation for their success. Mind the words of the Rah-hora, given to us by the Fathers-Of-Us-All."

"Please, Guardian," said Toniss. "Before you leave, I was mate to Straf'Tor at one point. You have not told us much of Kthama. Where are Straf'Tor, Moc'Tor, and your mother, E'ranale? The last we knew of Straf'Tor is that he and Tyria left for Kthama."

"My father sacrificed himself for Etera. As for Straf'Tor and my mother, their bodies rest with my father's in the Chamber of the Ancients, sealed deep within Kthama Minor."

Though Toniss and the others likely expected that Straf'Tor was dead, she gave them a moment as she could see the expression change on Toniss' face. Hearing it would have made it real.

"As you probably realized immediately after the Rah-hora, all memory of the location of Kthama, Kthama Minor, and the other communities was wiped from the memories of the Sassen. That was the point of the Rah-hora, to keep the Sassen and the Akassa separate. The Akassa must live free of the threat of those who would destroy them, who still hold bitterness in their hearts over their very existence."

"But what of those of us who followed Straf'Tor?" asked Toniss.

"The rift between Moc'Tor and Straf'Tor was based on a disagreement over how much of the Others' bloodline was to be brought in," Pan answered. "There was never deep-seated animosity between the two brothers. Each believed he was doing the best for Etera. The Rahhora was put in place to keep the Sassen from the Akassa, should they bear hatred for the Akassa in their hearts. As for the Mothoc at Kayerm, only you know if they bear ill will toward the Akassa. If so, it is up to you to try to heal those wounds before we are reunited; because if not, they will surely bring trouble into our upcoming alliance. We seek unity, not more division."

Pan turned to Kyana, who was standing next to Wosot. "Yours is a good match. Much greatness will come of it.

"Now, when I return to lead you to our new home. I pray that we will be able to live as one people again. In the meantime, it falls to you, Norland, to decide when to tell the Sassen that you will be leaving them. Trust the counsel of others, but ultimately trust yourself to know when that time is here."

Then Pan raised her hand in a blessing, turned, and walked away. As the others followed her, she slowly faded from sight in front of their eyes.

"Once again, the Mothoc are to leave their home," said Norland. "But we will be brave and strong. We are Mothoc, and above all, we honor the Great Spirit's guidance. We have been blessed by the Guardian's visit. Let us plan to meet later today after we have all had time to think about her words."

Kyana looked at her son. So young to be a Leader and yet so perfectly suited to it. Nothing like his father, what his father became. She hoped that wherever Nox'Tor was, his spirit had been healed, and he could take pride in the grown male his firstborn had become.

She took Wosot's hand. "A new start for us all. Perhaps it is for the best. Yes, this has been our home for a long time, but there are many stains here. The death of Ridg'Sor, the banishment of his followers, Ushca's murder—and more—all at the hand of the Mothoc. Perhaps, with us gone, the Sassen can come into their own. Our presence no doubt serves as a constant reminder of the turmoil we created."

"It is a sad irony, is it not?" said Norland. "That which we all desire above all else, to live in peace and harmony, has been the cause of so much strife among our people."

Having delivered her message to Kayerm, Pan was anxious to get back to Tala, but there was something she had to do first. As soon as she reached home, she went to the sacred meadow and joined with the Aezaiteran flow. Then she entered the Order of Functions, moving back through the Aezaiteran stream before returning to her body. She did her best to shake off the despair from once again facing her father's presence trapped in the Order of Functions. She could sense him there but could not communicate with him. She prayed that he also sensed her presence and knew she would do everything she could to free him.

After a day's rest with Rohm'Mok and Tala, and after arranging once more for her offling's care—this time for longer—she packed supplies and turned in the direction of the abandoned Mothoc camp Hatos'Mok's sentries had discovered.

CHAPTER 5

Across all the communities, the Mothoc Leaders revived their efforts to engage their Akassa counterparts. Though the Akassa were reluctant, this time, the Mothoc did not relent. More and more, they included the Akassa in decision-making, having long conversations about the running of their communities, pushing them to select those best suited for particular stations and prepare for the changing seasons. Working the plan they had agreed to at the last High Council meeting at Kthama, the Mothoc took their time laying a solid foundation for when they would no longer walk among the Akassa.

During Pan's absences, Rohm'Mok and Dochrohan worked together to lead Kthama. It was well known that Rohm'Mok had been groomed to accept leadership of the Deep Valley, and the people readily sought out and accepted his guidance.

Just as Pan had asked each of the Mothoc Leaders to do in their communities, Rohm'Mok met on her behalf in private with all the Mothoc at the High Rocks. He explained that they would be leaving Kthama at some point. Everyone listened politely, and Rohm'Mok knew it would take them time to adjust.

One day, as he sat at morning meal, Takthan of the House of 'Tor approached Rohm'Mok and asked to join him.

"I need your guidance. I have been unable to decide between two for the choice of High Protector. What qualities should I look for?"

"What does your own counsel tell you?" Rohm'Mok asked.

"That he must be someone the other males look up to. Accomplished in many areas. Fair-minded. Quick to decide, but at the same time not impulsive. Able to weigh all factors and come to a plan of action."

"All solid answers. I am not sure why you are confused?"

"I do not know if I should choose someone who is desirous of the position. Someone who pursues it over someone who is less—driven, so to say," Takthan'Tor answered.

"That is a common quandary. Who is best suited

to lead? The one who seeks it and makes it his goal in life? Or the one who carries the mantle more lightly, who is satisfied without control and influence over others."

"Exactly my problem."

"There is no simple answer. And one is not necessarily always the right choice over the other. Perhaps the choice lies not between the two different temperaments but is more wisely based on the integrity of each of the candidates. Above all, the welfare of the people must always be the guiding factor behind any decisions made by those in leadership. Not the acquisition of more authority, fame, or admiration. Those who are able to set aside their own self-interests, even with an internal struggle, will always be the better choice in a position of authority."

When Takthan'Tor had thanked Rohm'Mok for the wisdom of his direction and left, Tyria and her Helper Jhotin joined their Leader, as they often did at mealtime.

"Where is your offling?" Rohm'Mok asked Tyria.

"He is with Tensil, the Akassa Healer. We are taking her and the Helper she has chosen out to gather supplies."

"They will be joining us shortly; we told them we would meet them here," Jhotin added.

Rohm'Mok looked at the sturdy young Mothoc male who had become Tyria's Helper. He had often heard Pan remark that she hoped the two would eventually pair.

A moment later, the Akassa Healer and her Helper approached.

"Please, get something to eat and join us," said Rohm'Mok.

He watched them walk away, sensing their hesitation at returning to sit across the table from the Mothoc Leaders. But, to their credit, after they got their food, they did return to sit with him and the others.

The contrast was striking. On one side sat the Mothoc, large thick-coated giants with deep-set dark eyes. On the other, the Akassa Healer and Helper. A quarter of the Mothoc's size, relatively hairless, so the elderly, young offling, and females often wore wraps of hide and fur. Though their muscular build was developed from hard work, they were frail by comparison. For a moment, Rohm'Mok saw himself through their eyes.

My mate is so right. The Akassa would never accept themselves as the Mothoc's equals.

Pan had been gone for some time. She missed her mate, her daughter, her friends. She worried what Dak'Tor was up to in her absence, and she wondered how the training of Akassa replacements was coming on. She had nothing to do as she walked but to think, pray, and reflect.

She trudged up a steep incline, following the flow of the magnetic current far beneath her. She knew by its increasing strength that she was nearing her destination. Though she was not afraid, she did stop to gather her thoughts and say a prayer.

Great Spirit. Guide me in what to say. We have all suffered pain, loss, and disappointment, but we all seek the same blessings, to live in peace, to love and be loved. To live a life of contribution and satisfaction. But in that quest, we have all caused harm to one another. Please grant me wisdom.

Pan reached the ridge and looked down. In the distance stretched several mountain ranges. As she quieted herself, an overwhelming feeling of sadness came over her. But more than sadness. Despair, heartache, anger. It was as Hatos'Mok's sentries had reported. There was much loss and devastation here. But where had they gone? She must find them and try to make peace; the future of Etera might depend on it.

Pan quieted her soul and once again reached out to the Great Spirit. She closed her eyes and waited. Within a few moments, she heard the caw of Ravu'Bahl. She opened her eyes to see a very large black crow eyeing her from the top of a nearby locust tree.

She stared at the crow, "Greetings, Ravu'Bahl. You have come as a reminder of the Great Spirit's love and our sacred duty to the laws. I am on a quest to serve the Great Spirit. Do you have a message for me?"

The crow took flight, making a sweeping circle and then returning to roost in exactly the same place.

"I hear you, Ravu'Bahl. Lead the way."

The crow flew off again and perched in another tree as if waiting for Pan to catch up.

Days passed with Ravu'Bahl patiently leading the way. Pan had no concerns; she knew the crow was being guided by the Great Spirit. She noted the stars overhead at night and the position of the sun during the day. She occasionally paused to eat and rest but never faltered in her willingness to be led to the group of rebel Mothoc.

After nearly a month of travel, one day, as the sun hung low in the late afternoon sky, Pan could feel the magnetic tributary strengthening. They had never left its path. That night, sleep came easy to her, visions of home, as always, in her dreams.

When she woke up, a dusting of snow greeted Pan. She rolled out from under the covering of fir branches and squinted against the morning light. Up overhead, Ravu'Bahl waited in a large tree, staring at her with an unblinking black eye. Then the crow flew off, circled once, and came back to roost.

"We are nearing there, then. Thank you, Ravu'Bahl. If I do not see you again, I bid you farewell with my gratitude and blessings." As she finished speaking, the large black crow took off and disappeared from sight.

Pan said another prayer before climbing to the nearest high point to survey the horizon. Along the base of the mountain range, she could make out a fairly large outcropping, under which the entrance to a cave or cave system could often be found. Out in front, several Mothoc were moving, apparently going about their morning duties. This had to be the new camp of the Mothoc rebels banished from Kayerm by Straf'Tor.

Again, I ask you for the words to say to open their minds to unity. Let there be peace among all our people again.

Pan shook a few remaining leaves and sticks off her striking silver-white coat, and in a moment of vanity, smoothed it down. Then she started walking toward the Mothoc encampment.

Gard's mate looked up to see the unmistakable approaching figure of the silver-coated Guardian of Etera. She ran inside and called to everyone. Their Leader, Laborn, was one of the first to make it outside. Smaller than most Mothoc and an unusual ruddy color, he stood transfixed, his heart pounding more than he would ever admit as he waited for the figure to reach them.

Pan raised a hand in greeting. "I am Pan, daughter of Moc'Tor, Guardian of Etera. I come in peace."

Gard had just reached Laborn's side. "The Guardian has come to us. What can it mean?"

"We will find out shortly," Laborn answered. He looked fearlessly at the Guardian. "I am Adik'Tar Laborn. What is your business here?"

Pan continued her approach until she was standing just a short distance away.

"You are the group that left Kayerm," she said.

"Thrown out of Kayerm is more accurate," Laborn answered.

"I found your earlier home. It appears there was a disaster there; is that why you left?"

"There was a huge cave-in," Laborn replied bitterly. "My mate, as well as a fair number of our community, died in the collapse. That site is now sacred ground. Some of my people return there occasionally to pay homage since we could not give them a proper Good Journey. It seems we have suffered nothing but loss since we followed Straf'Tor."

Pan watched as more Mothoc came through the entrance. "I grieve with you at the loss of your loved ones," she said. "I know the importance of family, and that is why I am here. I come in hopes of reuniting our people. When we split up, families were divided. Loved ones lost contact with each other because of a difference in philosophy. Time has passed now, and perhaps wounds have healed. It is my fervent prayer that we may overcome the sins and pain of the past and move forward together toward a common future."

"So, you have come to your senses and annihilated the abominations, the Akassa at Kthama?" Laborn asked. "And what of the Sassen at Kayerm?"

"The Akassa and Sassen are part of creation. They were created with the Great Spirit's guidance. To harm them would go against all we, as Mothoc, are charged with."

"As you are a daughter of Moc'Tor, I should expect to hear nothing else," Laborn retorted.

"I am not here to debate the wisdom of what the Fathers-Of-Us-All decided. I know there are strong feelings on each side. I am here to invite you to set aside the grievances of the past and rejoin the Mothoc community. As equals, as brothers and sisters, as family."

The bitterness in the rebel group over the death of Ridg'Sor at Straf'Tor's hand had run deep, but after they had settled into the blessings of the first cave system, a flicker of hope dawned that the anger might be relinquished. However, the disaster that claimed many of their loved ones was all the fuel Laborn had needed to incite anger against all except those of their own community. And he had used his gift of persuasion to twist grief into hatred and blame.

"The past cannot just be swept clean with words, Guardian," said Gard. "Too much has happened for that."

"They are not just words," Pan said. "They are my heartfelt desire, and that of the other Mothoc, for our reunion."

Laborn turned to address his group and pointed back at Pan as he spoke. "We have been deceived by the House of 'Tor before."

He turned back to Pan, "We will not fall for your lies again. We will not rest until Etera is purged of the abominations created by your father and Straf'Tor—the Akassa and the Sassen alike."

"The Sassen carry what is left of our blood. If you destroy them, you destroy Etera. The Rah-hora—"

Laborn cut Pan off. "*Va!* We do not speak of any Rah-hora here."

All those assembled looked at each other nervously. In all this time, the Rah-hora had never been spoken of, though each one still clearly remembered witnessing the message to the Sassen and Akassa through the formation of the One Mind.

"An agreement forced upon us by those who betrayed us holds no weight. Now leave. Do not return. If you come back, you do so at your own peril —Guardian or not," Laborn snarled. The older adults gathered close to him in a show of unity. Many raised fists in the air to demonstrate their rejection of Pan and her message of reconciliation. Some of the offling tossed small sticks and stones at her. Only a small group of adolescents and the older female named Useaves stood apart, not partaking in the demonstration.

"I can see that bitterness has taken root in your hearts. You have nursed your resentments until they are all you know. But your souls are still Mothoc, and embedded within the core of each of you is the duty to serve Etera," Pan said, not giving up. "In time, the Promised One will come to bring peace to all Etera."

Laborn did not know what she meant by the Promised One, but he could not show his ignorance in front of his tribe. And the last thing he wanted was for them to look beyond him for direction.

"Eliminating the Akassa and the Sassen is how we will bring peace to Etera," Laborn retorted angrily. "We will continue to grow in strength and numbers until we can make right the sins of the Wrak-Wavara."

Pan felt the animosity rolling off of them like a heatwave, some of their lips curled enough to show their canines. "I will leave. But I will not give up hope for a united Mothoc family. My prayer is that in time your hearts will soften, and you will turn from the path of destruction you have chosen."

Pan turned and walked back the way she had come, her heart heavy with disappointment.

The Mothoc rebels' thinking was twisted, but they were committed to their cause. In their isolation, they had become convinced that their intention to rid Etera of the Akassa and Sassen was somehow in service of the Great Spirit. And Pan had no doubt that, barring contagion or other cause of an even larger reduction in their numbers, they would one day attempt to carry out their threat.

Even though the magnetic current and the stars would guide her without his help, Pan searched the cold winter skies for Ravu'Bahl. She missed his company and wished for his return, his reassurance that she was walking the path the Great Spirit expected of her. As she placed one foot in front of her other, she spoke aloud to her mother.

"Oh, how I wish I could talk to you again, Mother. I had such hopes of being able to reach the rebels. But they have gone far down the path of darkness, perhaps, I fear, beyond where the light of redemption even flickers. Their thinking has been warped. We both know that Etera cannot survive without the Sassen or the Akassa."

Rohm'Mok was sorely missing Pan, so one morning he trudged through the deep snow to the sacred meadow above Kthama, the place where he had once fallen to his knees and beseeched the Great Spirit to return her to him. If it was wrong to go there, he never felt it.

The morning was bright and clear. Though the newly fallen white blanket covering everything gleamed in the sunlight, the cool temperatures were a delight, giving relief from the summer's heat.

Rohm'Mok walked to the spot where he had cradled his fallen mate. Once again, he knelt down in the snow and closed his eyes.

Great Spirit, hear my prayer. Wherever Pan is, guide her on her journey and protect her. She wants only to serve you and to help your offling find their way back to unity.

His reverie was broken by the flap overhead of a bird's wings. He opened his eyes to see that a black crow had landed only a few feet away, its tiny feet making sharp indentations in the snow.

"Ravu'Bahl, what sacred duty have you come to remind me of?" Rohm'Mok asked out loud. He looked closer and saw something red in the crow's beak.

"What is that?" he asked, and as if on cue, Ravu'Bahl dropped the object onto the snow where it sank and disappeared. The crow cocked its head to look at Rohm'Mok once more before taking off into the winter sky.

Rohm'Mok leaned over to uncover the object the crow had dropped. Expecting to find an acorn or a nut, he was surprised to see it was a round piece of red jasper.

"The stone that represents the Great Spirit's love for us. And our personal love for each other," he said out loud, gently fingering the smooth red object.

"Thank you, Great Spirit. Thank you for hearing me," he said, then rose and made his way back to his quarters, the precious reminder clasped safely in one hand.

Back in their quarters, Rohm'Mok placed the red stone in plain sight on a small piece of hide on Pan's personal work area. He remembered Pan telling him that her mother had kept a similar stone on her bedside in the Leader's Quarters, a gift from Moc'Tor. Though theirs by rights, Pan and Rohm'Mok had never moved into the Leader's Quarters; Pan hadn't felt comfortable to do so.

Satisfied with its placement, Rohm'Mok went to retrieve their daughter from Tyria and the wet nurse who had been watching her together that morning.

CHAPTER 6

Tyria had just finished examining Ei'Tol when Rohm'Mok announced himself.

The Healer went to the door, "I am sorry, I am busy with someone. I will bring your daughter to you in a little while if that is alright."

"Yes, of course."

Ei'Tol sat up, "Who was that?"

"Rohm'Mok," Tyria answered, helping her to her feet.

"I thought so. He is a good mate to the Guardian; I am sure he misses her."

"I am sure he must," agreed Tyria. "Your offling is due soon, so, as you know, watch for the signs. I do not expect any problems but make sure Dak'Tor does not wait too long to send word, especially when your water cradle breaks."

Tyria noticed Ei'Tol's face fall at the mention of her mate, and she turned to Jhotin, who had been waiting in the background, watching Tala and Fahr playing safely in the back of the room. "Please leave us for a while," the Healer said before turning back to Ei'Tol.

"What is wrong?" Tyria asked when the Helper had left.

"My mate is not happy about my being seeded. We rarely speak any longer, and he sleeps elsewhere. When he does come home, he just eats and goes. I fear the distance between us will only grow once the offling arrives."

"Has he said as much?" asked the Healer.

"Dak'Tor is not the kind to be blunt or rude. He is more mannerly than that. Though sometimes I find it to be a fault, as I am often unsure of how he feels. However, sometimes I can tell that behind the mask he puts on, he is irritated. I am certain this is one of those times."

Tyria tried to console Ei'Tol. "He may feel differently once he meets his son or daughter."

"I do hope you are right."

A few weeks later, Ravu'Bahl returned to Pan. She cried out in glee at seeing him circling above her against the bright blue sky.

"I am so glad you are back. I hope you will stay with me for the rest of the journey." The black crow landed on a nearby branch and perched there as if waiting for her to begin her journey once more.

Ei'Tol did not have to wait long. Within a few weeks, she had delivered a daughter. Tyria's Helper, Jhotin, found Dak'Tor and gave him the good news.

"Tell my mate I will be along later. I have something I am working on that I need to take care of first."

Jhotin waited a moment, thinking he had not heard Dak'Tor correctly. "You are not coming now? Your mate will be expecting you. This is a happy moment for you both. What could be more important than this?"

"When you have your own mate and offling, maybe you will understand. This will change everything between us. I have seen it before. If you think it is such a happy event, you go and be with her. As I said, I will be by later," Dak'Tor replied.

Jhotin scowled at Dak'Tor but returned to the Healer's Quarters. "He is not coming. Not yet, at least," he told the Healer.

Ei'Tol looked up from nursing her newborn, having heard Jhotin's report, then she looked down again and arranged the offling's hide wrap. "If I have to raise you alone, I will," she said. "I will do my best to make sure you want for nothing."

Before Moc'Tor had made pairing mandatory, when it was still uncertain who the father was, for generations, females had raised their offling by themselves. Though there was communal support, it was not until the pairing of one male to one female that the true concept of fatherhood became commonplace.

Ei'Tol continued. "At least you are not a male, needing a father to teach you."

Jhotin watched, his heart sad for the new mother. Then his compassion turned to anger.

"I have something I have to do," he told the two females and strode from the room.

Dak'Tor was spearfishing down in one of the icy shallows of the Great River.

A strained voice interrupted him from behind. "This is what was so important that you could not go see your daughter?"

Dak'Tor turned around to see Jhotin. Again. Irritated and not able to mask his reaction this time, he barked, "How dare you seek me out and challenge me. I do not see that this is any business of yours."

"Perhaps not from another male. But I am the Healer's Helper. It becomes my business when I see a new mother heartbroken at a time that should be filled with joy. I have heard about you, Dak'Tor. Until now, I have ignored the stories that, though you are clever with words, you are self-centered and selfish.

But seeing you now, I am starting to believe them to be true," Jhotin said.

Dak'Tor threw his fishing spear onto the river-bank. "Who are you to criticize me? I am the son of Moc'Tor, brother to the Guardian of Etera."

"I do not care who you are," Jhotin retorted. "You are not above the law. Our law calls us to revere our females and look out for them. Your behavior is despicable."

"You have said your piece; now leave. I will be by later, as I said," and Dak'Tor turned his back on the Helper.

Jhotin hesitated and then started to leave. He got a few steps away before turning back. He said loud enough for Dak'Tor to hear, "You may be the son of Moc'Tor, but you are nothing like him. Moc'Tor was a male of honor and devoted to his family. If he were alive, he would be ashamed of you for how you are acting."

Dak'Tor showed no reaction to Jhotin's remark, though inside, he was seething.

He did come to the Healer's Quarters later. The sun had long set, and it was well past evening meal. Tyria was sitting at Ei'Tol's side, lost in thought, keeping her company while she and the offling slept. The clack of the announcement stone startled her, and she rose as quietly as she could.

"I am here to see my mate. And my daughter," Dak'Tor said.

"It is late, and your mate and daughter are sleeping. They need their rest. Perhaps you could come by in the morning?"

"I am here now, and I am not going to be further criticized for not coming to see them on the day of my offling's birth." Dak'Tor pushed past Tyria and went to wake Ei'Tol.

Ei'Tol looked up sleepily. "You finally came."

"I was tied up in some things that could not wait," he said, ignoring the hurt look on her face. "Is she healthy?"

"Yes. The Healer says she is perfectly healthy. Do you want to see her?" she asked hopefully, preparing to clear the wrapping from the offling's face.

"No. Let her sleep. I should not have disturbed you. I will see you in the morning. How long before you will come home?"

"I will be home sometime tomorrow. Tyria will stop by now and then to see if I need any help," Ei'Tol said.

"Alright then. Get some rest." Dak'Tor turned and left without as much as a kiss or a hug for his mate.

Ei'Tol was glad to be back in her own quarters. As was the custom, some of the other females had prepared a nest for the new offling. They had also brought in and hung dried lavender to create a soothing environment. After both were settled, Ei'Tol's friends left her to rest and get further acquainted with her offling.

"What will I name you?" she said out loud, playing with her daughter's little fingers. "I cannot tell yet if you will have any of your father's silver coloring or if you will favor mine?"

She held her offling up in front of her, letting the little feet dangle free. "I am going to name you Diza, after the yellow flowers that bloom first in the spring."

Diza gurgled and seemed to smile, her chubby fingers clenching and unclenching.

Just as Ei'Tol was about to set Diza to nursing, someone arrived at the door.

Jhotin had come to visit them, bringing some fresh food for first meal. "I intercepted one of your friends bringing this; I hope you do not mind. I was coming to check on you anyway." He placed the foodstuffs next to Ei'Tol.

"How is she doing?" he asked.

"She seems to be a very calm offling so far."

"So far," Jhotin chuckled.

"I named her Diza."

"That is beautiful. After the bright yellow flowers that rim the riverbanks," Jhotin said. "I will leave you be. I am sure Tyria will also be in to check on you before too long. I hope you can manage to get some rest between so many visitors."

All the way back, Pan had more than enough time to think. The sparkling snow-covered landscape was evidence of the Great Spirit's artistic hand. The sound of the snow crunching under her feet, the winter birdsong, the mild rush of water around frozen ice all served to deepen her faith in the Great Spirit's love.

Ravu'Bahl stayed with her for the rest of the journey, only disappearing for short periods of time. At night he perched above her, and he greeted her each morning with his throaty caws.

Her return was more direct than the route that had taken her away, for which Pan was grateful. Finally, the mountain tops that cradled Kthama were in view, and she quickened her pace. The watchers sent word that the Guardian was on her way home, and Rohm'Mok thanked them profusely as if they were somehow to be credited with her return.

Just past twilight, Pan finally arrived at the High Rocks.

Before walking into the Great Entrance, Pan stomped the snow from her feet and legs and gave her whole body a shake to loosen the rest of it. Her mate was there waiting for her, holding little Tala in his arms. Behind him, a crowd, including her sisters, waited at a respectable distance to allow them space to greet each other first.

"I knew you would be safe, but I am still so relieved you are home," Rohm'Mok said. Pan stretched up to give him a discrete kiss and then took Tala from him.

"She has grown," Pan exclaimed, pulling the wrapping back to look at her daughter.

"It is possible." Rohm'Mok chuckled. "You have been gone quite a while."

Pan thanked everyone for coming to meet her. As she scanned the group, she noticed it was made up of Mothoc alone. "Only the Mothoc are here," she said to her mate.

"The Akassa were told you were returning," he said.

Again, more proof that the Akassa did not see everyone as part of the same community. Did they think they were not welcome? Surely it was not that they did not care.

"Why did none of them come?" Pan could not help but ask.

"The disparity between how they see us and how they see themselves widens despite our efforts otherwise. I suspect that, in their minds, they have elevated us to the point where they almost feel unworthy of joining us as equals. I fear that is why they did not come."

Trying to set aside her sadness at hearing this, Pan addressed the group. "Tomorrow, I will be glad to tell all of you about my trip. But right now, I want to eat something larger than a snowberry and spend some time with my mate and my daughter."

Everyone understood, and she and Rohm'Mok went to the Great Chamber.

"I am famished and sick of nuts and dried fruit," she said, looking down eagerly at the hearty serving of venison the servers brought her. It was one of her favorites, and she said a prayer of gratitude before finishing it off quickly. While she ate, Rohm'Mok filled her in on what had been going on at Kthama, including the healthy birth of Ei'Tol's offling.

Full at last, and after bidding the few others in the room a good night, Pan retired to her quarters with her family.

After she had Tala settled down, Pan told her mate about her journey to find the rebel Mothoc, their bitterness, and their threats against both the Sassen and the Akassa. When she mentioned how the black crow had led her to the rebel's home, Rohm'Mok told her how a black crow had come to him when he was praying for her safe return.

"Could it have been the same crow?" he wondered out loud.

"It would not surprise me," Pan replied.

Then Rohm'Mok stood up and went to her workspace. He told Pan to hold out her hand and in it placed the round red jasper the crow had dropped.

"A red jasper. My mother had a stone like this that Father gave her," she gasped, turning it over in her fingers, the deep red glinting against them. "Where did you get it?"

"Ravu'Bahl brought it. When he landed near me in the snow, he dropped it in front of me."

Pan closed her eyes and smiled. "The more I learn about the Order of Functions, the more I am in awe of the intricate workings of creation."

The next morning, as promised, Pan called all the Mothoc together for a private meeting.

"I know you are anxious to hear the details of my trip to Kayerm. A great deal has happened there, and I am sorry to say, much of it tragic."

Pan went on to tell them about how Straf'Tor's group had found the rebels already living at Kayerm, the poisoning of Ushca by Ridg'Sor, and his execution by Straf'Tor. Then she told them how she had found the rebel camp and described their hostile reception. That they had no interest in rejoining the Mothoc community.

She talked until she had covered everything she had been told, including Nox'Tor's death and that his son, Norland, was now Adik'Tar of Kayerm. She told them about Toniss and her mate Trak, both of whom many remembered.

When she finally stopped talking, Dochrohan asked, "How did they react to the news that they need to leave Kayerm?"

"Each according to their nature, as is the way of things. Those who accept change as an unavoidable part of life were positive. Those who struggle with change were less receptive. But, eventually, they will all come to see it as a blessing. They will be leaving behind a difficult and sad history and making a new start."

As time passed, the Mothoc in all the communities finally succeeded in drawing their Akassa counterparts into the meetings and discussions. Without telling them what was happening, the Mothoc discussed everything they could think of that the Akassa would need to know about or be able to do on their own once the Mothoc were gone. They spoke to individuals according to their skills and discreetly quizzed them on simple things from sowing and planting to stocking the water holding areas with fish for the winter and reading the stars. All the time they were testing the Akassa, the Mothoc were realizing more and more just how fatally dependent the Akassa were on them. Whatever resistance existed to Pan's proclamation that the

Mothoc had to withdraw from the lives of the Akassa was soon dispelled.

At the High Rocks, Tyria and Jhotin spent days on end with the Akassa Healer and Helper. Other Mothoc oversaw as the Akassa gathered, prepared, dried, tanned, wove, chopped, and sorted—then started all over again with the next season's provisions—silently assessing their abilities and readiness to move on without supervision.

Now that the Mothoc were paying dedicated attention to the differences, they became acutely aware not only of the Akassa's lack of strength but also their poor night vision. They could adapt to low light, but they had nothing near the acuity of the Mothoc. Though they had been warned not to do it, one experiment with a small fire inside for warmth for the young and the elderly soon proved that smoke was hard to dispel into the outside due to the high ceilings throughout Kthama. After that, the Akassa, chagrined, agreed that fires would only be allowed on the approval of the High Protector or Leader.

But where the Mothoc were superior in size and strength, the Akassa had their advantages. It had long been demonstrated that they were far more dexterous than the Mothoc, able to weave baskets and strips of hide more tightly. They could make needles out of bone for sewing hides together.

As promised, the Mothoc were taken in groups to the new location, which the High Council had named Bak'tah-Awhidi. When they returned, they gave their opinions to their Leaders, to be shared with the High Council when it next met. The trip was long, even for the Mothoc, but it mattered little as time was what was needed to prepare to leave their communities. Pan had decided that, though the Mothoc at Kayerm would eventually be joining them, they would not be involved in the preparation of their new home. There were so few Mothoc at Kayerm that the absence of any of them would be noted and not easily explained to the Sassen.

As time passed, Pan grew more and more aware of the need to return to Kayerm to see how they were progressing in their preparations.

While there were gains, there were also losses. The rift between Dak'Tor and his mate Ei'Tol grew wider and did not go unnoticed. Dak'Tor spent most of his time among the community or in isolation, and he took no interest in his daughter. In contrast, the Helper Jhotin had become a trusted friend of Ei'Tol's, a fact that was not lost on Dak'Tor and only advanced his dislike of the Healer's Helper.

CHAPTER 7

In the time that had passed since the Guardian's visit, the Leaders at Kayerm had focused on what Pan had charged them to do. But they were becoming anxious as they awaited her return.

Norland was up on the ridge, looking out at the sunrise breaking over the horizon. He was restless and feeling the need to take a mate. He was past the age when other males were usually paired. But when he looked around Kayerm, he saw no females he would want to pair with. He had grown up with them; some were his cousins and others simply friends. He hoped that the Guardian's leadership would mend the differences between the estranged Mothoc. Perhaps when the communities were reunited, he would meet a female who appealed to him.

Coming up behind him, Dotrat broke Norland's reverie. "It is beautiful."

Norland looked over at him and laughed. "When did you get so tall?"

"You are so involved in what has been going on that you have not realized how much time has passed. I am not your little brother any longer."

Norland smiled. "Time is passing quickly, it seems. How do you feel about leaving Kayerm?"

"A bit sad, which I think is natural. We grew up here. We have memories here, and since mother and Wosot were paired, I have never seen her so happy, and it has brought our family peace and security. However, many of the memories are unhappy, and in the end, I will be glad to leave. And another thing, there are no females here that I would want to be selected by."

"You too?" Norland asked. "It would just seem wrong to me. Like being paired with your sister!"

"If the Guardian brings all the remaining Mothoc together," said Norland, "there should be a large number of us. I am confident that in all that crowd, there will be someone there for each of us. And the same for our sisters. All in all, this will turn out to be a blessing; I am sure of it."

"But what will become of you?" Dotrat asked.

"I have thought of that. I am Adik'Tar here. And there are Adik'Tars at each of the other Mothoc communities. Who will become the head Leader? People are used to following the Leaders of their own communities. It will take the wisdom of Moc'Tor to resolve that one."

"Let us pray the Guardian is as wise as her father was." Dotrat paused. "I will miss my Sassen friends."

"We all will. Change is hard for us, but change is the nature of life."

In silence, they stood together a while longer.

Lorgil was sitting at Kyana's side watching her daughter playing with Kyana's daughters, who enjoyed their roles of big sister. Pagara was with them as the three had become good friends.

Kyana sighed. "I am sure everyone is wondering why I am not seeded yet."

"It could be his seed," the Healer offered. "He is older. It might have nothing to do with you at all."

"I doubt very much the problem is with him. He is very virile. But, it does not matter; it is happening to both of us," Kyana said.

"We are not the most fertile of species, but you have had four offling! Since the contagion, many of our females have had trouble becoming seeded. Do you know if Wosot sired offling before?"

"I try not to think of that, of who they are and where they might be. But yes, he has," she said.

"There is another possible reason," Pagara added. "It could simply be the will of the Great Spirit for you not yet to be seeded."

"I would accept that happily if it were the reason.

I just pray that I am not barren now and unable to give Wosot the family he deserves."

"You have given him a family; he has been a father to your offling far more than Nox'Tor ever was."

"I know," said Kyana. "I know what you are saying. But it is also me. I want to bear his offling. I want to know that once I am gone, there is a part of us, together, still here. An offling of ours who will be able to carry on the 'Tor bloodline."

The Healer leaned forward and rested her chin on her hand. She sighed. "Do you have the feeling that we are just waiting for something to happen?"

"The Guardian's return. Yes, we are all waiting for it, and it does seem as if the time is near. The Sassen are well established now, and Raddoc will make a fine Leader. He is respected and looked up to. I only hope that when we leave, it will not shake him as Straf'Tor's leaving shook us all."

Back in the tunnels of Kayerm, Wosot, Teirac, and Raddoc were taking a tour, looking for areas that might need to be shored up. Raddoc was the Sassen who would become the next Leader of Kayerm, though he had not yet been told.

"If there are issues," counseled Wosot, "they will show up on the westerly sides, as that is the direction the weather comes. Intense rain, snow, and winds can cause shifts in the ground above. But overall, you need have no fear. Kayerm has stood for a thousand years, and she will stand for thousands more.

"The direction of Kayerm's entrance is also to our benefit," he added. "The greatest threat would, of course, be a cave-in, but there is no reason to expect that unless the ground shakes."

"The ground shakes?" said Raddoc.

"It has happened. Sometimes the ground will shift under your feet," Wosot explained. "As if it is rocking. It does not happen very often, but when it does, that is the real danger. Even if there is no collapse at that point, the movement can weaken the structure, but the effects may not become apparent for some time.

"We are fairly high above the Great River and far enough away that we do not fear the rising of the waters in even the heaviest of spring melts. Though the waters overflow the banks, there is no fear of flooding within Kayerm. Just make sure the offling do not play there if there is any threat of flooding."

"Yes, none of us cares to get wet. We become so much heavier when our coats are soaked. And drying seems to take forever," Teirac chuckled.

"It is good to know this, but you will outlive us all," said Raddoc.

"The more everyone knows, the stronger the whole community is," Teirac commented.

Wosot looked at Teirac. "Come. We have spent

enough time on this. Raddoc will catch up with us later."

"Raddoc questioned why Teirac and I have been focusing so much on teaching him and the others since we will no doubt outlive each of our Sassen students," said Wosot to Norland.

"The Guardian left it to us to decide if and when the Sassen are to be told that the Mothoc will be leaving," Norland replied. "Knowing it would be a long while until the Guardian returned, I have not let them know. But perhaps it is time."

"I would say it is," said Wosot. "I can feel it coming; the time is not long now. But which is better, for them to be forewarned, or for us simply to disappear as Straf'Tor did?"

"Straf'Tor's disappearance affected us all, but it broke my father. He was never the same. He felt betrayed and abandoned. Though not everyone reacted that way, I would rather not run the risk. It will be hard enough on them as it is because they have looked to us for guidance, support, and protection all their lives. They have never known a time without us.

"Pan said it was my decision," Norland added, "but please find Toniss, Trak, Pagara, and my mother. I would like us to discuss this together."

Norland addressed his small circle. "I believe we are all feeling that the time is nearing when the Guardian will return to lead us to our new home. I know you have each done your part to prepare the Sassen for our leaving. I ask you now, is it time to tell them? I do not wish for us simply to disappear. I think that would cause more harm than good."

"I agree," said Toniss. "I think we break trust if we disappear. And it would create a mystery that no doubt some would wish to solve."

"We have prepared them in practical matters," said Pagara. "And I am confident we have done a good job. But we have not prepared them emotionally to live without us. That task still remains and cannot be done until they know we are leaving."

"The mantle of leadership, even if only self-leadership, can be difficult to bear," Norland mused. "Even I feel it. I admit I wish the Guardian had told me when to tell them. Making that decision on my own is difficult. So, I know that for them, in turn, having to take over and continue on without us will be even more difficult."

"So you are saying it is time?" Kyana asked.

Norland let out a long breath. "I am saying it is time."

Norland sent for Raddoc, the Sassen Leader, and Pallida, the Sassen Healer, whom Pagara had dutifully trained.

"Raddoc, I have watched you grow in wisdom and strength. I have seen you listen, learn, and seek knowledge from all who have it to give. And you, Pallida, I know from Pagara's testimony that you are an adept and compassionate Healer. Having been well prepared in the practical matters of life at Kayerm, it is time for you to take the next step."

"You are turning over your roles to us," said the Sassen Healer.

"I have seen it coming too," said Raddoc. "But it is more than that, is it not? It is worse than just handing direction to us."

"Worse is a matter of perspective," said Norland. "What one person sees as loss, another may see as gain. But you are right; it is time for you to begin leading Kayerm without us."

Raddoc sighed. "Without you?"

No one answered.

In the silence, Raddoc finally said, "I knew this was coming. And I knew it was something more than simply taking over for you and Pagara. Something far greater is happening. You are not just leaving us in charge; you are leaving us. Leaving Kayerm."

"Yes." Norland glanced around at the others. "We, as well as every other Mothoc here, will be leaving Kayerm."

"*Why*? And when?" Pallida asked.

"The fact is, you do not need us any longer," said Trak. "You are capable of guiding your own lives. Our presence here, while it was helpful until now, has become a hindrance."

"As long as we are here," agreed Norland, "you will not move into the future of your own making."

"But we do not want you to leave," exclaimed Pallida. "Do we have no say in it?"

"No. I am sorry, you do not; this is how it has to be." Norland spoke as kindly as possible.

After a few moments, Pallida asked again, "When are you leaving?"

"We do not know," Norland answered. "But we all feel the time is nearly here."

"This must be shared with everyone immediately," said Pallida. "They will need time to adjust to it, just as Raddoc and I do."

"In time, the sting will pass." Kyana spoke gently. "To the generations to come, we will be only a story, carried along into memory on the stream of passing time. But we recognize that we have relationships with you. Ties. We care deeply about you. It is also hard for us."

Norland nodded. "It is time to share this with the rest of the community, to help them understand that, as Kyana said, though we will be apart from all of you, we will still carry you in our hearts."

. . .

Standing side-by-side, Norland and the new Sassen Leader, together with the new Sassen Healer, addressed the community, explaining that in time all the Mothoc would be leaving. Many of the Sassen were stunned. Some were angry, feeling betrayed. Pallida was right; it would take them time to adjust. Just one more in what seemed like an unending assault of losses they'd had to endure.

When Kyana and Wosot were alone, relaxing on their sleeping mat, she asked him, "Do you still look forward to leaving here?"

"I am ready."

"What will it be like, to see your old friends? No doubt many will feel much joy, but I am sure there will also be difficulties. Many of those here left family to follow Straf'Tor. Relationships were harmed, feelings hurt."

"It will be hard on us all," replied Wosot, "though I have few ties from the past that I wish to revive. For our offling, and those to follow, it will simply be what is. For those of our population who left Kthama with the Sassen, the tearing away from yet another home will be painful."

"I wish we could already have seen our new home. I hope that there will be the same amount of space for everyone. I know that is a petty thing, but it will impact our lives, and I cannot help but think about it."

"We will be wise to approach this one step at a time. Once our basic needs are met—knowing where we will live, the water and food sources, getting to learn the weather patterns and the stars—we will all feel more comfortable. At first, everything will be unfamiliar. Here, we know every twist in each tunnel, every chip in the walls, where the footing or the slope changes suddenly, the best fishing shoals, the animals' migratory paths. We will have much to learn, but we will learn it together," and Wosot pulled Kyana tightly into his arms.

"There is something else worrying me," Kyana said. "Something unspoken between us for some time now."

Wosot fell silent, giving her room to speak frankly.

"I am ashamed that I have not been able to give you an offling. You deserve to have it all, and I have failed you."

"The reason could be mine. We both know I am a lot older than you. I am grateful that you have Norland, Dotrat, Lai, and Somnil."

"They are as much your offling as mine," she said.

"I know that, so now rest and put that concern from your mind. I have you, the desire of my heart. The fact that you are lying here in my arms is a miracle in itself."

Kyana tried to take comfort in Wosot's loving words. But her heart was heavy, and she could not seem to let go of her disappointment that she had not yet been seeded to give Wosot a son or daughter.

Pan and Rohm'Mok stood before the Mothoc High Council. It was a large gathering, and all the Mothoc Leaders, Healers, and Helpers from every community were there. Everyone knew in their heart what was coming; they were just waiting for the Guardian to declare it so.

"Greetings," said Pan. "And welcome. Thank you for leaving your homes so we could meet together at this very important time. Each of you has no doubt felt the leading of the Great Spirit that the time is close for us to take the final step in the vision inspired by my father to avoid the extinction of the Mothoc blood from Etera. There is one step left for us. In my father's wisdom, I believe he knew that at some point it would come to this."

Rohm'Mok spoke next, "Each of you has prepared those of the Akassa who will be taking over once we are gone. You have also prepared those Mothoc who are not part of the High Council for what is to come. As I look around, I see there is little left to do here at the High Rocks. And I know it is the same in your communities. The physical changes have been made. The only step left is the actual leaving. When you return, instruct your friends and family to decide what personal items they will take with them. Anything not to be taken must be destroyed. There must be no signs of us left."

After the High Council had finished for the morning, Pan called a meeting of the rest of the Mothoc of the High Rocks to do as she had just instructed the other Leaders.

When Pan had finished telling everyone that the time was coming for them to leave Kthama and how to prepare for that, a female voice rose from the crowd.

"What will become of the Akassa?" she asked.

"Emotionally, it will be hard for them—and us—but we have prepared them to take care of and lead themselves. In time, they will adjust. Have faith. It had to be this way. We may not see the Great Spirit's hand in what has taken place, but we must trust that everything is unfolding as it should. The Akassa must learn to walk without us, just as the Sassen at Kayerm must. There can be no possibility that in the future, after the pain of the Wrak-Wavara has passed from memory, the Akassa might affect the Sassen by their very existence. The Sassen blood must not be further diluted."

Throughout the time which had passed since the

Ror'Eckrah, it had never been spoken of openly. But now, in her heart, Pan knew it was time.

"At the time of the great division when the Fathers-Of-Us-All invoked the Ror'Eckrah, they spoke of the Age of Shadows."

A hush fell over the crowd.

"I do not know what the Wrak-Ayya, the Age of Shadows, is or when it will fall. But I do know that, in time, one known as The Promised One, the An'Kru, will come. When he attains his full power, he will usher in the Wrak-Ashwea, the Age of Light. Until then, we will continue with our lives. We will serve Etera as we always have. And in time, Bak'tah-Awhidi will become our home."

While everyone was reflecting on this revelation, Ei'Tol stepped forward from the crowd.

"Please, Guardian, for those of us who have not visited Bak'tah-Awhidi, how are the living quarters being assigned?"

"Bak'tah-Awhidi is a large system. Though I had not thought it possible, I am told it is more elaborate than even Kthama and well suited to our needs. There is no Mother Stream running through it, but there is a rich water source nearby, and the vortex is strong. There are multiple levels, as there are here, but with many more branches. There is no telling how far through Etera the caverns stretch. The entrance is secluded and not immediately notice-able. There will be more than enough room for all the people from all our communities as well as those joining us from Kayerm."

"Will we be separated from those who come from Kayerm?" someone else asked.

Dochrohan, the High Protector, spoke, "Great thought has been put into the planning. All the communities will be separate from one another, each housed in an area of their own. The Deep Valley, the Far High Hills, the Little River, the Great Pines, and so on, each under the authority of their own Leaders.

"After we are settled, we will look at improvements, and we welcome your input," said Rohm'Mok. "If you are unhappy with your assigned quarters, there is room for adjustment. We are luckily not short on space."

In the back of the room, Dak'Tor was in his usual spot as far away from Ei'Tol as possible. Pan occasionally glanced back at him, each time noting how his sour expression had seemed to take on a permanent set.

More questions were asked and answered, and Pan was encouraged by the interest, though she knew some of it was from anxiety and not all from positive anticipation.

As they were dispersing, Ei'Tol came up to Pan and Rohm'Mok, who were standing together.

"I realize this is indelicate for you, Guardian, as he is your brother, but I do not wish to be assigned living quarters with Dak'Tor."

Pan had seen the estrangement between Dak'Tor

and his mate as well as the time Ei'Tol and Jhotin spent together. Jhotin, having taken an interest in Ei'Tol's daughter, had effectively become Diza's second parent.

"Are you asking for a temporary assignment for you and Diza?" Pan asked.

"No. I am asking for a permanent separation from Dak'Tor. In every way."

"If what you are asking is for your pairing with Dak'Tor to be set aside, I believe this should be brought before the High Council," Pan said. "To my knowledge, it has never happened before." Seeing the distraught look on Ei'Tol's face, she added, "We are reconvening after midday meal. Please join us at that time and make your petition known."

Immediately after Ei'Tol had left, Dak'Tor approached his sister.

"What was that about?" he asked sharply.

Pan replied, knowing Dak'Tor would find out eventually. "Your mate wishes to have separate quarters officially assigned to her and the offling at Bak'-tah-Awhidi."

"Are you going to allow that? You are my sister; tell me you are not going to agree to it?" His voice rose, and he scowled angrily.

"It is not my decision. It will be brought before the High Council after midday meal," Pan answered, looking at her brother, whose attitude had inexplicably been growing progressively worse.

"Why did you not just refuse her? It is bad

enough that she cavorts around the High Rocks with that Helper. Now this? What is next? Will he move in with her and my daughter?"

"There is no reason to deny her; there are more than enough spaces for her and your daughter to have their own room," Pan said. "Now, please drop it; this is High Council business."

As the High Council members came back to order, Pan scanned the room. Near the entrance stood Ei'Tol, watching Dak'Tor leave. As soon as he was out of the room and the High Council had settled down, Pan announced that one of the members of the High Rocks community wanted to address the council and then signaled for her to speak.

Ei'Tol stepped forward and faced the group. "Earlier, I approached the Guardian and Leader of the High Rocks to tell her that I want a permanent separation from my mate, Dak'Tor. She told me I would have to ask this of you, the High Council."

Everyone was very still. Dak'Tor slipped back into the room unnoticed by all except those standing at the entrance.

Ei'Tol noticed Dak'Tor and swallowed hard. "I want to apologize for putting the Guardian in an awkward position since my mate is her brother. Had I known that this was the proper place to bring my request, I would not have gone to her," she said, looking over at Pan.

"You do not need to apologize," Hatos'Mok said. "Pan is the Leader of the High Rocks and would ordinarily be the one to approach with a question that directly affects her community. But because this situation has not happened before, it should be decided by the High Council. So, to be clear, what you are asking for is for your pairing to Dak'Tor to be set aside?"

"What!" Dak'Tor exploded from the back of the room and came rushing forward. Before he could reach Ei'Tol, Dochrohan and Bakru stopped him.

"What are you talking about?" Dak'Tor said as he wildly tried to shrug off their restraint. "You no longer want to be paired with me? That is not even reasonable. There is no provision for such a thing!" he shouted.

Pan had never seen her brother so openly out of control. "I ask that you calm down, Dak'Tor. That is why I asked Ei'Tol to bring her request here to the High Council. To my knowledge, no one has asked for this before."

Hatos'Mok stood. "Ei'Tol, I do not mean to make light of whatever issues there are between you and your mate. But all pairings go through good and bad times. There is probably not one of us here who at some time has not wished they had never been paired."

Several in the group nodded and chuckled,

welcoming the break in the tension.

"You may change your mind in time," he added.

"Perhaps a new start will help," counseled another. "There is no need for such a drastic move on top of the upheaval we are about to go through."

"With all due respect, I will not change my mind," Ei'Tol said firmly. "For some time, Dak'Tor has not been a true mate to me in any way. He has no interest in our offling and has not had from the day she was born. Our estrangement is not a passing phase; it is the only life my daughter knows. It is no secret that he took separate living quarters almost immediately after her birth. Moving to a new location is not the cause nor the solution to this problem," Ei'Tol answered. "I find it fitting that our new home will be called Bak'tah-Awhidi, which in part means *new beginning*, for that is what I am asking you to grant me."

"Do not blame me for this," Dak'Tor shouted. "Everyone at the High Rocks knows that this is not about *me*. This is about Jhotin's interference. *He* is the reason for our problems. Surely you can all see what has truly happened here?"

Pan spoke up again. "Part of what my brother says is true; it is no secret that Jhotin and Ei'Tol are close. Jhotin spends time with Ei'Tol and her daughter. Even now, he is caring for Ei'Tol's daughter and mine in the Healer's Quarters. Regardless, is that not the nature of the calling of the Healer and Helper? It is a relationship of support and shared dedication.

Yes, they appear to be close. However, there has never been an accusation of unfaithfulness against Ei'Tol."

"Why are you taking her side?" Dak'Tor asked. "I am your brother. You should have refused her request when she asked you instead of taking the coward's way out and making her bring it here."

Pan's face fell at her brother's insult. "It is not within my authority to grant the dissolution of a pairing. It has never happened before, and whatever is decided will set a precedent for all our people. It would have been an abuse of my authority to decide such a matter myself, brother. Can you not understand that?"

"What I understand is that you do not care about what happens to me. You do not care how this will humiliate me. You have the power; you just do not want to help me. *I should never have put the Leader's Staff in your room and made you Leader!*"

The entire room gasped. Pan almost stumbled. Then a deafening silence fell over the huge chamber.

"What did you say?" Pan managed to ask. "You put the Leader's Staff in my room? You moved the 'Tor staff? From where?"

"Yes, I moved it from my room," he shouted, trying again to shake off Dochrohan and Bakru's hold on him. "I did not want to be Leader. I told Father that, but he would not listen. I thought you were the better choice. Now I see I was wrong."

"Oh, Dak'Tor. *What have you done*?" Pan could

not help it. She was overcome and turned to her mate at her side for comfort. Rohm'Mok put his arms around her as she leaned her head against his broad chest.

"Sacrilege," said Hatos'Mok coming quickly to his feet. "If what you are saying is true, you have committed a grievous crime."

Pan covered her hand with her mouth, reeling from her brother's confession. *My father did not betray me.* He had never intended for her to be the Leader of the High Rocks.

Tres'Sar from the Far High Hills stood up, his face contorted. "Dak'Tor, do you realize the consequences of what you have done?"

"If you were paying attention, what I have just done is tell you that my sister is not the rightful Leader of the High Rocks. *I am!*" Dak'Tor practically bellowed.

Many shook their heads at his response.

"What you have done," Hatos'Mok replied, "is admitted you have perpetrated a fraud not only on the people of the High Rocks but on all of us, the High Council included." In his anger, he took a step toward Dak'Tor.

"In addition, you have betrayed your sister's trust at the deepest level. We all witnessed her struggle to make peace with what she understood was your father's choice for her to lead. To her credit, she accepted the responsibility and has served with honor. There is no counting the damage you have done and the seriousness of the injustice you have foisted upon her."

"You are missing the point," Dak'Tor snarled.

"No. *You* are missing the point," Hatos'Mok said, then looked to his son Rohm'Mok.

"Considering the new information, I am asking for a vote on the matter of Ei'Tol's request for Bak'-tah-Awhidi," Rohm'Mok said. "Those who agree that her pairing to Dak'Tor should be dissolved, please stand."

Every single seated body stood.

Pan, as Overseer, declared, "*Kah-Sol 'Rin.* Your request has been granted. Go in peace."

Ei'Tol thanked Pan and the others at the front and then the crowd behind her.

Slowly, reason returned to Dak'Tor's mind. Seeing he had lost, it started to dawn on him what the other Leaders had been saying.

He clenched his teeth and forced himself to calm down. It took all his self-control to keep from watching Ei'Tol leave the room, and he realized that in one moment of anger, he had thrown away all the time and energy spent in concealing the truth. In trying to avoid the humiliation of his mate leaving him, Dak'Tor had put himself in a grave situation. He would have to think fast to undo the jeopardy his confession had just created.

"High Council. I apologize for my outburst. Please give me a moment to collect myself."

The room felt silent until Dak'Tor spoke again. "You must forgive me. I love my mate. Despite our problems, I never betrayed her. I have not been the best mate or father, but it grieves me deeply that you would allow our pairing to be dissolved. Set aside. As if it never existed. Nevertheless, you are the Leaders, and I must bow to your decision."

Everyone waited for him to continue.

"As for my so-called confession. Again, I lost control and allowed my emotions to take over. What I said about putting the 'Tor Leader's Staff in my sister's room was a lie. I only said that to hurt her. I realize now that it was a terrible thing to say."

He turned to face his sister, "Forgive me. I never moved the Leader's Staff. You are and have always been the rightful Leader of the High Rocks."

Pan's mind was reeling. All that struggling to understand why their father had chosen her and not her brother had been resolved in the instant of Dak'-Tor's confession. Now he was saying it was not true. But in her soul, she knew it was devastatingly true.

Hatos'Mok spoke up, "I am glad that reason has returned; however, the fact that you said it, even if untrue, is in itself a serious crime. And if what you confessed is true, the consequences should be well known to you. We need some time to discuss the situation and come to a resolution about your behavior."

"Dochrohan, Bakru; escort Dak'Tor to his quarters while we discuss what will be done about this situation," said Rohm'Mok.

"Do you wish him restrained?" asked the High Protector. Rohm'Mok looked to his father for help. This was his mate's brother, after all.

Hatos'Mok thought of Pan and how devastated she already was at her brother's betrayal. He did not want to deepen her anguish, "No. We will trust him to behave himself for the short time we will be in session. He is in enough trouble; I doubt he wants to bring any more down on his head," Hatos'Mok said, locking his gaze on Dak'Tor's.

Dochrohan and Bakru took Dak'Tor to his individual living quarters. Once inside, he turned to them.

"You have been at their meetings. You have seen the High Council in action before. Are they going to banish me?" Dak'Tor asked.

Dochrohan looked at Bakru, then back to Dak'-Tor, "Considering what you have done, you had better pray that is *all* they do to you."

The room turned to chatter as soon as Dak'Tor was gone.

Hatos'Mok spoke first, "Now that he has been removed, let us decide what the punishment will be for Dak'Tor's betrayal of us all, but most of all his sister."

"If I may," Pan said, "emotions are still running high right now. For myself, perhaps more than anyone. I ask that any other matters be considered before we move to my brother's actions."

Hatos'Mok looked closely at Pan and could see her exhaustion. "Then let us also take a short break."

Pan was too upset to return to their quarters and did not want to collect her son from Jhotin in her present state. She asked Rohm'Mok to escort her to the meadow above Kthama.

"Are you going to enter the Aezaiteran stream?" he asked as they walked.

"No. There is no time for that, and I do not want to keep everyone else waiting. I just want to be away from all the others, and I know I will not be disturbed here. Stay with me, please? I will not take long."

Pan walked away from him to where she usually discharged her duties as the Guardian. But instead of sending her consciousness down into the vortex, she lay down and closed her eyes in prayer. *Please, Great Spirit. This has been such a long and difficult journey. I am not sure I know what to believe any longer. My role, my decisions, my belief in the Order of Functions. Help me find my way. Help my disbelief.*

Fuming, Dak'Tor paced around his quarters for a while. Filled with anger and fear, he decided he would not give them the satisfaction of banishing him. He would leave on his own.

He poked his head outside. Seeing no guards, he crept down the hallway toward the levels that led to the Mother Stream. But before he had gotten far, a thought occurred to him. They were no doubt still discussing his punishment. They had not had time to decide, let alone announce it to the community. No one outside the High Council knew he was in trouble, so he did not need to slink around.

As he continued on, another thought occurred to him. The crystal. *Father said the crystal was powerful, that it was invaluable.* Perhaps he could figure out how to use it. It was meant for him, anyway.

Dak'Tor changed direction and headed down the tunnel to Pan's quarters. He listened at the door. Hearing nothing, he carefully opened it and entered. He sighed in relief when he saw the staff in plain sight and grasped it to feel around for the seam. He finally found it and pried off the cap. The crystal was safely encased in its recess at the bottom of the small chamber. He tried to remove it but found it was stuck. Using both hands, he finally popped it out of place. Although his fingers were shaking, Dak'Tor set the crystal aside and hurriedly attempted to re-assemble the staff, being careful to match the grains of the two pieces and then to put the staff back where he had found it.

He left and ducked into someone else's empty quarters. Looking around the room for something to protect the crystal, he grabbed a carrying basket. He tucked the crystal safely in the bottom before going into the food preparation area and packing all the food he could find. On top, he placed an empty gourd for collecting water. Then he walked confidently toward the lower levels.

Within a few moments, he was on his way up the Mother Stream.

Pan opened her eyes to a place of indescribable depth and beauty. Where colors were more vibrant, textures deeper, sounds richer and more pleasing than anything on Etera. *She was back in the Corridor.* She blinked, and in the place where there had been no one, once again stood her mother, E'ranale.

"Mama!" She flew into her mother's arms, as she had the first time.

"Thank you, thank you. Oh! I need you now, so much."

"I know. It is not often we interfere in anyone's life journey in Etera's realm. But in certain situations, it is allowed," E'ranale said, resting her chin on her daughter's head.

"Dak'Tor betrayed me. Not Father. Dak'Tor was Father's choice to lead the High Rocks. Did you know that?"

"Yes. I knew that."

"Why did you not tell me?"

"My dearest daughter, each of us has our own path to walk. And the experiences along that path, especially the difficult ones, prepare us for what is to come next. If I prevent you from going through what is yours to experience, I cheat you of the growth that should have come as a result. And that growth from that experience, no matter how hard, prepares you for the next step.

"Life on Etera is one of transformation, change, growth," she continued. "Unfortunately, that growth sometimes only comes from situations brought to us that we would not willingly choose."

"What am I to do now? What will become of Dak'Tor?" Pan asked.

"Your brother has chosen a difficult path. Remember this in your moments of worry and compassion for him. They will come, I assure you. After the anger and pain of his betrayal fade, your heart will soften toward him. It is then, when the shell of your anger breaks, that you must be careful not to excuse what he has done or what he does in the future."

Pan hid her confusion. "Father did not betray me.

He meant for the mantle of leadership to pass to Dak'Tor."

"Your father knew that you did not wish to lead Kthama. He knew that you would be carrying a great burden by being the Guardian and that his death alone carried the potential to crush you. He sought to spare you the additional burden. But the Great Spirit had other plans. The leadership of the High Rocks is yours, as it should be."

"Dak'Tor moved the Leader's Staff from his room to mine. But he touched it first, so the mantle passed to him. So how can I be the rightful Leader?"

"Your father was and is a great soul. I have always loved him with a depth that perhaps only a few can understand. However, as with any of us, he is not infallible. But this is the power and the love and the amazing benevolence of the Three-Who-Are-One. Ahead even of the mistakes we are yet to make, the All-That-Is has already laid out a new path."

E'ranale continued, "Dearest Pan, the mantle of leadership is not transferred by touching the Leader's Staff. The staff itself is only a symbol. It is a physical representation of the trust and authority placed in one as Leader. The Leader's Staff is only a representation of the position. Something physical to hold on to and to display, part of ritual and tradition, as both are important for any culture."

"So there is nothing magical about the Leader's Staff," Pan said, almost sadly.

"That is not what I said. Yes, there is magic within

the Leader's Staff. By virtue of the people's belief in it, by their trust in the one who carries it, therein lies its power. So it is with the staff of each Leader. Though, in the case of the staff of the House of Tor, there is more to it than that, as I have told you."

"You are speaking of the crystal within? That is why Father never told me about it. Father told Dak'Tor because he had chosen him to lead, not me. Mother, help me understand. What happened to Dak'Tor to make him so? We were both raised by you and Father; we both had the same siblings."

"While it seems that, being in the same family, you all should have had the same experiences growing up, if you were not distraught right now, you would know the answer. But aside from the fact that no two experiences are ever the same, seen from different viewpoints, no two souls are alike. What crushes one may only incentivize another to grow stronger. Your brother was never strong within himself; you know this. He often took advantage of his position as the son of the Leader and never pushed himself past his limits. But I do not disparage him. I love him dearly, as does the Great Spirit, and we all have our strengths and weaknesses.

"But you have asked, so I will answer your question. Dak'Tor is very clever in how he speaks, he uses well-chosen words to cover up his real intentions, so it may not be obvious what the truth is. He will try to manipulate a situation rather than to figure out a way to resolve it openly and directly."

E'ranale paused, aware that Pan could not handle much more.

"Your brother could have accepted your father's decision. He could have tried to grow into the leadership. Or, he could have approached the High Council and asked to be excused, for lack of a better word. Instead, he chose a more difficult path. He is not without a conscience. The guilt at his betrayal of you, and your father, has weighed more and more heavily on him as time has passed. It is that which has caused the change in his behavior, the bitterness you have seen growing in him."

Despite the beauty and wonder of the situation and her mother's presence, Pan's heart was heavy, "Why is life so hard? Why does the Great Spirit not take away these struggles? Tell us what to do instead of letting us make mistakes."

"Is that really what you want? To have no control over your life? Not to have your own dreams, your own goals, and the ability to pursue them? Nearly every soul on Etera asks this same question at some point, but there can be no self-direction without free will, without the ability to make our own choices."

"You know all you need to know for now," E'ranale continued. "But understanding it is not enough; it is the test of living it that changes us. When all seems lost, remind yourself of the loving heart, will, and mind of the One-Who-Is-Three and that no matter the appearance, everything is working for the good of all who serve the Great Spirit. Help will come when you need it most, perhaps from an unexpected source.

"When you return to your body, you will find that more time has passed than the few moments we have shared here."

In the next moment, Pan opened her eyes. Overhead where before there had been a canopy of afternoon summer clouds and sky, now twilight was descending. She stirred, and Rohm'Mok immediately stirred from where he was curled up at her side.

"Finally, you have returned!" he exclaimed. "You worried me; I have never seen you so sound asleep. You must have entered the Aezaiteran stream after all?"

"No. And I am fine," she said, sitting up and rubbing her eyes. "Did I miss the High Council meeting?" she asked.

"No. When we did not return right away, one of the guards came looking and found us here. I thought you must, after all, be exercising your duty as the Guardian and asked him to tell the High Council. They did not wish to continue without you, so they are still waiting for your return."

Pan looked around. "It is later than it should be, as she said."

"Who said that?" Rohm'Mok asked, confused.

"There is much I need to tell you; It is time that

you know. I only pray you do not think I have lost my mind. But, for now, we must return to the High Council. I have kept them long enough."

It was nearly twilight by the time he surfaced. Dak'Tor looked left and right, not sure where to go next. He knew that the Great River snaked north, so there was little chance of getting lost if he followed her banks. Unfortunately, anyone looking for him would also think of that.

For once in his life, Dak'Tor pushed himself, still being careful that no one was following him, though he was nearly exhausted by his fear. As he walked, the seriousness of his situation surfaced yet again. Despite never having been one of great faith, in his fear, he did something he had seldom done. He asked the Great Spirit for help.

Pan apologized profusely to the High Council for keeping them waiting so long.

Honoring her earlier request, Hatos'Mok asked Pan to bring up the next subject.

"High Council, I am Leader of the High Rocks, Guardian of Etera and also Overseer of the High Council. I have come to accept that it is not only a great burden to have to carry so many responsibilities, but that, in some way, it is not appropriate. Once we are through this, I would like to suggest that a new Overseer be selected. That is, assuming that you do not set aside my position as Leader of the High Rocks based on my brother's statement."

"Regardless of your brother's actions and your father's intention, there is no doubt in my mind or my heart that you are the rightful Leader of the High Rocks," said Tres'Sar of the Far High Hills.

"I agree," said Pnatl'Rar from the Little River. "You often speak of the Order of Functions and how matters unfold as they should. Your brother would have been a terrible Leader—forgive me, but it is true. Where you are self-sacrificing, he is self-centered. Where you are wise, he is short-sighted. You live to serve Etera; he lives to serve himself."

Pan closed her eyes. Though what Pnatl'Rar was saying was true, it hurt to hear it spoken openly. "This is my brother you speak of."

Pnatl'Rar continued. "Yes, but truth is the foundation of service to the Great Spirit. It may be painful for you to hear, but it is necessary that you do. You must understand this in your soul; that which appears to be a mistake, at least in my mind, was the most beneficial turn of events possible."

Rohm'Mok leaned toward Pan and whispered. "Listen to them, Saraste', you must hear this, lest this betrayal cripples you—as your belief that your father betrayed you almost did in the beginning."

"As to the matter of the High Rocks itself," said

Hatos'Mok, "now that the Guardian has expressed doubt about her position as Leader, I am calling for a vote of confidence in the Guardian's continued position as Leader of the High Rocks. Practically, it is a moot point. Dak'Tor's crime makes him ineligible to be Leader, anyway. The duty, therefore, falls to one of the other siblings, and I doubt either of Pan's sisters would challenge her for the leadership."

Many in the crowd voiced their agreement.

"Those who support the Guardian in continued leadership here at Kthama, please stand. If you are already standing, please remain so."

Everyone in the room agreed that Pan should continue as Leader of the High Rocks.

That being settled, Rohm'Mok spoke. "There is one last item before we turn to the subject of Dak'-Tor. My mate has asked to be removed as Overseer. Before we consider Dak'Tor's punishment, I believe it would be wise to settle this matter before we set out for our new home. Are there any nominations?" he asked.

There was a moment of silence before Solok'Tar from the Great Pines, who had remained silent for the most part, spoke up. "As obvious as it is that the Guardian continue as Leader of the High Rocks, I think the choice for Overseer is also as obvious. Hatos'Mok."

Everyone immediately indicated their agreement without a vote being called for.

"In that case, I accept," said Hatos'Mok. "And I

thank you for the faith you are placing in me. It is unpleasant that my first task as overseer will be dealing with Dak'Tor. But before we turn to that, I must say that I no longer think Bak'tah-Awhidi is a suitable name for our new home. It will forever be tinged with the historic dissolution of Dak'Tor and Ei'Tol's pairing and the subsequent painful revelations. Do you agree, and does anyone have any ideas?"

A few names were called out, and finally, Pan offered, "Lulnomia."

The females in the group looked at each other, and Tyria finally asked, "*Precious basket*?" to which several chuckled.

Pan welcomed the break in tension and even smiled herself. "I was going for *sacred weaving*. As in, the weaving of our lives together again into one pattern."

"Ah, yes," Tyria smiled.

Hatos'Mok saw almost every face smiling and nodding, so he stated that Lulnomia would be the name to replace Bak'tah-Awhidi.

He let the moment of levity last as long as he could before turning to Pan.

"Guardian, do you have any real reason to believe your brother was speaking the truth when he said he moved the 'Tor Leader's Staff to your room?"

"That is a wise question. Perhaps it was as he said, he was just striking out to hurt you," offered someone.

"My brother said that he left the staff in the corner of my room. No one but the person who put it there would know that. I have never said that it was in the corner, only that I found it in the room," she said, her face now blank. "You can ask anyone."

"But," said someone else. "Is not the Leader's Staff always kept in a corner? It is an obvious place to prop any upright tool."

"This is true!" Pan let out a long sigh, relieved that it was a lie after all. Then her face fell.

"What is it? You must tell us, no matter how difficult," said Solok'Tar.

Pan continued with what she had just realized. "It is a common practice, as you say, to prop a tall tool in a corner. But the Leader's Staff is not a tool. There are rituals Leaders must observe with the sacred staff. A Leader's Staff is always propped in the most eastward corner. Even though sunrise does not reach into our quarters, it is a symbolic placement. It is put there so the dawn of each new day greets it. This reminds the Leader to seek anew the wisdom and guidance of the Great Spirit. Every Leader here knows this. Dak'Tor left the staff in the western corner. It did not occur to me until just now when you asked. My father would never have left the staff in the waning corner."

Tres'Sar said, "I can affirm this. That would be a dreadful start to new leadership. No Leader would put the staff in any corner but the east. And certainly not Moc'Tor. I am sure Moc'Tor taught Dak'Tor that, but he himself has demonstrated, Dak'Tor does not think clearly when his emotions are high. In his haste, no doubt sneaking it into Pan's room, he forgot the proper placement."

Hatos'Mok hung his head for a moment, "With that revelation, there seems no doubt that Dak'Tor's confession was the truth. I do not need to belabor the seriousness of what he has done, nor, I think, do any of you. So, I will give you a moment, and then I will call on each of you to state what you think the punishment should be."

Pan interjected. "I hope you will not see it as weakness that I ask to be excused from voting."

"No one here will look down on you for your request," Hatos'Mok said.

"Thank you." Pan looked at him with gratitude.

Then she reached down deep and steeled herself. Dak'Tor's was a crime without precedent, and though the most likely punishment was banishment, she could not be certain. Today seemed to be the day for the High Council to set new precedents.

One by one, each of the High Council members stood. Nearly to a person, the vote was for banishment. Toward the end, however, one member stood and called for Dak'Tor's execution. It was Pnatl'Rar, Leader of the Little River, who had introduced Dak'Tor to Ei'Tol.

Pan could not help it and jumped to her feet,

"Please, no. I do not challenge your opinion, and this may well be the just response, but I am asking for mercy. We are on the brink of a new beginning. Let us not stain that new beginning with blood."

"I understand, Guardian," said Pnatl'Rar. "I will amend my vote to banishment, to match the others."

Pan let out a huge sigh and sat back down, covering her face with her hands.

The vote was unanimous.

"Dak'Tor will be banished from all the Mothoc, Akassa, and Sassen communities," stated Hatos'Mok. "I respect the pain this causes you, Guardian. We will allow a day or so for him to prepare himself. Unfortunately, there is no way for it to be kept a secret, nor do I believe you would ask us to do so. It is too likely that the truth will be distorted if it is not spoken of openly."

In retrospect, the decisions made that day were the fastest decisions the High Council had ever made. All were grateful that all three resolutions passed had been reached unanimously. All had peace in their hearts and minds that they had made the right decisions, however difficult.

However, had there not been such a delay in reconvening, the consequences that followed might have been very different.

Finally, too exhausted to continue, Dak'Tor decided that since it was late and he had come a considerable way, he should try to sleep for a little while. They might not yet know he had escaped, but, regardless, as no one had caught up with him by now, he felt confident they would never do so.

CHAPTER 8

With the last item decided, Hatos'Mok sent Dochrohan to bring Dak'Tor to hear his fate. But before long, the High Protector returned to say he was not to be found. Another search for him around the immediate area outside came up empty. Dak'Tor was nowhere to be found within or outside of Kthama.

After some time, the High Council reconvened.

"He was certain he would be banished, or worse, so he left instead," said Pan.

"Where would he go, I wonder?" Rohm'Mok mused.

"I do not want to think about it," said Pan, sick at heart. "Whether banished or off on his own, he is not suited to either. He has basic skills, but he did not take the time to hone them. Do you think someone helped him escape? Went with him, perhaps?"

Rohm'Mok said, "If so, we will know in time. If

someone else is missing, their family will say something."

He turned to the other High Council members, "Should we send scouts to try and pick up his trail?"

Pan knew Rohm'Mok was trying to give her some hope that Dak'Tor could be found.

She slowly shook her head. "But to what point? What would happen if we did find him, only to banish him again? It is pointless."

Pan knew that the sentries would not pick up his trail. The single thing her brother had found intriguing and had taken the trouble to learn was how to track, and therefore how to evade trackers. He would have traveled along the stream bed and have varied his methods so no one would be able to follow him.

Some of the other Leaders spoke up and agreed it was senseless to try to find Dak'Tor only to banish him. Since that was the expected punishment, Dak'Tor would have resigned himself to it and so left ahead of time. Hatos'Mok dismissed the High Council, and Pan and Rohm'Mok collected Tala and returned to their quarters.

"I do not know if I can feel any worse than I do right now," Pan said to her beloved mate.

"None of this was your doing. And what could you have done to stop it?"

Pan shook her head. "I feel I should have been able to do something, and now we are getting ready to leave for Lulnomia. He does not know where it is."

"He is banished. He cannot join us at Lulnomia either, even if he did know where it was." Rohm'Mok tried to say it gently, realizing she was distraught and not thinking clearly.

The items Dak'Tor had stolen from the empty living quarters had gone unnoticed. When the occupants realized that items were missing, they did not connect them to Dak'Tor's disappearance.

Dak'Tor had positioned himself so the sun's morning rays would wake him the minute they came over the horizon. However, it was not the morning rays that awoke him but the piercing screech of a hawk circling overhead

He shielded his eyes from the early summer sunrise and searched for the source of the cry that had disturbed him. He spotted it, circling far overhead, the largest hawk he had ever seen. The hawk cried out again, its call piercing Dak'Tor's soul.

"Why are you here, Kweak?" he called out.

The hawk screeched again.

"Go away. You are no use to me. Unless you have come to lead me to a safe place."

The hawk continued to circle overhead. Dak'Tor waited for it to move on, but it seemed to be there intentionally. Then he remembered his prayer for help.

"Is this a sign? Is this some type of divine help sent to lead me to safety? If you have come to bring me a warning, it is not necessary. I already know I am in grave danger."

Suddenly, Dak'Tor thought of the crystal he had taken from the 'Tor staff, and his father's words about its power came back to him. Though never one to place much faith in such things, at that moment, it occurred to him that perhaps the crystal had summoned help.

As the thought occurred to him, the hawk glided to the top of a nearby tree.

Dak'Tor chastised himself for not paying more attention to his mother's teaching about the messages the Great Spirit sent through the creatures of Etera. However, he found himself addressing the hawk again. "Have you come to help me? I suppose perhaps you have. I certainly have nothing to lose. If you have come to lead me somewhere, then show me by taking off again and coming back."

When the hawk did just as he had asked, Dak'-Tor's eyes widened, and he picked up his carrying satchel and slung it over his shoulder. He had better get moving before the day started to heat up.

"Well, it seems you understood me. Since I have no idea where to go, let us see what happens." Kweak flew off, never going far enough ahead for Dak'Tor to lose sight of it. The farther he followed the hawk, which often circled back as if allowing him to catch up, the more convinced he became that this was help sent to him by the Great Spirit.

Confident he was not being followed, and having put his faith in Kweak, Dak'Tor paid little attention to where he was going. He was only aware both of the magnetic currents under his feet and that the hawk never flew out of his sight. Whenever he stopped to rest, the hawk alighted in a nearby tree. Each morning, he woke to see Kweak still with him.

During one stop, Dak'Tor made a spear and used it to catch fish whenever he was close to any waterways. He always remembered to toss some to his escort in gratitude for its help.

They had been traveling for quite a while. As each step of the journey continued, Dak'Tor realized more and more how much trouble he was in. There was no doubt that if Kweak was not truly leading him somewhere, he would die alone out in the wilderness. Having little else to do, he reflected on his past and realized he had spent his life controlling his anger, never letting anyone see the truth of it. By hiding the truth, he had lied to manipulate others to get what he wanted. But now, he could see that this strategy, which he had felt protected him, had only made him more fragile. All of his relationships had survived on lies. And so, when he could no longer keep up the mask of deceit, every connection that might have saved him dissipated.

Weeks passed, and Dak'Tor realized that his path had turned west. He was growing weary and struggled to fight off the occasional fear that he was deluding himself and the hawk was leading him nowhere. But despite his fears and because he had no other plan, he continued to follow the hawk.

Then finally, from the top of a hillside, Dak'Tor could see off in the far distance a large rock overhang along the base of the next range. Rock formations such as that were often host to caves of varying sizes. If nothing else, there would be some shelter.

He had lost weight and was tired and drained because he had not eaten well for some time and had gone too long without water during extended stretches when it was not available. The range was too distant for him to go any farther that day; he had to rest. But in the morning, he would cross the valley and pray he did find a cave.

The stars moved in their patterns overhead until finally, the sun broke over the horizon. Dak'Tor decided he had just enough strength to make it and headed in the direction of the overhang. He could see from the surroundings that there was provision there and that if he was lucky enough to find shelter and could hold on a little while longer, regain his strength, this location could provide enough to sustain him.

His heart was pounding as he got closer. He felt a glimmer of hope that this might be his salvation. His whole countenance brightened when he could indeed see an entrance to a cave.

But once outside the cave's entrance, a sense of sorrow came over Dak'Tor. Something terrible had happened there. He took a deep breath and stepped inside.

If the bad feeling had not been enough to warn him off, whatever was left of the hope Dak'Tor had for this cave being his chance at survival were dashed immediately. Inside its mouth, boulders were piled and scattered everywhere. There clearly had been a cave-in. What appeared to be several tunnels were blocked with more rubble. The sense of devastation was overwhelming.

Dirty, hungry, broken, Dak'Tor felt rage rise within him. "Curse you, Kweak," he shouted. "This is what you brought me to? There is nothing here for me. Nothing but death. I was a fool to believe in you!"

Then his thoughts turned to Kthama, and his sister, Pan. Safe and secure among their people, revered, and admired.

Though he was exhausted, Dak'Tor used his rage to force himself to climb to a high spot. As he looked down into the ravine below, he angrily hurled his spear, knowing he would not live long enough to make any more use of it.

Then he reached into his satchel and found the crystal his father had told him was so precious. His fingers closed around it. As for you, Pan, he thought, she who had it all, there was one thing she did not have and now never would. What kind of a great Leader would she really be when she needed the power of the sacred crystal. In a moment, it would lie shattered at the bottom of the ravine.

Just as Dak'Tor was about to remove it from his carrying bag, a voice called out from below.

"Guardian. Why have you returned to this place?"

Dak'Tor turned and looked down to the front of the cave. Three males stood there, clearly Mothoc. One was much taller than the others, and the middle one was very dark in color.

"That is not the Guardian," said the tallest, apparently realizing when Dak'Tor turned toward them that only the top of his head and his back were silver.

"What is your business here?" cried out the shortest. "This is sacred ground!"

Dak'Tor blinked and stared at them.

"Perhaps he is addled," the tallest one remarked.

"Look at him. He is about to die more likely than anything else," said the dark-colored male. "What should we do? Kill him? It would not take much."

"Let us not be hasty," said the tallest again. "He

appears to be alone and is certainly no threat to us—and we could use some new seed. If we kill him, Laborn may be angry. Though, of course, if we bring him back, Laborn may be angry anyway; it is hard to tell with him."

Then he called out to Dak'Tor, "Come down here."

Realizing he was likely to die one way or the other, Dak'Tor carefully yet slowly made his way back down. At least at their hands, it would be a quick death.

"Who are you, and why have you come here?" the tallest one asked.

"I was led here by Kweak. I am looking for a new home," Dak'Tor answered.

"Why? Have you been cast out?" the tallest one asked, looking Dak'Tor up and down.

"I am from Kthama. Let us say that the Leader and I do not see eye to eye."

"The Leader of the High Rocks, is that not the Guardian? You are not a friend of the Guardian sent here to spy on us?"

"I assure you, I am no friend of the Guardian. I want only what we all want, to live in peace among our own kind," Dak'Tor said.

The three Mothoc glanced at each other.

"Come with us," said the tallest. "We will take you to our home. It is not far, but we will hunt for you along the way so you do not die before we get there. What happens to you then is up to our Leader.

But at least you have a few more days to live, even if worst comes to worst. I am Krac."

Thinking better of it, Dak'Tor did not give his name, only falling in step with them. Overhead, Kweak let out a long, piercing cry before disappearing into the distance.

The three did as they said and kept Dak'Tor alive. Barely. He tried to pay attention to the terrain they were crossing and the direction they were traveling in, but his mind was almost too tired to think. When they approached their home, several of the offling playing outside ran in to announce that Krac and the others were back and that they had brought a stranger with them.

Kaisak and Laborn came out to meet them.

"We found him at the sacred place. We thought you should decide what to do with him," said Krac. "He says he is from Kthama but that he is no friend of the Guardian."

Laborn stood in front of Dak'Tor and looked him up and down. "No. He is indeed no *friend* of the Guardian. From his markings, I would say he is the Guardian's *brother*!"

Laborn reached up and grabbed Dak'Tor by the throat. "Why are you here? Did she send you to spy on us? How could she be so stupid as to send her own brother; with your markings there is no mistaking you, *Dak'Tor*, even though you were an offling when I saw you last."

Dak'Tor struggled, trying to escape Laborn's hold on his throat, but in his weakened state, he struggled in vain. Then a wizened old female came out of the entrance, supporting herself with a thick branch.

"Let him go," she ordered.

Laborn turned to see Useaves, the oldest of their females who was also as close to a Healer as they had. He released Dak'Tor, who stooped over, coughing.

Useaves raised her stick and waved it toward the Leader. "Your anger is your worst enemy, Laborn. Would you destroy a gift sent to us from the Great Spirit?"

"How do you know he is a gift? He could just as well be a curse. Or a spy," Laborn answered.

"You can see he is no spy," she said. "If Kthama had sent a spy, they would have prepared him. They would not have sent him out in such a state to arrive as he is, half dead. And he has no spear for protection, only his food satchel. Clearly, he set out on his own."

Laborn frowned at Dak'Tor, at the moment not daring to frown at Useaves.

"I suggest you find him a place to sleep and some

decent food before he perishes from your nonsense," she added.

Laborn nodded to Kaisak, who motioned to Dak'Tor to follow him. Several of the younger females who had been watching appeared eager to help Kaisak get the handsome though unkempt and scrawny stranger settled in.

"He is the Guardian's brother," Laborn repeated.

"The greatest divides are often between family members," answered Useaves. "Whatever drove him from his home must have been a serious disagreement. Or a crime. Regardless of the reason, it makes him more an ally than an enemy."

"We will see," was the most defiant thing Laborn dared let himself say to the old female.

Grateful that the old female's words had calmed everyone down, Dak'Tor sank onto the sleeping mat, the coolness of the interior a relief. He tucked his satchel against the wall behind his back where it would be out of sight.

Luckily, he had thrown his spear into the ravine before they had seen it, and his traveling satchel was a simple design used to carry only food and a water gourd.

Iria had waited for the stranger to wake.

"I am Iria, of the House of 'Del. I am here to help you get better," she said. She could not keep her eyes off his remarkable coloring. Though he was dirty and scraggly from being without self-care for so long, the silver in his coat was striking and in great contrast to her own dark coloring

The stranger frantically gobbled up the food she had brought him, almost choking himself in the process. When there was nothing left, he washed it all down with the water, ran his forearm across his mouth, and thanked her. Then he lay down and quickly went back to sleep. Iria picked up the gourd to refill it for later.

While she was down at the spring filling the water gourd from the clear, flowing water, several other young females came over to her.

"Lucky you, to be chosen to take care of him. Who did you ply with what favors to be chosen?" one of them teased Iria.

"Stop it; I do not know why I was chosen. And you know I am a maiden still, so hush."

"Did he speak to you? What is he like?" one of them asked.

"He is exhausted," Iria said. "He woke long enough to eat, drink, and thank me. Then he dropped back off to sleep. We did not have a chance to talk. But he is handsome. I imagine he is a very striking male when he is not so skinny and such a smelly mess."

"I wonder which of us he will pick," said one of them. "How exciting to have new seed in our community. I wonder if his offling will have his coloring!"

"He is the brother of the Guardian. Could he possibly sire another Guardian?" wondered Zisa, Iria's best friend.

"Let us see if he survives before we start worrying about that," another chuckled.

Iria did not blame them; she'd had all the same thoughts herself.

"Well, it is your job to keep him alive," said someone else. "Do not fail us!" she added.

They all had a good-natured laugh over their common interest in the Guardian's mysterious brother.

Dak'Tor had been left alone except for the visits by the lovely young female who had apparently been assigned to care for him. He was still recovering and spent a lot of time sleeping. But instead of the female, this time he woke to see standing over him the tall male who had brought him there.

"Wake up," said Kaisak. "The Adik'Tar wants to talk to you."

He slowly rose to his feet and followed Kaisak outside to where Laborn was waiting.

Dak'Tor was surprised to see it was nighttime. A

large fire was burning, and around it sat the one named Laborn, the one named Gard, and the older female they called Useaves.

"Are you feeling better?" asked Useaves.

Dak'Tor nodded and took a seat next to her.

"You have had several weeks to rest. You have put on some weight; Iria must be taking good care of you," Laborn said.

"She is. Thank you."

"Why did you leave Kthama?" demanded Laborn. "And in such a hurry. You had few supplies with you. It almost looks as if you were forced to leave."

"I was not officially told to leave, but I believed it was coming. In the eyes of the Mothoc leadership, I committed a grievous crime."

Laborn waited, staring at him.

Though he was being nursed back to health, Dak'Tor knew he was still in grave danger. Laborn seemed hot-tempered, and Dak'Tor had the impression he would never know where he stood with the Leader. The smartest thing to do was to listen and learn and to talk as little as possible.

"I touched the Leader's Staff. No one is allowed to do that. They were about to banish me, so I left instead."

"You think I am a fool. Yes, that is a grievous infraction, but there has to be more to it than that," Laborn sneered.

"Alright. The truth is that Father chose me to lead Kthama. But I did not want to. So after he died, when

I found the Leader's Staff, which he had left in my room, I moved it to my sister's quarters so she would think he had chosen her. Then, years later, in a fit of anger, I told everyone the truth, that I am the rightful Leader at Kthama."

"Moc'Tor is dead?" Laborn asked.

"Yes, and my mother, E'ranale. Straf'Tor, too. It has been some time now." He waited as Laborn fell into silence.

Eventually, keeping his voice low, Dak'Tor said, "I have answered your questions. Would you answer some of mine?"

"Go ahead and ask. I will decide after I hear the questions," Laborn replied.

"Who are you? You seem to know about the High Rocks and the Guardian, but you did not know my father and mother had returned to the Great Spirit."

"We did not agree with your father's giving the females so much power, so we left Kthama for Kayerm. Then, when Straf'Tor came there with his followers and the Sassen, we left Kayerm as well."

Dak'Tor knew there was more to the story. He would have to bide his time and try to learn as much as he could. It was not as if he had anywhere else to go.

"I thank you for taking me in. Once I am well, I hope I can be of service to your community."

"If I decide to let you stay, I am sure you will be; the females are already circling you. We are in need of offling by new blood."

At the irony, Dak'Tor had to stifle a chuckle. He had never wanted offling and had abandoned Ei'Tol after she was seeded. Now here he was, his safety and perhaps even his existence tied to providing the one thing he did not want—offling.

But this could be different. He had cared for Ei'Tol. He would not let himself care about any female again.

"Do you pair here?" he asked.

"Va!" Laborn spat out. "We have returned to the true ways. We do not allow the females to choose which male mounts them," said Kaisak.

"But I am 'Tor. Are you not also all 'Tor?" Dak'Tor asked. "How will my bloodline help?" The moment he said it, he knew he had made a mistake.

"Some of us are 'Tor but not all of us. Our original Leader, Norcab, and one of our others, Warnak, were murdered before our eyes by your father for speaking out against him. We found Kayerm and made a home there, where we gathered some additional followers until Straf'Tor murdered our new Leader Ridg'Sor and banished us from Kayerm. Like you, we seem to have a problem fitting in," and Laborn smiled just enough to reveal his sharp canines.

The more Laborn talked about how Dak'Tor's father, Moc'Tor, and Moc'Tor's brother, Straf'Tor, had murdered two of their Leaders, the more convinced Dak'Tor became that he was a likely target on which Laborn could seek revenge. His life here would be short-lived unless he could find a way to be of use to Laborn.

"Then you could benefit from my seed. I have sired many offling," Dak'Tor lied.

Laborn's gaze flickered up and down Dak'Tor's body. Then he said, "I will confer with Useaves. If she agrees, then we will select a female for you. Being of your line, they will be able to mate our future offling more safely. We lost many families in the cave-in, which you discovered at our first location. We must be careful now so our community will grow in numbers, but healthy numbers, and live long enough to accomplish our purpose," said Laborn.

Though he had vowed not to say much, Dak'Tor could not help himself. "What purpose is that?"

"We live to serve the Great Spirit. We will not rest until the abominations your father created are eradicated. We will not rest until the Sassen and Akassa are wiped from the face of Etera."

The time away had made Dak'Tor realize how comfortable Kthama was. He had grown up playing in the corridors, and he knew every tunnel, every turn, every marker. He knew every path that snaked around the High Rocks, each twist and turn of the Great River. He knew who he could trust and who he could not. Everything here was different. He could not find a way to be at ease here and missed the feeling of home, despite his troubles there. And always in the back of his mind was the knowledge that Laborn was watching him and that as long as Laborn was Leader, he could never drop his guard. There was nowhere else to go, so somehow, he had to win Laborn's trust or escape, and—although highly improbable—somehow find a way to redeem himself in front of both his sister and the High Council.

Iria continued to care for Dak'Tor, and in time his health was restored to the point that Laborn decided it was time he started mating. The Leader had consulted with Useaves, and they had decided that Iria, being of the House of 'Wok, would be selected to be seeded by Dak'Tor.

When she was given the news, Iria tried to hide her pleasure at being picked. The young maiden had grown fond of the stranger as she took care of him every day. He seemed pleasant enough, though quiet, and she hoped that in time, he would open up to her and become a true companion. She had no doubt he would be a good provider, being strong and robust of build.

Laborn had made an exception to his disdain for pairing and conducted a brief public pairing ritual which made it clear that Dak'Tor and Iria were from then on only to mate with each other. They had been given their own quarters, and the first private chance

Dak'Tor had, he carved a small recess up in the shadows, as high as he could reach, and tucked the crystal into it.

After the pairing ceremony, Dak'Tor performed his duty with Iria and prayed she would prove as prolific as Ei'Tol and quickly become seeded.

Iria tried to hide her disappointment with their mating. She had hoped for an emotional connection with Dak'Tor, but he seemed distant and somewhat removed. When he had finished, she turned her back to him and tried to sleep, not wanting to create problems between them on their first night together. She knew her friends would be waiting to ask her about their lovemating.

When she awoke, her new mate was already gone. She got up and went out to join whoever was at the morning gathering.

Dak'Tor was sitting in the circle with a group of males who leered at her while some of them slapped Dak'Tor on the back. Iria ignored them and went to join the females' group.

The younger females had hardly given her time to grab anything to eat before they started pelting her with questions. *So how was it? Did he satisfy you? Did he show you any mysterious lovemating secrets?*

"How should I know if he knew any secrets; I have never been mated before. It was fine. It was fine," she answered, playing with her food.

"Fine?" one of the females rolled her eyes at another.

"Yes. Fine. How am I to know? I have nothing to compare it with," she answered.

"You have heard the older females talking about it. We all have. What do you mean you do not know anything about it!" asked Visha, Krac's daughter. Visha had never liked Iria and took every chance to put her in a negative light.

"Leave her alone," said Zisa, Iria's lifelong friend. "Stop trying to make her feel something is wrong just because you are jealous of her."

"You are right," said another. "But to be fair, he is not some young male. He should know what he is doing by now. After all, I heard him tell Laborn that he had sired many offling."

"That does not mean anything," Zisa answered. "Any male can mount a female. It does not mean he knows how to bring her pleasure or even cares about it."

Iria picked up what was left of her meal and stood up. "I do not want to talk about this any longer." She left to find her mother.

After Iria had left, Zisa turned to the others. "That was mean. Laborn picked Iria for him. Being cruel to her because you were not who he picked is unfair. You might want to be careful how you treat her. Someday, when they are grown, you may want her offling to mate with yours."

"Ha!" Visha scoffed. "Is Laborn ever going to let any of us younger ones mate? Sometimes I think the fact that we lost so many families when our first home collapsed is just an excuse. Maybe he wants to deprive us because his mate is dead."

"What a horrible thing to say," Zisa replied, even though she had no love of Laborn.

Iria made a vow to try and break through Dak'Tor's wall of silence. She went out of her way to learn what he liked and did not like, testing him with one food or another. She made sure their room was tidy and comely. She offered to help him learn about the community by answering his questions the best she could. But despite her efforts, he still remained distant, and their lovemating did not progress beyond the mechanics.

Then finally, one day, when they were alone in their room, she could not stand it any longer and spoke her mind, "Dak'Tor. We have been together for several months now, yet you do not open up to me. You ask me questions about life here, but you do not ask any about me. Do you not care to get to know me? Are we never to be companions? Or are you just hoping to seed me to secure favor with Laborn?"

"I am sorry, Iria. I do not mean to shut you out. I am not sure who I can trust here and who I cannot."

"Surely you feel you can trust me? I am the one who cared for you and brought you back to health. Why would I betray you, especially when I am paired to you for life?"

Dak'Tor put his head in his hands, buying time to think.

"Tell me what I can do to win your trust?"

He raised his head and looked at Iria. "Tell me how to fit in here. Tell me how to ease Laborn's suspicions about me."

His young mate came and sat down next to him. She let out a long breath. "Laborn is easy to understand. All you have to keep in mind is that he cares about only one thing since his mate was killed in the cave-in. And that is destroying the Akassa and the Sassen. He blames them for everything that has gone wrong in his life."

"I thought he blamed my father and Straf'Tor?"

"Oh, he blames them as well, though originally for giving the females too much power. But, I am told, after a string of mishaps, it became something else. Now he believes that if he can destroy the Sassen and the Akassa, the abominations as he calls them, then the Great Spirit will again favor him. Who knows, he might also have some grand idea of even more power."

"Does everyone here believe as he does?"

"Not everyone. Many of my generation do not share his hatred. But we have learned to hide our opinions and never voice them except in our very small circle."

"Who are closest to Laborn?" Dak'Tor asked.

"Gard, the one with the scar on his face, from an altercation with Laborn. Then Kaisak, who, along with Gard, is also often in close contact with him."

"What about Useaves, the old female who stopped Laborn from choking me to death?"

"After all this time, I do not know what to say about Useaves. She does not speak much, and she keeps to herself. I do not know if she shares Laborn's vendetta to destroy the Akassa and the Sassen. But Laborn's bitterness has put a dark cloud over our lives."

"He seems to have contaminated everyone with his hatred for all but the Mothoc," said Dak'Tor.

"My friends and I think his quest to destroy the Akassa and the Sassen is an empty one. None of us believes he can do it because he would not have the numbers. But you are part of that solution. With your seed, our numbers can grow. Other offling will have a new line to breed with," Iria explained. "Now tell me, do you agree with Laborn that they should all be destroyed?"

Dak'Tor weighed his options. He needed his mate's allegiance to teach him about the ways there. But he needed Laborn's trust.

"No, I do not think they should be destroyed. I only know the Akassa, and they are peace-loving. But, I will play along as the rest of you do."

Iria finally found the courage to ask the question she had wanted to ask from the first moment she saw him. "At Kthama, did you have a mate?"

"I did, but I just lost her before I left."

"Oh no. I am so sorry. What happened? Did she have an accident?"

Dak'Tor thought for a moment; admitting that Ei'Tol had left him did not present him in a good light. "She died trying to give birth to our offling. I lost them both," he lied. "I am basically alone in the world."

"But you have other offling you said. You said you sired many."

Dak'Tor ran his hand across his chin, realizing how easily he had lied again. "It is too hard for me to talk about this right now. Why not tell me about yourself? Why were you not already mounted by some male?"

Iria absentmindedly drew little figures in the sand on the floor with her toe.

"We lost a great number of families when the cave-in happened. Laborn is worried about the bloodlines becoming too entwined. He says he needs time to figure it out, so we just wait. Your coming along was an answer to his prayers—not that he prays or even believes in the Great Spirit any longer. He and so many others are angry and bitter. If they pray to the Great Spirit, none of the rest of us knows it."

Then Iria got up, stepped into the tunnel outside, and looked around before coming back and sitting next to him again. She whispered, "What was it like at Kthama? What are the Akassa like? Do they look like us? Are they friendly?"

Dak'Tor spent the next few minutes telling her about Kthama. About the positive relationship between the Mothoc and the Akassa. He described them to her, told her about typical days there. Then he told her what he knew about Kayerm and about the Sassen. What he did not tell Iria was that the Mothoc were preparing to leave Kthama and Kayerm and move to a new location. Considering Laborn's hatred of Sassen and Akassa, he thought it best no one there knew they would no longer have the protection of the Mothoc. At least not until he decided if it would be in his favor to do so.

When he was done, Iria thanked him. "I am glad we talked. That is the most time we have spent together since we were joined. Other than, you know—"

"It is late," he said. "Do you want to go and join the others at the fire?"

CHAPTER 9

As Dak'Tor was trying to make peace with his new life with the rebels, the Mothoc at Kthama and Kayerm continued their preparations to leave.

To keep her mind occupied, Pan joined Dochrohan and met tirelessly with the Akassa Leader, Takthan'Tor, and their Healer, Tensil. Pan made sure they had the laws memorized. She had struggled long over the laws, and with everyone believing Lor Onida's scroll lost, had modified the ninth law to reinforce the Rah-hora. Where the Ninth Law had ordered them to have no contact with Outsiders, which would have ruled out the Brothers, Pan proposed to the High Council that they change it to *honor all agreements with the Brothers.* After much debate and consternation over changing the laws that Moc'Tor and Straf'Tor and the original Leaders who stood with him had agreed upon, it was accepted.

And so it became that both the Sassen and the Akassa, under the direction of the Mothoc Leaders, each inherited a slightly different set of laws. To the Sassen, the ninth law was now *Avoid all contact with the Akassa* in alignment with the Rah-hora. And to the Akassa, it was *Honor agreements with the Brothers*.

The longer the Mothoc Leaders talked with the Akassa Leaders, they came to realize that the Akassa needed additional laws as a foundation for their culture. And so seven additional laws, which became known as the Second Laws, were born. These laid down the structure for leadership, specifying the positions of High Protector and Second and Third ranks.

In times of crisis, the High Protector could supersede the authority of the Second and Third Ranks, working directly with the Leader to address urgent issues. The law specified that the Leader could choose his own mate, and should that mate prove barren, could petition the High Council to take a second or third mate if need be. The Leader had to produce offling so the bloodline would continue. On the off chance that there was still no blood heir to leadership, the High Council could select a male relative instead.

Where Pan had failed in convincing the High Council to forbid all Healers and Helpers to pair and have offling, she succeeded with the Akassa leadership. So the fifth of the Second Laws stated that Healers and Helpers could neither pair nor reproduce. Next to the last stated that pairings were arranged by the High Council and also allowed for Bak'tah-Awhidi, the setting aside of a pairing for cause.

The last of the Akassa's Second Laws became *No contact with outsiders*.

But while the Sassen were aware of what was about to happen, the Akassa were not. They only knew that changes were being made at Kthama, and the changes alarmed them.

Dochrohan approached Pan. "The Akassa are becoming restless," he said. "They know you have frequently been meeting with Takthan'Tor and Tensil. They have been watching the changes and are convinced we are leaving them."

"They are right, we are," she answered.

"Should we not hold a gathering and tell them? Explain why we are leaving? To reduce their worry?" Dochrohan asked.

"Yes, please arrange it. You are right; it has been wrong of me to let it go on for so long."

Pan looked around for what she needed. Finally, being drawn to a specific tree, she studied its branches. As she was considering which to use, Ravu'Bahl lighted on one of them.

It was perfect for its purpose. She reached up to Ravu'Bahl's perch, at which he hopped up to a higher branch. Then she broke off the original one and spent the rest of the afternoon making it ready. When Pan was done, she raised it over her head and reverently asked the Great Spirit's blessing on it.

Pan and Rohm'Mok stood at the front of the Great Chamber to explain to the Akassa what was going on. She looked out across the crowd as she had on occasions before. But now, there were just the Mothoc and the Akassa. The variations in the Akassa that had previously existed had been bred out long ago. Other than varying shades of hair color and the usual differences in build, the Akassa were a fairly homogenous group.

Pan spoke first. "Many of you are asking about the changes being made to Kthama. The new doors which are more suited to your use. Replacing all the service baskets with those woven by your hands. And in the next few days, there will be even more changes. Eventually all the seating boulders we use will be removed. Some of you have rightly guessed the reason for these changes, that before too long, all the Mothoc, including me, will be leaving the High Rocks and all the other communities."

The crowd broke up into anxious chatter, and Pan patiently waited for them to quiet down.

She did not have her Leader's Staff with her. In fact, she had not been able even to look at it since Dak'Tor had disgraced himself in front of the High Council. The sight of it only brought heartbreak at his deep betrayal of her. Instead, she had the new Leader's Staff for the House of 'Mok that she had spent the afternoon making. Smaller and more suited to the Akassa, she held it at her side instead.

When she could, Pan continued, "As well as we are able, we have prepared you to go on without us. You are as adept as us at the skills you need to survive on your own. And so, it is time for us to move on. It is time for us to leave you to the future of your own making," she said.

"But why? Have we offended you?" shouted someone from the crowd.

"You have not offended us. We care for you deeply. But our presence here overshadows too much of your culture. You need to be free to discover on your own who you are. Your lives will go on without us. And you will be the better for it."

"Where are you going? Will we be able to find you if we need you?" asked a female.

"The time is not immediately at hand, but before very long, we are going far away. We will let you know before we leave. But you will not need us; you will be fine on your own, you will see. Trust the Great Spirit. Trust the Order of Functions. Remember the First and Second Laws. Take care of one another and let all talk of us fade into history."

Then Pan called Takthan'Tor to come forward. He stood beside her, dwarfed by her immense size. She turned to him and held out the new Leader's Staff.

"The leadership of the High Rocks is now yours. Take the staff of the House of 'Tor. Lead with wisdom. Lead with honor."

As Takthan'Tor clasped the wooden staff, Pan released her hold on it.

Many voices rose, but Pan held up her hand and proclaimed, "*Kah-Sol 'Rin*." A great silence fell over the chamber. Concerned faces, creased and pinched, looked back at her. Her heart was breaking, for she could already feel the distance that would separate them.

Then Pan led her family and all the other Mothoc from the Great Chamber.

Dochrohan caught them as they were walking away. "Thank you for that. At least now they know the truth. They will still be upset by our leaving, but I am glad you told them, and they did not have to wake up one day and find us gone."

"If you think it helped, I am glad," said Pan. "I cannot bear to see any of them suffer, so I was putting it off. You had better send messengers to the High Council members that, if they haven't, it is time they do the same with their communities. All the Akassa need to be prepared."

After a while, Pan returned to the Great Chamber. The last few stragglers realized she was waiting for them to leave, and finally, the Great Chamber was hers alone.

She scanned the expanse. The high ceilings, the massive stone walls. The rock slabs and benches were next to be changed out, sized down so the Akassa could move them around. The storage rooms had been modified to shorten the wood structures that held the extra goods so the Akassa could reach the top shelves.

She walked out of the Great Chamber and down through the main branch of tunnels. She tried to memorize the feel of the rock floor under her feet, the faint sounds of offling playing in the background. The familiar smell of lavender and pine, used in ritual and for pleasure. At night, fluorescent stones would light the lower levels; removed, re-charged, and replaced daily as part of the ongoing chores. Pan believed that in time the Akassa would realize they did not need the extra lighting other than for its beauty. But for now, it gave them a sense of comfort.

There were tasks she still had to take care of, but she allowed herself the luxury of reminiscing about her life here. Her father, her mother, and now even her brother—all gone. Little Liru, daughter of Oragur, and Lor Onida, who had died giving birth to her—the offling Pan had thought would be hers to raise. The heartbreak and shock when Oragur told her he wanted the offling back. Pan had not seen Liru since Oragur had returned with her to the Deep Valley. But she would be able to see her when they made Lulnomia their collective home.

There was never a time when the responsibility of leadership had weighed heavier on her. And as Pan walked through the rest of Kthama and finally outside, she found herself at the Healer's Cove, staring up at the massive stone that marked the sealed entrance to Kthama Minor.

Pan felt a deep connection with this place, for good reason. Deep in the tunnels of Kthama Minor were the discarded shells of what had been her father, her mother, and Straf'Tor. She wondered what their last moments had been like. Her mother had connected with her in the Corridor, and having proof that life continued was a great comfort to the Guardian. Except that her father was trapped in the Order of Functions, and if Pan failed, would remain there forever. She could not fathom such a terrible fate. To be stretched to the edges of eternity, split into an infinite number of pieces, with no escape. He had been far more experienced in the Order of Functions than she was. Was it possible that even in this place of nowhere and everywhere, he had some sense of self left? And if so, did he have hope she or someone would free him? She prayed that he did.

"Somehow, you thought me capable of this," she said to the Great Spirit, "that by your hand, the leadership of the High Rocks was passed to me and not my brother. And that it has fallen to me to close the rift my father created. To reunite the Mothoc once again into a single community. Please give me the wisdom to know what to do and the faith and strength to do it."

Pan stayed a while longer before fetching her guards and going up to the meadow, once again to fulfill her duties as the Guardian of Etera.

Afterward, when Pan opened her eyes, she knew what she had to do next. `

Once again, as the multi-colored leaves painted the landscape, Pan set out for Kayerm. Before long, Norland and his close circle were on their way to meet her, the welcome cooler fall air making their walk easier.

"We have awaited your return," said Norland as they drew close.

"It is nearly time for us to travel to our new home," Pan said. "Prepare what you will take with you; it will not be long now. But before I come to take you there, I need to meet with the Sassen Leader and Healer."

Pallida and Raddoc were summoned and soon approached the ridge behind which Pan waited for them. As they cleared the top and saw the Guardian standing next to Norland and the others, both Pallida and Raddoc stopped in their tracks.

Pan waited a moment for them to gather themselves, knowing they had never seen a Guardian before. She beckoned them toward her, and they moved forward hesitantly.

Norland also motioned them forward, and Raddoc kept his eye on his Leader until he was standing close enough to speak.

"I am Raddoc, Sassen Leader of Kayerm. This is my Healer, Pallida," he said, indicating Pallida now standing by his side.

"I am Pan, Guardian of Etera." She took a moment to look them over before continuing. "You are ready to take over Kayerm and lead your people into the future of their making?" she asked Raddoc.

"With the help of the Great Spirit, Guardian, I am," he answered.

"And you are fully trained and ready to be their Healer?" she asked Pallida.

"I will never be fully trained, Guardian. No Healer ever is," Pallida answered politely. "There is always something new to learn. I am ready, though."

"Good answers, both of you. A Leader must be willing to accept the mantle of leadership, and a Healer must always be learning. I believe the future of Kayerm is in good hands. Do you understand why my people, the Mothoc, must leave you?"

"Yes. Norland has explained it to us many times. As long as the Mothoc live among us, we will never fully rule ourselves," Raddoc answered.

"Before long," said Pan, "I will return to take them with me. But this visit is about you. I need to spend time with you both—alone," she said, turning to the other Mothoc standing with her.

"We will leave you then," said Norland. "Will we see you again before you leave?"

"Yes. For what I have to do, I will need to stay for a few days."

Norland nodded. "We will be honored, Guardian. We will prepare a private space for you."

⚜

Once they were alone, Pan turned to Raddoc and Pallida. "The Mothoc blood circulates to care for all of Etera. Even though we will be gone from you, our duty remains. Your Mothoc blood, though diluted by the Others, serves Etera as does ours. But aside from your physical duty to Etera, the greatest gift you can give your people is to help them forget about us. You must help your people turn their thoughts to the future. If you are faithful to this charge, by the next generation, there should be little talk of us, and in the generation after that, even less. Allow us to fade into history. Speak rarely of the Wrak-Wavara. Honor the Rah-hora. Have no contact with the Akassa and leave the Others to them. Teach your people to cloak themselves at all times. Your existence must remain a secret."

"But the Others know of our existence," said Raddoc.

"They have memories of the Mothoc existence. They know nothing of you, the Sassen. In time they will; it is unavoidable, but by the time that comes, the similarities between the Sassen and the Mothoc will make it seem as if we are the same. They will not realize there was any other kind of Sasquatch."

"Sasquatch?" Pallida frowned.

"That is one of the names by which they call you and the Akassa."

"But we are nothing like the Akassa. The Akassa look more like the Others than we do. How can they think we are the same?" Pallida asked.

"You are not the same, but you are not all that different, either. The Akassa may look more like the Others than they do you, but you and they both have your pasts rooted in ours. Mothoc blood flows in the veins of you all; it is just that in theirs, it is less concentrated. The Others are wise in the Great Spirit. They will sense this truth in the Akassa."

Raddoc let out a long breath, and Pan continued.

"This is the message you must hand down to the next Leader, and he to the next, and so on and so on, even to the end of the age. Honor the Rah-hora lest you yourselves be destroyed. Have no contact with the Akassa. Leave the Others to them. Conceal your existence." She repeated it all again. "Anything else you need to know will be given to you at the time. But there is one thing I must teach you, and that is the Ror'Eckrah."

"The One Mind?" Raddoc asked. "We have heard it spoken of."

"The Ror'Eckrah is an ancient ritual. It is seldom used because there is rarely a need for it. It is a powerful tool and must never be used for wrongdoing. It is the joining of minds melded together as one and with one purpose as directed by whoever is trained and is strong enough to initiate the joining." Pan explained.

"The dream. The vision, the message you just spoke of," Raddoc said.

"Yes. My father called forth the One Mind to divide your people from the Akassa and theirs from you.

"Up until now, how to invoke Ror'Eckrah has been passed only from Guardian to Guardian. But I have seen that the time may come when it falls to the Leader of the Sassen to invoke the One Mind. But when and if that should happen is unknown to me. I have come to teach this secret to you, as Leader of Kayerm."

When she stopped talking, only the sound of acorns hitting the forest floor broke the silence.

Pan waited for Raddoc to agree. When he said

nothing, she added, "We will start now if you are willing."

The Sassen Leader looked at Pallida as if questioning whether she should leave.

"Pallida needs to hear this too," Pan said. "The Leader and the Healer must work together in all things."

Pan then led Raddoc and Pallida to a secluded spot she had seen on the way there. She told them to sit while she explained how to invoke the One Mind. She was prepared to work tirelessly with them. When she had returned from her last engagement with the Order of Functions, she knew this was her next step, but she was still unsure that Raddoc would be able to do it.

Before long, it was twilight, and Pan could see the Sassen were tiring. "Come, it is nearing end of day. You must be hungry and tired. We will begin again in the morning."

As Pan, Raddoc, and Pallida arrived back at Kayerm, all the others outside turned to watch. Though a crowd had gathered when she appeared on the ridge on her first visit, they had only glimpsed her from a distance.

"Thank you for your hospitality in allowing me to stay with you. Please go about your business and do not let me disturb you," she said.

Pan often forgot the effect her presence could have, and nobody moved.

Toniss spoke up, "We have prepared a variety of

foods for you and left them in the private sleeping space we prepared. We thought you might have need of some solitude and hope you will be comfortable."

Pan knew they probably had questions they wanted to ask, and it was only fair that she speak to them all before she left. But tonight was not the time.

"If you will forgive me, I do wish to retire. I will meet with you all before I leave Kayerm," she said.

Satisfied that they would see her again, the others relaxed, though they did not take their eyes off her until she was out of sight.

The next morning, after an early first meal, Pan continued her sessions with Raddoc and Pallida.

When she felt he was ready, she told Raddoc to invoke the One Mind. She was careful to block herself off from him so he could only attempt it with Pallida. The Guardian needed to know that her own powers were not in some way augmenting his.

After many attempts interspersed with more instruction, Raddoc finally succeeded in establishing the Ror'Eckrah with Pallida. At his success, a rush of relief passed through Pan. A part of her was disappointed in herself for that, as her doubt in him meant she did not yet fully trust the wisdom of the Order of Functions.

As she had instructed, Raddoc and Pallida moved

away, walked in a circle, and came back, leaving the damp fallen leaves trampled by their feet.

When Raddoc finally released the One Mind, Pallida shook her head and looked around. "I cannot say that was pleasant." She bent over and rested her hands on her knees.

"I could see and hear everything around me. But I had no will of my own. I was only a witness under Raddoc's control," she explained. "I did as he willed me to—as if I were an extension of him."

"Whoever initiates the One Mind," Pan said, "controls the bodies and the minds of everyone engaged in it. Joining others in the One Mind has always been done with their permission. It is a powerful tool, and in the wrong hands, it could be used for destructive purposes. Through the Ror'Eck-rah, you also have access to the creative power of the Aezaitera flowing in the blood of each of those joined with you. Strength. Will. Almost limitless energy. An army of Sassen would be a powerful force."

"An army of Mothoc even more so," said Raddoc.

"Exactly," Pan said. "That is why, until now, the secret has only been known to the Guardians of Etera. If one is powerful enough, it is even possible to bind the minds of the unwilling.

"I have no plans to return after I have brought the Mothoc from Kayerm," she continued. "So, Raddoc, you must tell me when you are confident that you have practiced enough to remember how to do it."

"Yes, Guardian."

"It will also fall to you to teach this sacred ritual to the next Leader, and so on and so on through the generations of Sassen leadership."

"And, Pallida, as the Healer, you must lead Kayerm with Raddoc and teach your future counterparts to depend on each other in the same way. Remember that when there is more for you to know, it will be given at the right time. Make sure those who follow you also understand that."

They stayed a while longer, and Raddoc established the One Mind more easily on his next attempt. Eventually, all three were satisfied that Pan had accomplished her mission. She ended their session with another warning that they must pass everything they had been taught and told on to their successors. That the future of Etera rested in their hands.

Twilight came early as the days were much shorter now. Having rested and eaten, Pan prepared to address the community of Kayerm at the evening fire.

The firelight reflected off Pan's silver-white coat, making it shimmer under the soft yellowish glow.

When everyone was seated, she began by addressing the Sassen.

"Great change is about to come to you, though for some of you, great change seems to have been the nature of your lives all along. As you know and have been preparing for, soon I will return to collect all the Mothoc among you. It will be before the end of the first night of the second full moon from now. I know this will be difficult for you, not in terms of survival, as I know you are capable of taking care of yourselves and your offling. But emotionally, it will be a great loss. You have bonds between you—shared experiences, both painful and happy. Even if you understand why it has to be this way, part of you will still grieve. It is important to respect that and give yourselves time for this deep wound to heal."

She glanced at Raddoc, then said to the Sassen in the crowd, "You are in good hands. You have a strong and wise Leader who has only your wellbeing in mind. Listen to him and respect him. And do the same to your Healer. Follow the Sacred Laws. Take care of one another. Respect our fellow creatures of Etera as has always been our way.

"After the Mothoc have left with me, you will, of course, need time to adjust. No doubt you will grieve. But the time will come when you will need to speak no more of their presence here nor speak of my visit. The other Mothoc and I must disappear from your daily life and daily thoughts. Allow this to happen. The future belongs to you now. Live your lives and let the past fall away. Be the protectors of Etera, as it is in your blood to do."

Pan looked over the group, each member gazing at her, spellbound. She had thought there would be questions but realized that the reverence of the moment overruled that.

"You know of the Wrak-Ayya, the Age of Shadows, which will at some point fall upon Etera. I cannot tell you what the Wrak-Ayya is or when it will come. But I can tell you that in time an age of light will replace the Wrak-Ayya. It will be issued in by the coming of the An'Kru, the Promised One. So take heart, and have faith in the hand of the Great Spirit, which is always upon us."

Feeling that her task there was finally complete, Pan raised her hand in farewell, and in a display meant solely to emphasize her message, slowly disappeared from sight.

Everyone at Kayerm gasped at the wonderful display. The little ones turned to their parents with wide eyes and open smiles. Even the Mothoc were astounded.

Pan walked far enough away before uncloaking herself. Only a Guardian could cloak his or herself from their own kind. It was seldom demonstrated and not widely known. She had struggled over making such an exit, having told them not to speak of her visit afterward, but decided she wanted it to stay in their minds so they would remember their obligations. Their obligations to their new Leader and Healer and to Etera herself.

⟨❀⟩

Kyana and Wosot were sitting together, and she turned to him. "I am a little scared."

"You know I will protect you. As long as I breathe, no harm will ever come to our family," he replied, smiling down at her.

"It is because I do not know what to expect," she said, leaning into the comfort of his broad chest. "This has become our home, our way of life. Now we will be living among only our kind, amid a much larger group that includes all the Mothoc who followed Moc'Tor. And there will be many Leaders, one from each community. How will the rights of leadership be resolved?" she said.

"That is a very good question and one that perhaps one that only the Guardian can answer. It is asking a lot for all past hurts to be released. Some are deep. But we will get through it, I promise." And pulling her closer, he kissed the top of her head.

What Kyana did not share with her mate were the fears she had barely acknowledged to herself. Fears about what offling he might have sired. Who are they? Do they know he is their father? And what of the females he mated with? And more and more, her despair deepened at not being seeded by Wosot.

CHAPTER 10

The Mothoc of all the communities were busy sorting and discarding in accord with Pan's orders that they should decide what to take and destroy the rest.

In the end, very little was taken that could be replaced. Baskets far too large for the Akassa were taken far away and buried, where, in time, they would return to the soil. Tools were difficult to discard in a way that they would never be discovered, so they were collected in the Great Entrance. Carrying satchels were packed with the items they felt they could not do without or which had sentimental meaning.

As the time to leave was approaching, Dochrohan had sent groups ahead to Lulnomia to prepare it for the arrival of the rest. Each group that left took either their own personal items with them, or some of the collection of tools, or both.

One group gathered food and prepared the store-houses to provide a comfortable cushion while everyone settled in. Another prepared sleeping mats and stored them in the entrance. They gathered and hollowed out gourds for water, as well as collecting fluorite and other stones for beauty and comfort. Whatever they could do to ease the transition, the teams did to the best of their abilities. Some then returned to their communities while others stayed to make further preparations. Those who did return made sure to share what progress they had made and much other information about Lulnomia.

Dochrohan and First Guard Bakru had made the long trek there and back many times. Vowing that no group would consider itself disadvantaged, they spent long stretches investigating the tunnels and branches, determining the most equitable distribution of space. They thought of marking each main tunnel for the specific community it would serve but thought better of it, leaving that for later should there be adjustments in how the space was allocated.

Eventually, Lulnomia was as ready as they could make her. Cold weather was setting in, bringing a break from the punishing heat. With their heavy coats, this would be the best time for the Mothoc to travel.

Dochrohan and Bakru had it all planned and measured so the Mothoc of each community would gather at appointed places where guides would meet them and lead them to Lulnomia. Despite the varying distances that had to be traveled, the people would arrive comfortably spaced out, allowing one community's members to settle a bit before another community arrived.

The same flurry of activity was taking place at Kayerm. Harvest season was finishing up, and the stores were full. Carrying satchels were packed with only the minimum of personal items and supplies for the exodus. Emotions were spiked with excitement and trepidation over where they were going and sadness over leaving their Sassen friends and family. For many, it was only the Guardian's authority that was making them leave. As had happened thousands of years before, families were being divided, never to see each other again. It was a heartwrenching time in many ways.

It was a beautiful late fall morning and Faeya, a Sassen female, was out with her offling looking for the last of the season's berries as a treat for the trip. The cloudy sky overhead warned of rain, and Faeya kept an eye on it as they searched. The usual patches had been picked pretty well, leaving the customary half for the birds and other fellow creatures. Not wanting to take what remained there, the two wandered off their usual path.

"I think we have gone far enough; we need to go back," Faeya eventually said to her daughter, looking around and realizing how far they had accidentally gone.

"Did you hear me?" she asked.

Her daughter stood frozen, staring at something through the brush.

"What is it?" Faeya asked and immediately realized they were not alone.

She slowly eased up behind her offling and put huge protective arms around her, peering through the brush to see what she had seen. They stood motionless for a while until, suddenly, a small brown figure darted up and ran off as fast as it could, crashing through the brush and scattering birds and wildlife everywhere.

Faeya was terrified of what she might just have done. Not sure if it was an Akassa or one of the Others, her first thought was that she had broken the Rah-hora. She dropped her carrying satchel, picked up her daughter, and hurried back to Kayerm.

Trying not to cry out, Tocho ran as fast as he could back to his father. "Papa! Papa!" he finally yelled. Tocho's father dropped his bow and arrow and ran to embrace his son.

"What is wrong?" Yutu asked.

"I just saw something. Someone," the young boy gasped, all excited, pointing back toward the way he had just come.

"Who? Is there another tribe traveling through? Where was it? How many?"

"One. Then another, even more huge," Tocho explained. "We stared at each other for a while, and then I came to find you."

Yutu relaxed his embrace. "We must return to the village and tell Chief Chunta what has happened. If there are others traveling through, we need to be aware in case they are hostile."

The Brothers' village was nestled among the trees and firs, and relative to the size of the area was not that far from either Kthama or Kayerm. Unlike tribes in other areas of Etera, the Brothers here did not migrate when the colder weather approached, as food sources were plentiful year-round. Snowfall made it easier to track and hunt animals and to preserve food. Firewood was easily accessible, and the nearby lakes provided opportunities for ice fishing. Many of their shelters, constructed of tree poles and covered with bark and animal skins, housed entire families.

Chief Chunta looked up as Yutu and his son were escorted into the Chief's shelter by Sitka, the Medicine Woman.

"Tocho and I were out practicing his shooting skills, and he saw someone in the brush," Yutu explained.

"Describe him to me; what was he wearing?" the Chief asked.

"He was not wearing anything," the young boy stammered.

The Medicine Woman looked at Chief Chunta and raised her eyebrows. There was no known tribe that did not wear at least a breechcloth.

"Are you sure?" Yutu asked. "It is getting too cold to be out with no protection at all."

"No, he was all covered in dark scraggly fur. There were two of them. First, a big brownish one and then a huge darker one appeared. Taller than any of our people and enormous," he explained.

"Did they speak to you?" the Chief asked.

"Speak? No. We just stared at each other," Tocho said, looking up at his father for reassurance.

"You have received a great blessing," said the Chief. "And brought wonderful news to our people as well. You have seen Sasquatch, or Oh'Mah, the Master of the Forest. Our people across Etera have many names for him."

"It has been a long time," the Chief continued, "since we have been blessed to see any of them."

Sitka reassured the boy further. "They will not

harm you. They are our protectors, sent by the Great Spirit to watch over us. Describe them a bit more, Tocho, please."

Tocho spoke of the first one he saw, who was very big but nowhere near as huge as the second one. "Dark brown eyes, hair everywhere except his face and maybe the palms of his hands. When the second one came up, it stood right behind the smaller one and wrapped its arms around him.

"So, I saw Sasquatch? I really did?" he asked, his fear now replaced by excitement.

The Brothers had long known that the Sasquatch inhabited the mountains. Both treated each other with respect, and though contact was infrequent, it was considered a great blessing. Many ages ago, there had been talk of a huge, silver-colored Sasquatch. Like all white creatures of the forest, it was considered by the Brothers to be even more sacred.

After Tocho and Yutu had left, the Chief called all the Elders. They sat and considered for some time what the visit of Oh'Mah might mean.

As for the rest of the village, word quickly spread that Tocho had seen one of the sacred protectors. Yutu cautioned his son not to let his experience lead him to believe he was more important than anyone else in the village, but humbly to accept the blessing that the Great Spirit had bestowed on him.

For the rest of his life, Tocho never forgot that moment. And though he had other encounters later on, he returned to that first experience many times when he felt he had lost his way. It reassured him that he had a purpose and each time re-ignited his dedication to the Great Spirit.

Faeya hurried as fast as she could. Others saw her rushing toward Kayerm and went to greet her. She was out of breath and clearly upset and immediately went to Adik'Tar Norland.

"I fear I have done something terrible, Adik'Tar. Not intentionally, I promise you," she added.

Norland silently waited for her to continue.

"I have broken the Rah-hora. I—I came upon an Akassa," she stammered, standing with her head lowered. "We were looking for berries, and we wandered too far away. Perhaps if you punish me, no harm will come to our people for my mistake."

"Sit," Norland said, and he sent for Raddoc and Pallida as he knew they should also hear the story.

"Now start from the beginning," Norland asked her. "Tell us what happened and exactly what you saw."

Faeya squatted, covering her head with her arms.

"Please try to calm yourself," Norland said. "You did not intentionally seek out an Akassa. I do not believe the law applies to accidental meetings."

The Sassen female then told them what had happened. She described the small offling she had seen, having had time to look him over while they were staring at each other, enthralled.

When she was done, Norland said, "That was not an Akassa. That was one of the Others."

"How do you know?" she asked.

"Toniss has described the differences between the Others and the Akassa to a few of us on many occasions. They do look similar to the Others, but you would not mistake one for the other. The Akassa are far larger than the Others, somewhere between our size and that of the Others. The Akassa are darker-skinned, and they have a soft coat, similar to our undercoat, but no long hair on top of it like we have."

When Norland had finished speaking, he realized that a good point had been brought up—something overlooked completely since the Rah-hora was given. Only the oldest of the Sassen had ever seen one of the Others, and none except the Mothoc had seen an Akassa.

When Faeya was finally consoled, Norland drew the community together and shared what she and her offling had experienced. Then he spoke of the unspeakable—of the Brothers and the Akassa and the physical differences between them. At the end, Raddoc reminded everyone to cloak themselves when they were away from Kayerm's immediate vicinity, and he set a boundary around Kayerm in the direction of the Brothers' village, which they were not to cross—cloaked or not. They would respect the Brothers' territory.

The days were growing shorter. And so was the time before the Mothoc had to leave their homes and Sassen relatives.

The High Rocks, being the largest community, had been divided up and the people left in smaller groups. The first left for Lulnomia, led by Dochrohan, who wanted to arrive with them and make sure all was in order before the next group showed up.

The trip was lengthy, but the colder weather made the travel much easier. Had anyone been able to see the caravan, it would have become a legend; however, they were all cloaked, and only another Mothoc would notice the slight shimmer that accompanied their movement. Days would turn into weeks before they arrived. The group was excited yet tearful, knowing they would never see their Akassa family members again.

Soon Rohm'Mok and Tala would leave with the last group, and at that point, Pan would go and collect those at Kayerm and start the long journey with them.

A similar process was taking place across all the communities, the Mothoc and their Leaders leaving their homes forever.

It was a difficult time. Emotions flared, and some

of the Akassa even pleaded with the Mothoc not to leave them. The strain was particularly wearing on Pan, and despite her heartbreak at leaving Kthama, part of her would be relieved when they had settled into Lulnomia and started to acclimatize to their new life there.

Pan had few belongings to take. There was the red jasper that Rohm'Mok had given her, and her keeping stone, which marked the major events of her life and roughly recorded her time on Etera. These she had sent ahead with Rohm'Mok. But there was one item only she could transport—an item she had not touched since Dak'Tor's betrayal of her. She had on several occasions reached to pick up the staff but could never bring herself to do so.

She had no choice but to take it with her. Not only was it the official staff of the House of 'Tor and would be handed to the next 'Tor Leader, but it housed the precious crystal that would be used to free her father. In addition, it was an artifact that would be a constant reminder to the Akassa of the Mothoc who used to live among them.

Pan stood in front of the Leader's Staff, which was still propped up in the corner from the last time she had carried it. She let out a long breath, reached out, and lifted it up.

The Leader's Staff was very familiar to Pan. She

knew the weight of it, the feel of her fingers wrapped around it, the balance of the length of it, the glimmer of the obsidian stone embedded in the bottom end. So, the moment she picked it up, she knew.

Something was wrong.

It was no longer balanced. A terrible thought ran through Pan's mind, and she squatted down with the staff.

She carefully found the seam and eased the cap off, knowing what she would find. Then she put the staff down and cradled her head in her arms, letting out a long, agonized wail. *"Noooooooooooooooooo."*

Her cry echoed through the corridors of Kthama. The Akassa everywhere turned and listened to the anguish that reverberated off the stone walls.

The crystal was gone.

Her father would never be freed from the vortex.

CHAPTER 11

Dak'Tor had taken the crystal. Pan knew this as well as she knew anything. No one else was aware of its existence. No one else would dare handle the Leader's Staff other than her brother. But why would he take the stone?

And when did he take it? Her mind raced. And then she knew; it had to be when the guards accompanied Dak'Tor back to his quarters, and the High Council had continued meeting to discuss his punishment. He knew he would be banished. *So, he took the crystal, believing it had some value to others? Or perhaps to barter with it for forgiveness for his crime?*

The time she spent with her mother in the Corridor had bought him the space he needed to get away.

When her emotions subsided, Pan picked up the staff to put the cap back on. She peered into the recess where the crystal had been snuggly fit into place.

Sadly, she stuck her finger into the crevice and felt around to see how it had been designed. It was smooth and deep, and as she finished circling the depression, her finger touched a rough edge. Pan peered down into the chamber and saw something curled up inside the cavity. Carefully, she used her fingernail to coax it up out of its place. As it came loose, up, and out, something clattered to the floor. Pan looked down. Her mother's red jasper stone. She picked it up and held it tenderly in her palm for a moment.

My father put this in here. Then she turned her attention to the hide that had been hidden inside. She carefully coaxed it out and realized it had to be the lost scroll of the Sacred Laws. Lor Onida's scroll. *So, Father had it all the time. But why hold it back from the community?*

It was nearing time to go. Moc'Tor knew he had only a few moments before he and E'ranale must make their way to Kthama Minor to engage the Ror'Eck-rah. He reached up high into the recess carved into one of the rock walls. Most living areas had such a place where special items were kept, well away from offling's curious hands and eyes.

There, Moc'Tor found the scroll that Lor Onida had given him for safekeeping. He lifted it down, carefully unrolled it, and gave it one last look.

Then, placing E'ranale's red jasper stone in the center, he curled it back up.

Saying a prayer to the Great Spirit, he gingerly removed the cap and carefully popped the crystal out. He slid in the curled-up scroll with the stone captured inside it. Then he returned the crystal, snugging it into position, and replaced the cap, being careful to line the grain of the bark so the seam would be barely perceptible. Satisfied that it was properly done, he returned the staff to its proper corner in his quarters.

"Are you not going to leave it in Dak'Tor's room?" E'ranale asked, her voice weak. "Have you not chosen him to lead?"

"I had at one time. And he was the one I prepared. Will you think less of me, Saraste', if I admit that for once I do not know what to do?" He came and sat down next to her, taking her hands in his.

"Even not knowing what to do is wisdom, my love," she said, looking up into his eyes. "You really do not know who to choose?"

Moc'Tor thought back to his conversation with his son about the staff.

"As part of your preparation to be Leader, I must reveal to you a great power that is contained in the 'Tor Leader's Staff. This sacred secret is only shared from one Leader of the House of 'Tor to the next. It is an ancient gift from the Great Spirit, and it is said that one day in

the future, this powerful tool will be needed by one who is yet to come."

"Does Pan know about this?" Dak'Tor had asked.

"Pan is not chosen to be Leader, so no, she does not. You are to be the next Leader of the High Rocks. You must guard this secret with your life, and you must at all costs protect the Leader's Staff. That is why no one but the Leader is allowed to touch or handle it."

"But that is true of the staff of any Leader," Dak'Tor argued. "For anyone but the Leader to hold it or touch it is punishable by banishment."

"It is true of any of the staffs because to make it apply only to the staff of the House of 'Tor would have created too much curiosity about why only this one was to be so revered."

"Father, I have seen the staff. It is just a large piece of carved tree branch," Dak'Tor scoffed. "You talk about it as if it is somehow magical,"

Moc'Tor had closed his eyes for a moment, taken a deep breath, and slowly let it out. "Inside the top, the thickest end of the staff, is a special crystal. It is this which must be protected at all costs. It is hidden inside because that is the safest place for it, inside an object that no one would dare to touch."

.   .   .

"Is it valuable?" Dak'Tor asked.

"It has value beyond measure. There is a prophecy with it that someday the Promised One, the An'Kru, will come to save Etera. The crystal is somehow tied to him."

Moc'Tor heaved a deep sigh. "Now go. Enough questions. Prepare to accept the mantle that will fall to you and carry it with pride."

Moc'Tor brought his thoughts back to his mate and the present. "Both are reluctant. Dak'Tor partly because he is wise enough to know that, though by tradition it should fall to him, he is not the best choice. And I do give him credit for that. And partly because he has never accepted responsibility, preferring to let others bear that burden. Pan, because she doubts herself. And that is something only she can resolve."

He ran his hand up and over the top of his head.

"And I know that what is about to happen, what we are about to do, is going to hit Pan hardest of anyone. Can I place this burden on her, along with the load she will already be carrying?

"But now, it is too late. I have already prepared Dak'Tor, so I will leave it in his room. I will wake him early from the Ror'Eckrah, so he has time to pull himself together and come to terms with his responsibility. The minute he sees it, he will know what has happened. He does not want the mantle of leadership, but I can only trust that somehow he will find it within himself to accept it."

E'ranale sighed and leaned her head back. "And so your last act as Leader is the deepest act of faith of all."

Moc'Tor leaned over and kissed her lips, then her forehead. "Not quite my last act," he said sadly, thinking of the painful decisions that lie ahead.

Pan sat holding the Leader's Staff, overcome with despair at the loss of the irreplaceable crystal. *Wherever he has ended up, alive or not, the precious crystal is with him.*

Suddenly all the wear and strain of the events since the deaths of her father and mother came storming in over her. Their loss, her brother's betrayal, and now leaving the High Rocks and everything that represented home to her. What had kept her going was her faith in the Great Spirit. And the belief that someday she would free her father from the Order of Functions.

Something inside of Pan broke, and she stretched out on the cold floor of the quarters she had shared with Rohm'Mok and Tala and slipped into deep despair.

Dochrohan knew that before long, the group from the High Rocks that he was leading would be within sight of Lulnomia. They had made the long journey without grumbling, though he knew they were tired of it and were missing home. As he was about to lead them around the end of the mountain to where they would have the first sight of their new home, he turned to face them and called out loudly.

"Listen to me. We are almost there. Much work has gone into preparing our new home. Please be appreciative of those who have come before and toiled so hard on our behalf."

With that, he walked on ahead and then turned back to watch; as the path curved, it gave them, one by one, their first sight of Lulnomia's grandeur.

And it truly was one of grandeur.

The snow-topped mountain beneath which Lulnomia curved and twisted was even taller than that of the High Rocks. The rocky overhangs sparkled in the mid-day sun. The first snow of the season had left a white blanket, which lent a celestial aspect to the scene. Tall firs and pine trees lined the base of the mountain and continued up the face on both sides, providing dark green relief to the white everywhere else. Small winter birds hopped from tree to tree, eyeing the Mothoc who were now to be their neighbors. Overhead, Kweak circled and cried out.

"Look, there is Kweak!" someone shouted. "A good sign, Kweak has come to tell us our journey is complete and that we have found our way."

Dochrohan felt their spirits rising, giving them the boost needed to press on the rest of the way.

Then the family members who had gone ahead to help prepare their new home were coming out of Lulnomia to greet the newcomers.

As Dochrohan entered, his eyes lifted upward to the sprawling rock ceiling and then down the sides and circled around the wide expanse. In so many ways, Lulnomia echoed the feel of Kthama only on an even larger scale.

It must be how the Akassa feel at Kthama, dwarfed by its size, he thought. He had not considered it until now.

But where moisture constantly dripped from the stalactites overhead at Kthama, the entrance here was dry, and without the dampness coming up from the Great River, the humidity was lower.

As delighted reunions were taking place, Dochrohan pulled aside the Leaders in the group and spoke with them first, pointing out specifically those who would show them and their people to their quarters.

Eventually, conversation slowed, and Dochrohan felt comfortable addressing the group again.

"I know you are weary," he announced. "Please go with the guides here, who will show you to your section. As explained earlier, we are placing each community into its own area. This will help us all adjust as we will have those we know the best closest to our own living quarters. There is one large chamber that will be used for eating, and your guides will point that out on the way. There are more than enough living quarters, and they are all roughly the same size. Any that were disproportionately large have been reserved for storage or meeting areas.

"Rest if you need to. A horn will sound when it is mealtime, but if you are in need of food or drink now, please let your guide know. In time, when all members of the High Rocks have arrived, Pan and Rohm'Mok will address you. Welcome home."

Dochrohan would give this same speech to each group and each community and their Leaders as they arrived.

Slowly everyone went with their way-showers through the tunnels and winding corridors. Some side-tunnels were closed off, which raised questions in everyone's minds. But they trusted there would be a general assembly before too long, during which they could get all their remaining questions answered.

⁂

Jhotin and Ei'Tol, with Diza on her hip, were part of this group. Ei'Tol was overwhelmed with the new sights, which, though so familiar, were also so not. The tunnels had been worked on; she could see the tool marks. They had been smoothed, leaving no rough projections along the walls or trip hazards on the floors. She felt a deep appreciation for all the work that had been done to prepare the place.

As they made their way down the tunnel to Kthama's section, chatter gave way to silence as they peeked and peered into the various living spaces, the stone doors of which had been pushed open so they could readily be entered. Their guide pointed out which had nests and offling areas already prepared for those with young. Once curiosity was satisfied that the quarters were all basically the same, each excitedly picked a space and set their things down.

Just as at Kthama, there were large living areas set aside for those unpaired males who preferred to live communally. Though Jhotin was unpaired, as Helper, he had his own living space not far from the Healer's Quarters.

Ei'Tol walked into her space and looked around. The walls had not been whitewashed, so it was mostly rock grey. Before she made herself at home, she tended to her daughter, placing her in the cozy nest that someone had set up. After soothing Diza and being assured that she was content, Ei'Tol walked around the living area. *I am the first to live here.* She felt safe. Protected. She said a prayer thanking the Great Spirit and the High Council for her freedom from Dak'Tor. Then she said a prayer for him, wherever he was, and hoped that he was not dead or suffering.

Dak'Tor was neither dead nor suffering, though he did have doubts about his future place with the rebels. Try as he had, Iria was still not seeded, and the more time passed, the greater pressure he felt. Which did not help his performance with his mate.

Though Iria did not comment about Dak'Tor's inability to seed her, Laborn certainly did.

"It has been long enough, and yet the female is not seeded. Are you mounting her regularly?" the Leader demanded.

Dak'Tor wanted to say it was none of Laborn's business but knew that would not be received well. "Yes. I am," he said. "You know that sometimes it takes a while for a female to become seeded. We are not the most prolific of species."

"But you proudly stated you had seeded many offling. So the problem must be with her!" Laborn said, looking to Useaves standing next to him.

"Perhaps that is true," she said. "Perhaps Iria is barren. We do not have time to waste. Laborn, pick another female for this male. Then we will know if the problem is with him or with her."

Off to the side, Iria had heard the conversation. She cautiously approached Laborn and Useaves. "Please, it has not been all *that* long. Please give us a while longer. Perhaps the fault is mine; perhaps I am too young and need a little more practice."

Useaves scoffed, "Practice? How good you are at

mating has nothing to do with it. Whether you enjoy it or not is between you and him."

Then Useaves turned to Laborn. "Give them a few more months. Then if there is still no offling growing inside her, we will give him another female."

Dak'Tor was trying to remember how long he had been paired before Ei'Tol was seeded. His mind was spinning, his usefulness to the community in danger of evaporating if he did not seed Iria and soon. He was grateful to Iria for not telling them about his recent inability to enter her. It was embarrassing enough without everyone knowing about it.

"Thank you," Iria said. Then she took Dak'Tor by the hand and led him back to their quarters.

When they were alone, Useaves spoke privately to Laborn. "You do not like him."

"I do not."

"Because he is the Guardian's brother."

"Yes. And I am not convinced he was not sent by her, despite what you said about his lack of preparation for such a journey. I get no feeling of loyalty from him and not even much affection for Iria," Laborn answered.

"You have not cared about affection since Shikrin died."

Laborn glared at the older female. No one else dared to talk to him as bluntly as she did, and no one else dared to raise the topic of his mate's death. He respected her for her brazenness but also hated her for it.

"Not for myself. But for others. Affection binds one to another. Why do you think I picked Iria? She is the one who has cared for him since he came. She has tended to him, looked after him. Now he mounts her. If affection does not grow in him for her now, then he is dead inside.

"Besides," he continued, "One who cares for another is more easily controlled. You were right, but not for the reason you stated. They need more time together. Involving another female would be wrong. I must give them time to bond. Only that way, when he cares for her, will I have leverage over him."

Laborn spat on the ground and walked away.

〈𝕫〉

Once inside their living quarters, Dak'Tor thanked Iria for her silence.

"I would not do that to you," she said. "I understand that it is of bigger concern to you than to me and is therefore embarrassing for you. And I know you are not comfortable here. Perhaps that is contributing to—the problem."

"I am glad you do not blame yourself. You are beautiful. Any male would want to mount you," he said.

It was the first kind thing he had ever said to Iria,

and a little spark of hope flared within that he might be warming to her.

"You are right," Dak'Tor continued. "I am concerned about my future here. Laborn does not fully accept me and never will. When I lose my usefulness to him, he may well throw me out, or worse."

"Try to relax. It will happen in time. How long did it take for the other females you lay with to become seeded?" she asked.

Dak'Tor frowned. Lies only brought more lies. Suddenly, he felt immensely fatigued, and a wall inside him dropped.

"I lied," he confessed. "I have only seeded one offling. I have only been with one female, and she only had the one."

"What about the one who died giving birth?" she asked.

"That was also a lie. She did not die giving birth. She is the one of which I speak. When I said I lost her, I meant that she asked for our pairing to be set aside."

Iria did not know a pairing could be set aside. Though it bothered her to know he had lied to her, she was afraid to ask any more questions. She was afraid he would close her off again, and besides, she was not sure she wanted to know the answers.

"Let us not worry about that now," she said. "Let us walk down to the shallows and spear some fish.

The temperatures have dropped, and it will be a pleasant task."

She picked up their hunting spears and handed one to him. He nodded and took it from her hand, and together they went to take their minds off their troubles.

꙰

As the couple made their way to the river, Iria could feel the other females' eyes on them. Those who had overheard the earlier conversation must have told the others. She was sure that every maiden was now wondering if she might be the next chosen to be mounted by this handsome and mysterious stranger.

Not if I can help it, Iria thought.

The couple spent the rest of the day down by the river. They made a good catch and were pleased to have enough extra to share with others. Iria suggested they should give some to both Laborn and Useaves, as a thank you for giving them more time.

"You are wise," Dak'Tor said. "How did you get so wise?"

Iria chuckled. "Race you back?" she said. Then to her surprise, her mate grabbed up his portion of the catch, his spear, and took off.

"Wait!" she laughed. "I did not say to start yet!"

Dak'Tor turned back enough to see her and laughed. Finally, he slowed down for her to catch up with him. "I won!" he declared.

"You cheated!" she parried.

"Not my fault. You were not clear about the rules," he chided her good-naturedly.

Iria drummed her fingers on his chin and smiled. "Hmmm. Well, I will not make *that* mistake again."

After they had shared their catch and eaten and were back in the privacy of their own quarters, Iria vowed she would leave it up to Dak'Tor to make any advances about mating. She was pleasantly surprised when he woke her up in the middle of the night and successfully and vigorously mounted her. For the first time, she felt as if it was lovemating and that he might be developing feelings for her.

But the next morning, when she awoke, he had already left their bed.

Later, when Iria found Dak'Tor, the wall had come back up. The closeness they had shared the night before was gone. She wondered what had happened to him or what secret he was hiding that he would shut everyone out, even her.

CHAPTER 12

Pan did not know how long she had lain on the floor of her quarters. Finally, she pulled herself up on one elbow and rubbed her face. *I must go to Kayerm.*

It was now the night of the second full moon since her previous visit, and they would be expecting her. But Pan's heart was not in it, and it was only through sheer will that she forced herself to her feet.

She picked up the Leader's Staff and took one last look around the living quarters she and Rohm'Mok had shared. Then she walked down the hallway and through to the Great Entrance, purposefully not entering the Leader's Quarters where her parents had lived. More goodbyes, more loss. That was what Kthama had come to mean for her. Pan hoped she would never have to return.

Then, as another would do thousands of years in

the future, Pan cast off the mantle of leadership of the High Rocks and left Kthama.

The trip to Kayerm was not long enough, but at the same time was too long. What Pan did not want now was time to think. She forced herself to focus on the present, putting one foot in front of another. She allowed no other thoughts to enter, none but the duty that lay before her.

Nightfall was upon her by the time she arrived. She could see the evening fire with many gathered around it. The Mothoc bodies cast much larger shadows than the Sassen, and it was an eerie sight with the flickering of firelight upon them all.

Someone pointed, and everyone turned as she approached.

"Greetings. As I said I would, I have returned before the end of the first night of the second full moon. Say your goodbyes this evening and make ready your belongings. We leave at first light."

No one dared ask anything else. Norland approached, and understanding that she had said all she wanted to say, he led her to the same quarters she had used before.

Alone with her thoughts once again, Pan placed the Leader's Staff in the eastern corner, turned away from it, and willed sleep to come.

The next morning at daybreak, led by Pan, the Mothoc group from Kayerm set out for Lulnomia. There was little talk among them. The Elders were silent, their hearts filled with grief at once again having to leave what had become their home. Out of respect for them, the younger Mothoc kept their thoughts to themselves.

During the day's travel, the group began to lighten up. Talk started to turn toward what lay ahead, and there was much speculation about what their new home would be like. For those who had followed Straf'Tor from Kthama, there was concern over the reunions to come. Pan could feel the energy of the group rise and fall and knew that this would not be an easy transition for them. In many ways, it would be harder for them than any of the other communities.

The first evening, when they were getting settled down for the night, she spoke to them.

"I know you understandably have questions about where we are going. I have told you that it is very much like Kthama, for those who knew it. However, it is a far more elaborate system than that of any of the communities. Each community and their Adik'Tar will have a separate area of Lulnomia.

The leadership structure will stay intact. Those of you who were born at Kayerm will learn about the High Council and the High Council Overseer and how we come together to collectively decide issues that affect all the Mothoc.

"I am sure you will find it hospitable, but I know you also have concerns about the reunions that will take place. Much time has passed, and I pray there has been healing on all sides. Please try not to let your imaginations run away with you and anticipate problems where they may not exist. The first few months will be the hardest, as everyone will be trying to adjust as they also deal with feelings of loss and grief. In time, those will shift and turn to the united future we will create together."

Kyana leaned back against Wosot while they were listening to Pan. The warmth of his chest on her back and his muscular arms wrapped around her were comforting. She could feel the strong ka-thump of his heartbeat and his warm breath. She considered herself blessed to have a mate such as he.

As with the other groups, when the Mothoc from Kayerm got their first view of Lulnomia, they all fell silent. It truly was a majestic scene. Their hearts sped up as they made the last bit of the journey and first walked through the entrance.

By the time Pan and the Mothoc of Kayerm

arrived, the other communities had already settled in. A sentry, in place to watch for the approaching group, alerted Dochrohan, Hatos'Mok, and Rohm'Mok.

By design, the entrance was mostly empty. Pan wanted to be in her mate's arms but held herself back out of respect for her position as Guardian. But the looks they exchanged said everything that needed to be said at that moment.

Once they were all gathered together inside, this time, in place of Dochrohan, Hatos'Mok addressed the newly-arrived community. "Welcome home."

He watched their reactions to get a feel for everyone's state of mind. Some smiled, others exchanged glances, and some unconsciously moved closer to a loved one, looking for comfort or reassurance.

Hatos'Mok introduced himself as the High Council Overseer and explained what the High Council was and why it was formed.

As there were no questions, he continued on. "In a moment, Dochrohan, High Protector of the High Rocks," and Hatos'Mok pointed him out, "will explain more about Lulnomia's layout and features. You will have your own section to settle into, and I want to assure you that you belong here as much as any other community, though I know it may take time for that to sink in."

"Thank you, Overseer," said Norland. "I am Kayerm's Leader. In time I am sure we will get to know each other well. My people and I appreciate your words of welcome."

"At some point, we will all meet together as one community," Hatos'Mok explained, "but it will be a while. Settle in. Learn the layout of your section. The guides are here to answer whatever questions you may have."

And with that, Hatos'Mok turned things over to Dochrohan. After Dochrohan was done, the guides led them down the tunnel to their section of Lulnomia.

Great care had been taken to assign the different areas. If anything, favoritism was given to Norland's community to ensure they did not feel disadvantaged by being the only followers of Straf'Tor. Pan was anxious to speak to them again, not in her position as the Leader of the High Rocks but as Etera's Guardian. However, she knew they needed time to adjust and for emotions to settle before they were ready for that. Like love, trust and unity had to be nurtured and given time to develop.

Once everyone had cleared out, Rohm'Mok put his arm around Pan and took her to their new quarters, where Jhotin was waiting with Tala. Pan did not take time to look around the room but quickly used her abilities to determine which was the east corner and leaned the Leader's Staff there. Then she rushed to sweep Tala up in her arms and hugged her tight and examined her daughter's face, fingers, and toes, and kissed her profusely.

Rohm'Mok thanked Jhotin, who excused himself and left.

Finally, Pan looked around the space. "It is generous. I think this is even larger than the Leader's Quarters back at Kthama.

"It is hard to believe, but everything is on an even larger scale," explained Rohm'Mok. There are also quite a few sections we have had to block off as we have not had time to thoroughly explore them yet. The little that was done indicates that they go deep, deep within the mountain range, stretching underground for an unimaginable distance. There is more room here than we could ever imagine needing. Who knows, there might be a river running through it far below, just like the Mother Stream. There is much to discover here. Much to learn."

Pan set Tala down in the offling area that had been prepared for her and stepped into Rohm'Mok's waiting embrace.

"I am so glad to be here," she sighed.

Rohm'Mok enclosed her tighter and then asked, "What is wrong? Is it more than the travel and the change?" He released her and led her to the seating area.

"I so need someone to talk to," Pan said. "And therefore, I am going to tell you things that perhaps I should not. But I no longer care; I cannot bear this burden alone, and I need the counsel of others.

"I know you remember Dak'Tor's fascination

with the Leader's Staff? He walked in on me when I had taken it apart one day."

"Taken it apart? It comes apart?"

"Yes. It comes apart. There is a carefully designed cap. Inside was a special crystal that is critical to Etera's future and to freeing my father from the Order of Functions. When I picked up the staff just before I left, I knew the balance was off. When I opened it, the crystal was gone."

"You are saying Dak'Tor took it with him when he left Kthama? I suppose, since he was not detained in his room, and with the delay, yes, he would have had the time. No one else knew he was in trouble, so if anyone had seen him, they would think nothing of it. And I am sure he did not walk out with the crystal in his hand."

"Do you think he knew what it was for?" Rohm'Mok asked after a moment.

"I suspect so. Since Father intended for Dak'Tor to lead the people of the High Rocks, he would have told him," Pan explained. Then, before her mate could ask, she added, "My mother told me about it in the Corridor."

What followed was a long explanation about the Corridor and Pan's mother and about the Seventh of the Six, the Promised One who would come in time. Rohm'Mok had long ago accepted that he would never know all the secrets and abilities of a Guardian. So he took what she told him as truth, and mate or not was honored to be taken into her confidence.

When all was said, what Rohm'Mok did not dare ask was why E'ranale had not warned Pan so she could have stopped Dak'Tor. But with all her troubles, if the thought had not occurred to his mate, he was not about to add it to her burdens.

"You are tired and still wounded by Dak'Tor's actions. You need to rest and settle in. I will go and get you something to eat. Please rest until I return."

While Rohm'Mok was fetching some food for Pan, she said aloud to the Great Spirit, "My beloved is right. I am tired and overwrought, but it is more than that. I trusted you to guide me, to help me. And now, on top of my brother's betrayal, the crystal is gone, and no one has any idea where he is. How am I to succeed now? How am I ever to free my father from the Order of Functions. Have I failed you somehow, and this is the result?"

She wanted to cry, but did not as she knew Rohm'Mok would be back soon.

Before long, it was mealtime. Bakru, First Guard of the High Rocks, went first into one community tunnel and then the next, blowing into a bison horn signaling their turn for meals. He gave the first community time to get to the eating area and get settled before he moved to the next.

Long before, when several of the early Akassa females from the Far High Hills had wandered very far away from their territory, they came across a group of males like none had ever seen before. They were fascinated by their coloring, so very pale, their head covering the color of the sun. In a moment of terrible judgment, they used their seed and produced offling. But before they overcame the males, one of them had blown on a horn, perhaps calling for help. The females had brought the object back, and the Mothoc and the Akassa copied it.

The members of all the communities present showed respect toward each other, although, like Rohm'Mok, some chose to take the food and return to their own living areas to eat, either alone or with their families.

The community from Kayerm was not yet mingling, but across the other communities, there was much happiness catching up on gossip, meeting each other's mates or offling, and showing each other their living areas.

Pan's speculation that time would have tempered the harsh differences in philosophy that had split families and friends, leading some to follow Straf'Tor to Kayerm, was yet to be proven.

After a few days, Hatos'Mok called the community Leaders of the High Council together. It was the largest group of Leaders ever assembled. Present were even the Mothoc Leaders from the distant communities of the Far Flats and the High Red Rocks. It had taken a great effort to include them and get all their Mothoc to Lulnomia. Without their Healers and High Protectors, it was a small gathering, but it was important to Hatos'Mok that he address only the Adik'Tars themselves.

Because there were some new members there, Hatos'Mok re-introduced himself and explained the history and role of the High Council and the Overseer.

Then he added, "Never forget; you are still the Leaders of your communities. We have intentionally given you each a section of Lulnomia to call your own, and you still retain jurisdiction over your people. You have lost no authority, no power; nothing has changed other than that we are now living in close proximity. We all honor the same laws. On the off chance that there are disputes between Leaders, those disputes will be heard by the High Council, with the Overseer having the final say. If the dispute is with the Overseer himself, then how to resolve the problem will fall to the Guardian's wisdom."

Seeing the group relax, Hatos'Mok asked for a report from each of the Leaders on how their community was fairing. Overall, it was the same; everyone had mixed feelings. They were impressed and pleased with how spacious and comfortable Lulnomia was. There were positive reports about the abundance of resources from those who had ventured out to explore the area, and there were questions about the blocked-off corridors.

Pan had situated herself near Norland. He stood when it was time for his report. "First, I want to thank the Guardian for reaching out and including us in this community and for her efforts to help us feel as comfortable as possible. I know you realize that my people are experiencing a range of emotions, and some feel more uncomfortable than others. They fear rejection, perhaps even condemnation, for the differences in beliefs that originally divided us. We are few in number compared to the rest of you, the followers of Moc'Tor."

Pan did something she hardly ever did; she reached out and touched another, laying her hand on Norland's shoulder. He did not acknowledge it, but she could feel him relax under her touch.

"If this is not the time or place to ask, I apologize," Norland continued, "but I would like to know how you want to incorporate us into the general population when the time comes."

"This is the perfect time and place to ask," Hatos'Mok replied. "All of us recognize the difficulty of your situation. And I, for one, applaud your courage in reuniting your people with ours. All of our High Protectors have been given instructions that if any disparagement takes place, they are to notify the Guardian or me immediately. Each of us is here in peace, united as one family, and you are as welcome as anyone. Perhaps even more so."

Hatos'Mok looked at Pan, who added, "We have no timeline, and there is no rush for any of this. When your people are ready to reach out to their lost relatives and friends, it will happen. It may take some longer than others. Some may prefer not to engage at a closer level. Trust the rhythm of our new life here and let it unfold as it will." She heard the words come out of her mouth, but her heart was empty with despair. Still, she had a duty to do, and she was going to do it, no matter how betrayed and alone she felt.

Before they adjourned, Hatos'Mok thanked them and asked them to bring their Healers and their High Protectors to the next meeting, which would take place in a few days.

Before Norland left, Rohm'Mok came over to meet and welcome him. The two males hit it off immediately, which brought Pan one of her few moments of pleasure so far at Lulnomia. She was comforted to think that there would be someone else for Norland to turn to for support, and there was no better male to guide him than Rohm'Mok.

Kyana had settled into their new living quarters. They were far more spacious than those at Kayerm, and she was grateful she had stepped into a better life. Though she missed the Sassen she had grown up with and loved, the promise of an easier life at Lulnomia eased some of the heartache.

Being older, her sons were sharing quarters together. When Norland paired, his brother would no doubt move out, but for now, they enjoyed each other's company and the spacious Leaders Quarters. Kyana's daughters still lived with her and Wosot, though they often spent a lot of time either with Toniss or with Lorgil and her son, to whom they had grown close. Their time away gave Kyana and Wosot some privacy to enjoy time alone with each other.

Their lovemating was finished, and they lay together in each other's arms.

Wosot turned his head so he could look at Kyana. "Are you happy here?"

"So far, I am, with the usual sadness about leaving Kayerm, of course. But mostly, this feels like a great adventure. We have not mingled with the rest, but I do not anticipate any trouble."

Then she added, "Do you?"

"Not in the way you think of it," he answered. "There might be some—" He reached for the word, "—entanglements. But I will not allow them to affect us."

Kyana sat up on one elbow so she could look at

him, "You are talking about females you mated with?" There. It was out there. The dreaded subject neither had dared broach with any depth.

Now Wosot sat up, facing her.

"Remember that I was a friend of Straf'Tor. We were contemporaries. We were robust young males long before the time that Moc'Tor restricted pairing to one male and one female."

Kyana swallowed hard, afraid of what was coming next. "How many?" she squeaked out.

"Too many. I was no better than the others. I took pleasure where I could find it. But," and he paused, "never without consent. I never forced myself on a female as some of the males did. I want you to know that."

"But then after the rules changed, you did not mate after that?" she asked, not believing it could be likely that any male would go that long without mating. "And why did you not pair? Surely you were asked." She clenched her teeth against the answers that she did not want to hear.

"Yes. I was asked. By several. It resulted in turmoil and conflict, but there was no one I favored over the others. It was physical release only. So to quell the conflict, I accepted none of their offers. It was a long time ago. They have moved on with their lives, as I have, and they will give no more thought to me than to any other male. Much time has passed, and whatever interest they may have had in me is passed. Remember, you and I are paired. And nothing can come between us but what we allow."

Still struggling, Kyana was silent for a moment and then said, "So from that time, until you and I—"

Wosot tipped her chin up, so she had to look into his eyes, "Yes, from that time until you and I were paired, there was no one. It is true. Before that, yes, I shared pleasure with many females, Saraste'. But until you, never my heart."

Kyana reached up and caressed his face with her hand. "I love you so."

"And I love you." He pressed his lips to hers and then lay back down, taking her with him, pressing her up close and cuddling her.

CHAPTER 13

L ife moved forward at Lulnomia. The Leaders had decided that their High Protectors should join together to figure out how they could organize the work of maintaining Lulnomia. In the same vein, Tyria had suggested the Healers and Helpers start their own circle. Hatos'Mok looked upon this as progress, as the inter- mingling of the separate groups would foster the unity he knew was critical to the community's health.

Because of all the changes at once, the High Council had put any pairings on hold. If there was disappointment, it was not noticeable. There was change enough for now. When they did resume pair- ings, these would be the first celebrated at Lulnomia and even more in line with her name, *sacred weavings*.

Vel and Inrion had found their places at Lulno- mia, acting as unofficial leaders of the females of the

High Rocks. Just as the males had the High Protector and even Rohm'Mok to represent them, the females needed a way to put forward their questions or concerns.

Being the oldest sister, Vel was used to taking charge, and decision-making came easily to her. Inrion was a listener, more prone to deep thinking, so they made a balanced team.

When the High Council announced there would not be any pairings in the immediate future, Vel found she was relieved. Though she had asked long ago, seeing the strain on others and feeling it herself, she agreed this was not the time to make another big life change. Because the communities lived in one huge system, the opportunity to meet and establish a relationship with a potential mate was much higher. However, the pairings were to be decided by the High Council after examination of the bloodlines of the candidates. The possibility of emotional attachments independently forming complicated what had been intended to be a well-thought-out selection process.

With the height of winter upon them, there were fewer outside tasks to be done. Planting, tending, gathering would wait; now was the time for tool making and socializing. So it was a natural progression that the communities would start mingling.

Naming conventions for the primary areas of Lulnomia were practical. For example, the large entrance was called the Great Entrance, as it had been at Kthama, which had a similar expansive entry area. The common eating area was not the same chamber used for community meetings, only because the generous size of Lulnomia made it unnecessary. And also, due to the many available rooms, some had become dedicated to specific activities, such as toolmaking, which further encouraged members of the communities who shared a common interest to come together.

As the months passed, more and more friends and family members found each other. Those who did interact with others brought stories and news back to their individual communities. This stirred the desire in the hesitant to re-connect with their own lost loved ones.

Slowly the community of Lulnomia was becoming one, with the exception of the people of Kayerm, who still kept to themselves. Pan hoped she had been right, that time and distance had healed the bitterness among the original families who had been divided over the philosophies of Moc'Tor and Straf'Tor. But the test would truly come when the people of Kayerm began to mix with the other communities.

But not everything was as it seemed. Unbeknownst to Wosot and Kyana, at least one pair of eyes was watching them whenever they were out in public.

Wosot and Kyana were passing through the Great Entrance on their way to take a walk in the refreshing brisk winter air when someone called out Wosot's name.

He stopped and turned. "Lavke?"

The female came over to them.

"I would recognize you anywhere. You have hardly changed," she said and glanced in Kyana's direction. "I see you have a daughter?" The female brazenly looked her up and down.

"This is Kyana," he answered. "My mate."

"Oh," she said. "A natural mistake, I am sure you realize."

Wosot turned to Kyana, "This is Lavke of the House of Nil. We are old acquaintances."

"*Old* is not very kind, Wosot. And we were a little more than acquaintances," she said. And tilting her head at Kyana, she laughed unkindly.

"We must be on our way," Wosot said curtly.

"Do you not want to hear about Joquel?" she asked.

"Why should I? I never claimed Joquel as my own. We both know there is no way of knowing who seeded her," he scowled.

"I know that was always your position. And I say

as I always have, she is yours. As well as are many others, no doubt," she snapped.

"Our lives took different paths long ago. Be on your way now. Be happy with your life and your choices." Wosot took Kyana's hand and walked away.

As they left, Lavke called out to him, "Be sure to look up your other conquests. There are many things you need to know!"

Wosot tried to brush off Lavke's last comment but feared he knew what she was alluding to.

"I can see that time has not improved her personality," he said, to which Kyana gave a brief smile.

However, she could not so easily dismiss what had just happened. She tried to keep quiet but could only hold her silence so long. "So that was one of the females you used to mount."

Wosot appeared a bit shocked by Kyana's brusque comment but then agreed, "You are absolutely correct. And mounting her was all there was to it. There were no feelings involved and no affection. It was a physical release for us both, and do not let her or anyone else lead you to believe otherwise."

"I believe you when you say there was nothing on your side, but her reaction says that she did have feelings for you," Kyana said.

"Whether she did or did not makes no difference. That was very long ago, and nothing came of it. She is a person of no consequence to us. If anything, it is more likely jealousy because of your youth."

"And because you and I are paired," she added.

Wosot let out a long sigh. "Well, yes, there is that. She was one of those who wanted to pair with me, and there may have been more to it for her. But also, she might simply have wanted a protector, someone to provide for her and her offling because Lavke was not the kind of female who seemed to care who mounted her. If anything, she was often the one who initiated it."

Wosot stopped walking and turned to Kyana, "Please, Saraste'. Please do not let her get to you. Clearly, that was her intent. We love each other, and we cannot let someone else cause trouble between us. Promise me you will stay away from her, and if she corners you, not to believe anything she says. People who are unhappy are sometimes jealous of others who are."

"I know that," she said and briefly hung her head. "I just wish I was carrying your offling."

"Shhhhh," he said. "You are making far more of this than I. If we never have offling of our own, that is fine. I am even happier with our life than I ever expected to be. This is enough for me. More than enough," and he pulled Kyana into him and wrapped his arms around her.

Off in the distance, Lavke, who had followed them, had watched the entire exchange and was no doubt pleased to see that she had indeed managed to have an effect.

Somewhere along the way, Dak'Tor had made a friend. It started out as an assignment from Laborn, who sent him out on a hunting party with Dazal to teach Dak'Tor more about the area.

He struggled to keep up with Dazal, who had grown up all his life working for what he had. As the son of Moc'Tor, Dak'Tor had enjoyed the privilege of being the Leader's son; and had taken advantage of the generosity of others. He had not hunted and worked as an equal with the other males and knew that his father had frowned on this. However, he was now paying for his life of comparative ease.

"Wait up," he barked as he lost his foothold and slid back down the steep incline. Dazal stopped and looked back down the slope at him but said nothing.

Dak'Tor regained his footing, and huffing and puffing finally made his way up to where Dazal was waiting. When Dak'Tor straightened up, he looked at his palms, scuffed and bleeding. He glanced around, then reluctantly wiped them on his thighs.

"Are you sure this is the way?" He squinted at Dazal.

"I have no reason to make it harder on you than it is."

"Are you sure about that?"

"Our hunting together is not a trick of Laborn's to punish or try you if that is what you are thinking. Here, let us sit awhile."

Dak'Tor was relieved for the break, even though it meant longer time in the stranger's company.

"I have nothing against you," Dazal continued. "I was assigned to show you the hunting areas. Just as the female Iria was told to see after your health."

"Well, forgive me if I do not necessarily trust anyone here. In my position, would you?"

"Probably not." Dazal paused. "But you do not seem good at any of this."

"If you mean walking long distances, climbing up impossible heights, and whatever else we are about to do, you are right. I am not."

"Did your father not teach you? We have heard of the great Moc'Tor. Surely the son of Moc'Tor would be a skilled hunter, a great provider?"

"He did. He taught me everything we males should know. I just never kept it up. I concentrated on—other matters. But I am an excellent tracker and can hunt well enough to survive."

"By *other matters,* I can only assume you mean your preparation to take over as Leader of the High Rocks," Dazal said. "But we already have a Leader, and in case you had not noticed, Laborn is not one to give any quarter. He expects everyone to pull their weight. If he learned that at your age, you are not able to provide abundantly for yourself and any family you might have— I am not sure even those precious male seeds of yours would quell his anger."

Afraid Dazal would be giving a negative report to Laborn, Dak'Tor was about to lash out when Dazal said, "So we have to make sure he never finds out, right?" And he smiled.

"You are not going to tell him?"

"Not everyone here is loyal to Laborn. There are some of us who long to be free of his angry reign. But since that is not likely, we just stay out of his way and go on with our lives." Dazal stood up and brushed the snow from his coat. "So, whatever you do not know, I will be glad to teach you."

"Is there a catch?"

"There is no catch. I assume you would do the same for me."

Dak'Tor could only blink. For the first time in his life, he had a friend.

Iria was happy to see it and felt it could only be good for her mate to have someone besides her who was not against them. Dazal had a sister, Dara, and she, Iria, and Zisa all got along well. It was not uncommon for the five of them to be seen laughing together around their own separate evening fire. Laborn was not sure he was happy the stranger had found allies, but he reminded himself that personal ties only made him more vulnerable and easier to control.

Iria was still nervous over Laborn's threat to select another female for Dak'Tor to mate. However, finally, the day came where she was confident she was seeded, and she informed Laborn.

"Very well. I do not believe in coddling females,

but since this offling is so important to our future, another female will pick up some of your chores." Useaves, always present at important discussions, nodded her agreement.

"I appreciate that, but I do not think it is nec—" Iria started to object.

"It is not yours to think about, female," Laborn barked. "Another will take over your more strenuous tasks, and you can switch to mending and weaving and whatever else is less taxing."

Useaves nodded and walked off with Gard to find one of the younger females to take over some of Iria's daily chores.

When Dak'Tor and Dazal later returned from a brief foray looking for flint, Iria told them what had happened.

"As much as I hate to say it," said Dazal, "if you are seeded, I think that was a good decision."

"Why do you hate to say it?" Dak'Tor asked, frowning.

"Because I hate to give that miserable old PetaQ Laborn credit for anything."

They all laughed. Dazal was one of those in Iria's generation who did not think much of Laborn.

Dak'Tor thought back to his reaction when Ei'Tol had told him she was seeded. He realized that this time he felt none of the resentment he had then. Perhaps he was changing, or perhaps having a friend made it easier for him to accept it since there was more than one person he was close to. Or maybe he simply did not love Iria as he loved Ei'Tol, so it did not matter as much. However, he immediately put that out of his mind.

"A new offling due in the hottest time of year," Iria said. "Not what I would have chosen, but I am grateful—and relieved—regardless."

That evening there was even more gaiety at Dak'-Tor's fire. Again, it was not lost on Laborn, who watched from a distance.

As was always the case in a small community, word spread quickly that Iria was seeded. Some were happy for her, and some were happy for themselves as this meant a chance for their own offling to someday have offling by this one.

Some of the females were still jealous that Iria had the striking stranger all to herself. And some of the males were irritated that Laborn had chosen one of the most attractive females for Dak'Tor and that he was permitted to mate while they were not.

Whenever she was able, Useaves watched the couple closely, sizing up their exchanges, how they moved around each other, how often one touched the other. She could see that Iria cared for Dak'Tor, but she was not sure that Dak'Tor returned the female's feelings. The old Healer was not convinced of the affection for Iria that Laborn was counting on to make Dak'Tor more manageable.

One afternoon when they were alone, she told Laborn her thoughts. That evening Laborn called Iria and Dak'Tor to them.

"It is good news that you are seeded, but things can go wrong. Counting on only this offling is not wise. Gard, fetch Vaha and bring her here." Like Iria, Vaha was considered one of the most attractive young females they had.

Within a few moments, Gard returned with the maiden.

"You will now mate with Vaha," Laborn said to Dak'Tor.

"But I thought you said—"

"Do not tell me what I did or did not say. I am now saying that you are to mount Vaha. Often and frequently, until she is seeded. Once she is seeded, we will go from there."

Iria shook her head and glared at Laborn. "No, it is not fair. Dak'Tor and I are paired, and I am seeded. That is what you said you wanted."

"It was. Congratulations. And now I want something else. Do not argue with me; you have only your own selfish desires in mind. I am looking out for the health and future of our community."

Having tried to stay out of things, Iria's father could not take what he had just overheard and approached the group. "Laborn, do you honestly believe this is the best solution? We know nothing about the Guardian's brother. He may well seed offling with health issues. It would be wise to wait until my daughter's offling is born before seeding another female by him."

"You speak well, but you do not fool me. Your concern is not as high-minded as you would like me to believe. You are only trying to protect your daughter's heart."

Iria shot her father a look of gratitude before facing Laborn once more. "Where will she—is she—to join us in our living space?" Her voice was shaking with anger.

"That is not necessary. Vaha can continue living with her parents. There is no reason why this has to interfere between you and Dak'Tor," he added.

Not interfere? She wanted to scream. Her mate mounting another female was supposed not to interfere?

She clamped down hard on her emotions. "Are we dismissed?" she asked curtly.

Laborn waved them away.

Not wanting Dak'Tor to see how upset she was, and being afraid that he might not be, Iria hid until it was dark and went to spend the night with Zisa, who was always there to comfort Iria when she needed it.

Alone in their quarters, Dak'Tor had his own concerns. He had never had a strong sexual drive, and he was not looking forward to being forced to mate with another female. Iria's loyalty to him and her patience and understanding had helped him overcome his performance issues, and he was not sure this new female would react the same.

His welcome there was based on his ability to seed. Should his usefulness there come into question, what other bargaining chip did he have?

Dak'Tor's thoughts turned to the crystal from the 'Tor Leader's Staff. Some time ago, in a period of assured privacy, he had scaled the rough walls and carved out a hole near the ceiling, into which he had tucked the stone. Hidden by the shadows where the walls met the roof, it was not noticeable unless one was looking for it.

His father had said the crystal was priceless. But what did Moc'Tor mean by that? And he had said no one else knew about it, so why would anyone even believe Dak'Tor if he told them it was valuable?

The only other thing he could think of that would be of use to Laborn was the knowledge that the Mothoc had left the Akassa communities, making the Akassa very vulnerable. But once that information was given up, he had nothing else.

So, for now, he had to hope that Iria's offling would be born healthy. And that Vaha would turn out to be as understanding as Iria had and not tell Laborn of his problem.

It was very late, and the evening fire was reduced to a few faint embers. Useaves had waited for all the others to leave until she was alone with Laborn.

"Why would you give another female to Dak'-Tor?" she asked. "If you wish his affection for Iria to grow, it seems counter-productive."

"On the contrary. It is exactly the smart thing to do. It serves two purposes. One, it provides an opportunity for another of his bloodline to be born sooner rather than later. Secondly, it has been long enough. If he has any feelings for Iria, rokking Vaha will bring them out. If he feels nothing for Iria, he will not feel disloyal to her, and rokking a new female will be filled only with anticipation, no regret. Once one truly loves someone, it all changes, and taking another only makes one feel bad."

As Laborn talked, Useaves realized again how much he grieved the loss of his mate. She had never thought of him as having a heart but now saw the pain behind the rough and callous exterior. *He misses her. He truly loved her.* And that was why he had never taken another female since her death. Probably also part of the reason he was so opposed to anyone else finding a true mate.

Laborn could feel Useaves staring at him. "What are you looking at, old female? Whatever you think you have figured out about me, you are wrong."

He got up and stomped off.

Zisa was doing her best to console her friend. She had made Iria a soothing herbal drink and pulled as many hides up around her as she could, more for comfort than for warmth.

Then she sat next to Iria. "I know you are upset. I would be too. But my mother says that males do not think of mating as we do. To them, it is just for their own release. We are always hoping for lovemating, and I suppose it happens for some, but it is rare. There will be no emotional attachment to it for him, I can assure you of that."

"Why, why, do we have to feel affection for them? Why can we not just be practical and distanced?" Iria lamented.

"I wish I knew. Perhaps it is because we take the male into the most intimate part of ourselves. Some sacred act of acceptance, joining. On another level, it creates spiritual bonds for us. Why it does not do so for them, I do not know. In time perhaps—at least that is our hope—those feelings will become mutual."

"I cannot help but feel sorry for Vaha. Dak'Tor is handsome, but no female really wants to share her male. Maybe that is my mistake. I think of him as mine." Iria's voice dropped, "And he is not."

"Iria—"

She glanced up at her friend, "I know what you are saying. But I will never accept it. If he goes through with this, then he cannot care for me—not as I do for him. It is not just the pain of sharing him in that way, the most sacred way there can be between a male and a female; it is also knowing that he does not care how much it will hurt me. How can any male hurt a female he truly loves? If it is as meaningless to them as you say, how can it be worth it to them to hurt us so?"

Zisa had no words to dispute this. It was the greatest flaw, how differently males and females looked at the mating act. Neither was wrong, but they were irreconcilable viewpoints, and the exceptions were few.

"I agree," she said. "But in this case, I do not see that he has a choice."

Iria briefly put her hand to her mouth, and pushing back tears, looked at her friend. "You are right."

Vaha hurried as quickly as she could to tell her parents.

Her mother was horrified that Vaha would be used in this way, but her father had a different opinion. "This is an honor. You should be happy, not upset. Producing an offling of the Guardian's brother will elevate your status, which can only help you in life, not hurt you. Better him than someone else Laborn could have chosen for you. Or you might have gone a long time without being allowed to have an offling."

"How can you say that? The Leader is only using her. He is not doing this to help her," Vaha's mother retorted.

"Whatever the reason, that is still the end result. Your offling will not only be able to breed with any of the others, but it will carry Guardian blood. Who knows what might come of that?"

"The Guardian is only born of the 'Tor line," her mother replied.

"Well, exactly. Dak'Tor is 'Tor; you are not thinking clearly. It can happen. Imagine if the next Guardian was born here among us? Think of the power that would bring."

"I do not believe a Guardian would take part in Laborn's vision of eliminating the Akassa and the Sassen. A Guardian is the protector of all life on Etera, not here to do our bidding," his mate said.

"That is because they train each other. Without that influence, without another Guardian to fill that one's head with all that protector nonsense, a Guardian would be ours to mold into thinking however we want."

Then he turned to their daughter, his voice getting louder and louder with excitement at the possibilities. "You must do everything you can to please him. Make sure he mounts you frequently. This is an opportunity for you and for us. You are young; you could produce many offling, and one of them might well be a Guardian."

Vaha went over to her mother, who took her in

her arms. "Mama," she said, resting her head on her mother's chest.

"Shhhhh. The path is set. Short of running away, there is nothing we can do about it. And there is nowhere to run to. Try to make the best of it. Perhaps he will be kind. Iria seems to care for him, so let us hope for the best," and she stroked her daughter's head. "This is certainly not easy on Iria. Perhaps harder because she has feelings for him."

There were no preparations to be made, as Dak'Tor and Vaha were not to be paired. One evening, Gard simply brought Vaha to Dak'Tor and Iria's living quarters and presented her to him.

"Now that you have met, I will leave you to your responsibilities," Gard said before leaving.

Iria looked at Vaha, and Vaha looked at Iria. Then they both looked at Dak'Tor.

"Why are you looking at me? I do not know what to do about this either!" he blurted out. "This certainly was not my idea." Then he caught himself and added, "Not that you are not beautiful, Vaha, I did not mean that."

Seeing the look on Iria's face, Dak'Tor decided he had best shut up.

Iria rose and said, "I will leave you two alone. Dak'Tor, please let me know when I may return. For the time being, I will be staying with Zisa."

As she walked to her friend's quarters, she passed Vaha's parents. She and Vaha's mother exchanged looks, and suddenly Iria did not feel quite so alone. *She understands.* Even though it was her daughter who was lucky to be chosen, she understood what it was like for Iria.

Alone with Vaha, the pressure was enormous. Dak'Tor wanted only to disappear—at least to buy time until he could get his head together. He knew that pressure was the last thing he needed right now.

"You are a maiden, I presume?" he said.

"Yes, I have never been mounted," she answered quietly.

"I do not want to rush you. We can take it slowly. So, tonight, do not worry about it. Get some sleep, and I will be back in the morning," he said.

Vaha looked at him without understanding. "You are not going to —?"

"Not tonight. By the look on your face, it seems you could use a little more time."

Perhaps he is kind, after all. Vaha could not imagine many males taking their time with it. Maybe this was why Iria cared for him so. Apparently, he had a tender and thoughtful side!

Having bought some time, Dak'Tor sneaked out and went to find his friend Dazal.

He was disappointed to find Dazal's sister there,

too. Not knowing what else to do, he just blurted out, "May I speak with your brother alone?"

"Of course," and she left the two males.

"I need your help," Dak'Tor said.

"Of course, anything. What is it?"

"You are the only friend I have. The only friend I have ever had. I am trusting you with my life."

"What is wrong?"

"I know you know Laborn has given Vaha to me. Everyone knows." Dak'Tor swallowed hard. "I need you to mate with Vaha."

"*What*?" Dazal could not stop his reaction.

"Do not make me say it again."

"Why? Why would you need me to do that?"

Dak'Tor's heart sank. He was hoping not to disclose his problem. Then Dazal said, "Oh. I understand. You love Iria. And you cannot betray her this way."

A door of escape opened, and Dak'Tor quickly lunged through it. "Yes, I cannot."

"I have to say this is not something one gets asked to do every day. But how am I supposed to pull it off? Do not get me wrong, I would be more than happy to," and Dazal grinned widely.

Dak'Tor felt a huge sense of relief that Dazal was not going to refuse or go running to Laborn. "The new moon is up, and it is cloudy. It is dark. She is a maiden, so she would not know one male from another. If you sneak in while she is asleep and say nothing, she will not suspect."

"But we can see in the dark. And your coloring; will she not know the difference?"

"Do not turn your back on her; that is where the brightest of my light coloring is. But now that you mention it, I should find another place to take her. Someplace as dark as I can find, without any starlight even, where it is unlikely we will be noticed coming and going; she may even find that romantic. I can stand guard until you are done. If need be, we can dust you with chalk, enough to get through one brief rokking."

"You are not thinking straight. She would smell the chalk. If only you could just ask her to keep her eyes shut," Dazal suggested. Then seeing the look on Dak'Tor's face, he added, "I was just kidding."

"No. You might be onto something. I need another element of assurance." He walked around a bit as he thought. "I will ask her to keep her eyes closed."

"Why in the world would she do that?"

"I will tell her I am guilt-ridden for having to mount her when I am in love with Iria. That it will help me if there is no chance we could make eye contact, even in the dark. Make it less real."

"Well, this is the most interesting proposition I have ever received. Rok a maiden and not have Laborn know anything about it," Dazal said.

"Surely you have—?"

"No. Remember, Laborn has severely limited breeding to only those already paired from before or who have had offling. To begin with, the group that left Kayerm was made up mostly of relatives. Then on top of that, we lost so many in the cave-in, further reducing the number of bloodlines. That is why your coming holds so much value to him."

"Well, this is the only solution I can think of," Dak'Tor said. "And I can only put her off so long. If she does not become seeded, Laborn may suspect there is something wrong with her. But no one must know."

"Oh, absolutely not. For one, my sister and my mother would kill me if they knew I was doing this. Probably all the other females as well. Do not worry; I will not betray you. So, we will have to keep this up until she becomes seeded?"

Dak'Tor sighed heavily. "I had not thought of that. Apparently so. I will have to think of some excuse to put her off when the moon is brighter."

Dazal shook his head. "I cannot believe my luck. I hope that before I take my last breath, I can tell at least someone about this."

"As long as I am dead and gone, you can boast away. Though I suspect even then Laborn would have your head if he found out you had helped outsmart him."

"I agree, except it is not likely it would be only my head he would have removed."

"We have a deal then," Dak'Tor said and raised his palm in the sign of a Rah'hora. "You mount Vaha until she is seeded, and no one will know but us."

Dazal stepped forward and placed his palm hard against Dak'Tor's. "Rah'hora."

The new moon was not long off, and Dak'Tor had to scout secretly to find a place to use instead of the quarters he shared with Iria. Finally, he found a small cave hidden behind the rise that was home to their cave system. He spent some time there, making sure no one else was using it, possibly offling playing games. Then, so as not to be noticed, he very carefully prepared a soft sleeping area using dried grasses, leaves, and fir boughs. He placed it as far back as he could, in the darkest corner beyond a curve in the walls. It took him a fair bit of time as it was very dark in there, and even he had to feel his way. But the darkness was just what he needed.

The prearranged night came. Dak'Tor told Iria ahead of time so she would stay away and go to her friends. Then he told Vaha he had a surprise for her and led her out of his and Iria's quarters. Dazal was already hidden in place outside the cave.

"Where are we going?" Vaha asked.

Dak'Tor took her hand and said, "You will see. A special place just for us. It does not feel right being with you in the same place I was with Iria."

He led her to the very back and around a curve in the cave, to the soft area he had prepared. "It is so dark in here!" she said.

"I will explain why in a moment," he answered. He helped her to the mat and waited till she was situated comfortably. Then he sat down next to her.

"You know that Laborn chose Iria for me. But in our time together, I have grown to love her. I know I have to do this; it is my duty, and if I do not, who knows what Laborn might do. To her, to you, to me. But that does not make it any easier."

"I understand," she answered.

"I do not mean to insult you. You are very beautiful, just like Iria. I want to make this enjoyable for you. But the only way I can do that is if I can pretend you are her. So I need you to keep your eyes closed and not talk. It will make it less real for me. Can you understand that?"

"Yes. I can. And I think it is sweet of you."

"I have your promise then?"

"Yes."

Dak'Tor then kissed her and soothed her hair back, as he knew Iria enjoyed. He took some time trying to get her to relax. He kissed her a few times. When she eventually reached to wrap her arms around him, he was careful to keep his torso away from her. Since she seemed either ready or willing to submit, he paused and held himself still and said, "Shhhhh. Wait a moment. I think I heard something outside. I will be back."

Then, feeling his way out along one of the walls, he went to find Dazal.

"All the way to the back, like I showed you," he whispered to Dazal. "I told her I need her to keep her eyes closed and not to speak so I can pretend she is Iria. That this was the only way I could do it. Once she falls asleep, fetch me, and we will switch places."

"How can I ever repay you?" Dazal kidded.

"Be gentle. Do what you can to make sure she enjoys it. I do not want the reputation of being a selfish lover. If you think she can take a second filling, spill all you can into her."

"Not a problem," Dazal said and patted Dak'Tor on the shoulder.

Vaha rose up on one elbow when she heard soft footfalls approaching, but true to her promise, she kept her eyes closed. So as not to alarm her, Dazal whispered her name just loud enough so she could hear it but not tell it was a different male's voice.

He carefully sat down, took his place next to Vaha, and felt for her face. He caressed her cheek, then he pressed his lips against hers and kissed her deeply. With Dak'Tor's warning to be sure to make it enjoyable to her still in his mind, he made sure to hold and caress her. As he continued kissing her, a little more passionately, a little sound escaped Vaha's lips, and she snaked her arms around his shoulders and pulled him closer. He leaned her back on the mat and did his best to arouse her. Finally, he eased himself into her and moved as gently as he could so she would not have a bad first experience, as he had heard that sometimes this was the case. When he was done, he whispered, "Shhhhh," reminding her to be quiet. He positioned himself behind her, and gave her a little bit of time, and then took her from behind. When he was done, he laid down and pulled her down to him. He wrapped her arm around her waist, so she was facing away.

"That was easier than I even hoped it would be," she said, oh so quietly.

"I am glad," he dared to whisper in reply. "Now sleep," he said.

When Vaha was sound asleep, Dazal eased up away from her and went to find Dak'Tor, who carefully slipped in to take Dazal's place.

In the morning, when they awoke, Vaha thanked Dak'Tor for being kind and gentle with her. She asked how often they should mate, and he suggested a frequency that aligned with the darkest phases of the moon, lying that his sister, the Guardian, had once told him it was the best time for the greatest blessing on an offling.

Dak'Tor had been careful not to let Iria know he was not using their living quarters to mate with Vaha.

The fewer people who knew about the private spot, the less chance of exposure.

He also knew that the longer it went on, the more chance there was of discovery, so he and Dazal took great care to let no one suspect their travels. Dazal had even suggested that his sister, Dara, join up with Zisa on the nights when Dak'Tor and Vaha were supposed to be together, trusting that the two would keep Iria's thoughts occupied.

Each time, Dak'Tor and Dazal were concerned someone would see them coming and going or that Vaha would somehow discern the truth. But, within three moon phases, Vaha had good news. She was seeded; she was sure of it, as she never missed her moon cycle. Dak'Tor told her that they should not mate again until she was sure and prayed it was indeed true.

Vaha's father was overjoyed. He made a public display of both patting Dak'Tor on the back and celebrating his daughter's seeding. Seeing this, Iria was heartbroken and rushed off to find Zisa.

"How can this be? It took so long for me to be seeded. And—" she stopped short of revealing Dak'-Tor's problems in impregnating her.

"Do not make more of it than it is. She was probably at her most fertile. It can happen quickly, and just because it did not for you does not mean there is anything wrong with you," she said.

But nothing her friend or anyone else could say would take away Iria's heartbreak. Why did he have problems performing with her? Was she not attractive enough? Not attentive enough? He was just like any other male. Oh, how *she* wished she had never been born.

As happy as Laborn was to hear the news, he was disappointed that Dak'Tor had not developed enough feeling for Iria to prevent him from rokking Vaha. Though it meant another offling to breed with others, it also meant that his hold over Dak'Tor was not as assured as he wanted.

Since the first night Dak'Tor spent with Vaha, Iria had found it harder and harder to be affectionate with him. Though he had in total only spent very few nights with Vaha, it might as well have been a thousand. She withdrew from him emotionally, only going through the motions and doing the least she had to do for her part of the union. Dak'Tor noticed immediately but hoped that in time she would warm back up to him. He tried to convince himself that it must be because she was with offling, but in his heart, he knew he had hurt her deeply. And he was surprised to discover that this hurt him in turn.

One night he was being especially solicitous, trying to get her to talk to him. He brought her some of her favorite rocks after having rubbed them down with coarse particles fallen from the rock walls until they shone.

He left them on her side of their sleeping mat, knowing she would find them when she came in. "What's this?" she asked, picking up one of them and looking up at him.

"Just something I thought you might like. I know you like pretty things," he said.

She picked up the others and turned them over in her hands, then thanked him. She set them toward the top of the mat, where they would be out of the way but still visible. Then she lay down, and turning away from him, pulled the hide cover up over herself.

"I thought we might talk," he said, coming over and sitting behind her.

"About what?" she asked. She did not turn to look at him.

"About the situation Laborn has put us in. You do understand that I have no choice?"

"I do. But all the understanding in the world does not make it hurt any less," she answered.

"No, I suppose it does not." He reached out to put a hand on her shoulder, but she shrugged it away.

"Please," she said.

"I do not want you to be hurt. I do not know what to say."

She rolled over to face him. "The only thing you could say is that you did not go through with it. That you did not mount her. But we both know that is not true."

Dak'Tor's heart sank. It was then he admitted that he did care for Iria. Seeing how much she was hurt was more than he could bear. He did not want to love her. He never wanted to care about anyone again. But seeing how heartbroken she was, he realized he did. And very much so.

"I did not," he said quietly.

"Did not what? What are you talking about? She is seeded. *Somebody* did!"

"You are right. But it was not me."

"That is crazy. What are you talking about?" she repeated as she sat up.

Dak'Tor leaned over and stared at the floor. It was too late. There was no turning back. Now he had to hope she loved him enough to keep quiet about it, for all their sakes.

"It was not me. It was someone else. We switched places, but she does not know. She must never know."

"I want to believe you, but how can I? Who?" she asked, and then Dak'Tor saw from the look on her face that she had suddenly figured it out.

"By the Great Spirit. It was Dazal; it has to be." Her eyes were wide, and she turned so he could not see the tears of happiness that ran down her face.

"I am sorry I deceived you," Dak'Tor said, moving around to look at her. When he did and saw her tears, he felt even worse. Then he remembered what he had told Vaha as the reason.

"I could not bring myself to do it. I would have felt that I betrayed you. No one need ever know."

Iria pulled herself together. "Does Dara know?"

"No. Only Dazal and I, and now you. Luckily, we are about the same height and weight, so I doubt it will ever be discovered. I am not sure how it could be."

Iria put her arms out to him, and he readily accepted her embrace. "Thank you for telling me. I will not tell anyone. And I am sure Dazal will not either."

"He certainly has no motivation to do so. It is not like he got nothing out of it for himself."

"I feel so much better. I think I can sleep now if you can."

They both settled in; however, a sick feeling soon came over Dak'Tor for having broken his Rah'hora with Dazal.

Iria felt very bad for Vaha. She would feel terrible if Vaha ever found out she had been deceived. The good part was that Vaha would get her offling, and no one would be the wiser. But even though Dak'Tor was only meant to seed Vaha, not to be her mate, it was still deception, and Iria knew she would have to find a way to make peace with that.

The nightmare Iria had been forced into no longer had control over her, and she went to sleep knowing that Dak'Tor had refused to mate with Vaha because he cared. Being pure of heart herself, she believed him. It did not occur to her that it might have been his vanity and fear over his performance problems coming to light.

CHAPTER 14

Kthama felt empty. With the Mothoc gone, everything was just that much larger. The Akassa went about their business, but many were grieving, their hearts as hollow as the halls of the High Rocks.

As had become his morning habit, Takthan'Tor met with his closest helpers, Tensil the Healer, High Protector Vor'Ran, and Anthram, his First Guard.

"The cold weather is upon us," started the Leader. "The Protectors left us in good shape, and our stores are full. Plantings for spring are done. Even the Gnoaii is fully stocked. Other than a rock slide on the lower banks from the weather that moved through over the past few days, all we have to get on with is the matter of living. It is going to take a while to get over this. To feel normal again. Even though we are capable of taking care of ourselves, we must allow everyone to grieve."

"Perhaps in time, you should hold an assembly of some type. As Pan used to do," suggested Tensil.

"Yes. Not now, but before too long," Takthan'Tor agreed. "In the meantime, let us make sure everyone is occupied with something productive. Whether it is hunting, gathering, basket-making, it does not matter. Having a feeling of accomplishment will build everyone's confidence and keep their minds occupied. Even though we are in good shape, whatever the people want to do, let them do it. In the meantime, let us think of a reason to assemble."

"If we are to leave the Mothoc culture behind and create our own, perhaps we can form our own rituals," suggested Vor'Ran. "Something uniquely ours that our people can adopt and identify with. They could be subtle changes or more obvious ones.

"We could start involving the offling in the plantings and harvest. It would be good training for them, for one thing, and also involve them with the other adults. We can use the extra hands to help do what previously would have been done in half the time."

Takthan'Tor pondered Vor'Ran's words. "We will never be able to leave all the Mothoc culture behind because it is a part of who we are. But I agree, we need to establish new ways of our own. It is a good idea."

"One very important matter we have not taken care of is record-keeping," suggested Tensil. "We need to continue the work of Varos, the record-keeper, to ensure that our bloodlines are kept sepa-

The Secret of The Leader's Staff | 253

rated as much as possible. And the selection of who will be paired to whom.

"Perhaps that can be a type of celebration," she continued. "A periodic coming together of those who are selected to be paired. Instead of holding a pairing here and there, we could have them occur all at once. And the Overseer can pronounce Ashwea Awhidi over each of the couples. We could call it that—the Ashwea Awhidi—and all the communities could be invited," she continued.

"That would require a great deal of preparation," Takthan'Tor said. "Those who were ready to be paired would have to ask in advance. And if it were done here, we would have to house many guests and feed them. But we do have the room, now that there are so many empty living quarters; it is an excellent idea. Keep thinking, and we will discuss our thoughts. In the meantime, I will try to find a reason to bring everyone together sooner than that."

Alone with his thoughts after dismissing the group, and now that it had been brought up, Takthan'Tor admitted to himself that he needed to take a mate. It was not good for a male to be alone, and as the Leader, he had an obligation to produce offling and an heir to his lineage. But he was loath to make too many changes at once. Perhaps at the time of the Ashwea Awhidi, as Tensil had suggested naming it, he would have the opportunity to meet some of the unpaired females. But he would not allow himself to be rushed; he had learned from others' stories the importance of a good match.

Takthan'Tor left the room they had been meeting in and walked down the main corridor to the one that led to what had been Moc'Tor and E'ranale's quarters. It was expected that he would move into this space as it had long ago taken on the designation of the Leader's Quarters. Though he had been urged to move in some time ago, out of respect for Pan and her sisters, he had refused. If the Guardian had not taken them over, Takthan'Tor was surely not going to. But now they were all gone. Months had passed, and instinctively he knew it was important for the Akassa of the High Rocks that he step into the trappings of leadership.

He stood in the open doorway. It had been left open, at Pan's request, for those who wanted to express their wishes for the couple's Good Journey. They had simply disappeared, been taken away whole by the Great Spirit.

It was a large living space with plenty of room. It had a spacious work area for food preparation and storage and a separate personal care area. He noticed the sleeping mat had been replaced with a smaller one and felt a sadness fall over him. The years they had together and the love between Moc'Tor and his mate were legendary. For a moment, Takthan'Tor imagined them lying together at the day's end, sharing what they had done that day. Talking about their worries. Their dreams.

Suddenly he was filled with longing for such a pairing.

The Second Laws gave him the right as Leader to choose his own mate. At times he wondered if that was wise but equally did not want to leave such a match to other parties. It was ironic that now he had the right to choose, he had no idea who he would pick.

All the water baskets had been replaced with those properly sized for the Akassa. He reached up and gave one a spin. No doubt, some of the females had started preparing the space for his occupation. After a few more moments of reverence, he spoke aloud before leaving. "Soon. Soon. The day will come when I will take refuge here each night from the day's troubles. But today is not the day."

It had become his habit that after the morning meeting, he would visit the public areas. If nothing was urgent, he would eat first meal and then go on to meet with anyone wishing to speak with him. Throughout the day, he would be engaged in a multitude of conversations, some of which were only meant to show respect or friendliness, others that dealt with matters of the daily operation of the High Rocks.

His favorite part was checking in on the communal offling play area. It had occurred naturally that some of the mothers had started to congregate with their offling in one of the larger empty rooms. As word got out, more and more showed up each day. The females would sit and chat over their basket-making or other activities while they watched their offling play with each other and the various toys that had been made or brought in for them.

Each morning, Takthan'Tor savored the happy sounds of laughter and female chatter coming from the gathering as he approached. Those present would invariably look up at him when he walked in, and many of the slightly older offling tugged on his hand, begging him to play with them. And of course, the mothers would tell them no, that he was too busy to play with them, and they would go off as they were told and leave the Adik'Tar to go about his business. Once in a great while, he would get down and join them, much to their glee, but never long enough for their liking.

The males did not usually engage much with the offling until they were older. Their care and raising was left to the females in the community, with much communal parenting going on. If one female caught an offling misbehaving, it was expected that she would correct them in the mother's absence. The required conduct and manners were universal, and there was virtually never a dispute in how a female had handled a situation with another's offling.

When the males were old enough to begin learning skills, their fathers would engage with them with increasing frequency. All were taught how to track, kill with reverence for the animal's sacrifice, field dress, preserve, forage, and use tools. The Great

River provided ample opportunity for spearfishing, though, like the Mothoc, the Akassa did not enjoy getting wet. But they could fish from the banks and in the shallow shoals. Of course, there were often instances of young males pushing each other into the water as a prank, which in time became a rite of male adolescent passage.

As Takthan'Tor made his way back to the Great Chamber, Wry'Wry came rushing up and stopped him.

"Adik'Tar, my father needs help!" she said, out of breath.

Takthan'Tor looked down at her, trying to ignore the beautiful dark eyes and long thick brown hair. She was a light-hearted soul, full of fun and spontaneity, and everyone took to her immediately. But she was also the daughter of Vor'Ran, his High Protector, and despite how attractive and pleasing he had always found her, he felt she was now off-limits.

"Tell me about it then," he said as she stared up at him in return.

"The lower path to the Great River is blocked. Several of my father's males are down there trying to clear it, but they need more help and sent me to tell you," she said.

Vor'Ran had told Takthan'Tor earlier there were quite a few large boulders that had been dislodged by a recent storm. "Have they already started trying to move it?" he asked.

"Yes—but when they started to clear it, the pile started to slip, and more started coming down behind it from the hillside above. They barely got it under control and could not spare anyone to send for help!"

Having heard that, Takthan'Tor called out, "Anthram, I need you!" Very soon, the First Guard came running toward him.

Within moments Anthram had gathered the largest males available and headed down to the area in question.

Before long, they had safely cleared the huge boulders and rocks. Wry'Wry had watched from a safe distance.

"Thank you, Takthan'Tor," said First Guard Anthram. "We were lucky Vor'Ran's daughter came by."

"You were also lucky that so many of our males were close and not already off engaged in other tasks," the Leader said.

"Yes, we were lucky. The next time we might not be. If only the Protectors were still here, they could have removed this with ease."

"Well, they are not. We must stop thinking we cannot make it without them. We must find our own solutions to handle these problems," said Takthan'Tor.

"Perhaps, each day, we should have a set number

of males committed to tasks such as these," Anthram suggested. "So we always have a crew ready. And it will help our males bond, working side by side in different combinations."

"That is easily done. Speak to them and make the arrangements," Takthan'Tor answered. "We have more than enough males, and most should be able to spare a period of time out of their responsibilities. You are in charge of the male's activities, after all."

"There is always something that needs to be done here; the males will not sit idle," Anthram added.

Takthan'Tor could feel Wry'Wry staring at him and vowed he would not look back at her, no matter what.

"Thank you!" she called out after him as he walked away. He knew it would be rude to ignore her, so he reluctantly turned to acknowledge her with a wave and immediately regretted it. A bolt of electricity went through his center when their eyes met. *Bacht!* he said under his breath as he continued on his way.

Takthan'Tor did his best thinking when he was moving. He found physical work freed his mind to wander and find inspiration, so he decided to go for a walk outside before going in to check on the toolmakers.

Because, by comparison, they had far more

manual dexterity than the Mothoc, the Akassa were able to create finer tools. And lacking the effective cutting and shredding abilities of the Mothoc's thick nails, they had to compensate, so they practiced their craft until they excelled in making spearheads and cutting stones.

Both males and females of all ages were toolmakers, and good-natured competition between the genders and age groups was expected.

They made ropes out of various fibrous plants native to the area. Inside, these were helpful in raising and lowering the baskets and gourds used in the living quarters. Outside uses were limited only by the imagination.

Others were adept at tanning the hides that they put to various uses. Due to the cooler temperatures in the expansive cave system, some of the Elders, offling, and females wore some type of protective wrap. The males in their prime had such profuse hair over their hip area that they did not use any coverings.

As he stepped back outside into the brisk air, Takthan'Tor was drawn to the path that led to the Healer's Cove. He rarely violated the privacy of the area as visiting there was now seen as the prerogative of the Healer and her Helper.

It was a bit of a walk, and his thoughts returned

to the High Council meetings he had stopped attending. He now regretted it, wishing he had not given into his reluctance. Perhaps they should start holding High Council meetings and elect an Overseer as the Mothoc had. The Akassa communities needed to start depending on and helping each other. Once again, he found himself wishing he had a mate to discuss the idea with. Someone whose judgment he could trust. Someone he respected, perhaps even looked up to.

Wry'Wry's face popped into his mind, and he pushed it aside. "Stop it!" he said as if speaking to the Great Spirit. "She is not for me; it cannot happen." And he continued on his walk, planning to bring up the High Council idea with Vor'Ran and Tensil at evening meal if he did not see them both together beforehand.

Takthan'Tor was on a winning streak. As he re-entered the High Rocks, he once again ran into Wry'Wry, who turned in his direction when she saw him. He rolled his eyes at his own reaction to running into her *again*, but Wry'Wry quickly turned away.

He hurried to catch up with her. "Wait, please. Did you need to speak with me?"

"It is not important," she said and kept on walking.

"Wait, please," he reached out and grasped her forearm to stop her. She whirled around and looked first at his hand on her arm and then up at him.

"I apologize," he said and immediately let her go. "That was very improper of me. Please forgive me. I just thought—"

"I did not mean to be a pest, Adik'Tar. I just wanted to thank you again for helping my father. I am sorry I bothered you."

Takthan'Tor closed his eyes for a second, "You are not bothering me in the least, I promise you," he said, realizing she had seen his reaction and misinterpreted it. "Trust me. Is there anything I can do for you?"

"No, thank you," she said curtly.

"Well, then please carry a message to your father in case you see him first. Tell him I have an idea I wish to discuss with him and the Healer."

As Wry'Wry walked away, Takthan'Tor sighed with frustration. Now he had hurt her. And that was the last thing he wanted to do.

At one point, Wry'Wry had dared to let herself think that Takthan'Tor cared for her more than simply as a friend. Before he became Adik'Tar, there had been a period when they spent a fair amount of time together. They engaged in long conversations, and he seemed to enjoy her company. But all that must have been her imagination; whatever had seemed to be blossoming between them was no more.

Takthan'Tor shared his idea with Vor'Ran and Tensil, who both agreed wholeheartedly. The Leader was proposing a meeting at the High Rocks on the first day following the next full moon. Vor'Ran said he would send a messenger to the communities up the Mother Stream and have him bring back their responses.

The day came, and the Leaders from the other communities arrived. Lair'Mok of the Deep Valley, Culrat'Sar of the Far High Hills, and Tar'Kahn, Leader of the now nameless small community that was closest to the High Rocks. Takthan'Tor was disappointed in the turnout, as only the Leaders of the three closest communities had come, but he realized perhaps it might take time to prove the benefit of their meeting together.

After making introductions and welcoming everyone, the first order of the meeting was for each Leader to share how his people were doing. There was a guarded response, and Takthan'Tor felt the other Leaders were not being very candid. It was as if they did not know how to be with each other.

After a few paltry responses, he decided to try a direct approach. "I find I am having trouble dealing with the Mothoc's absence. I am trying to adjust but catch myself looking for them. Then it hits me again that they are no longer here. I feel a great loss."

Lair'Mok, Leader of the Deep Valley, nodded and then said tentatively, "I can relate to your situation."

"I know we must move forward," Takthan'Tor continued. "We must create our own culture—not erasing what the Mothoc gave us, but modifying it to our own. We have also been left with a heavy responsibility—creating a relationship with the Brothers. None of us knows if they have any idea how they were used. Taken advantage of, as what was done to them was *without their consent*. It does not matter if the means were pleasant or not. It was still a betrayal of the Mothoc's role as their protectors. So it falls to us now somehow to reach out to them and establish ourselves as people who mean them no harm. Who mean only to help."

"The Mothoc had no active relationship with the Others—the Brothers, excuse me. I find it hard to believe that they knew what the Fathers did. But I do wonder where they will think we come from," Tar'Kahn said.

In all his thinking, Takthan'Tor had not thought of that. "A very good point. And at present, I cannot think of an easy solution. I would never want to base our relationship with them on a lie. So the other possibility is that the truth will come out at some point, and that betrayal will be difficult to overcome."

"Perhaps difficult for the males, but maybe not so

difficult for the females," suggested Culrat'Sar of the Far High Hills.

Culrat'Sar had a point. Females seemed to bond more quickly than males. Whether it was the universal language of motherhood or just their more trusting nature, there appeared to be fewer obstacles to female rapport.

"Let us consider Culrat'Sar's point. For those of you who are aware of a tribe of Brothers nearby, think of how we can arrange a 'chance' meeting of one or more of our females with theirs. Perhaps a Healer, since, with their seventh sense, they would be more tuned in to any potential problems."

The group then made a plan to meet at the next full moon, this time up at the Far High Hills. Takthan'Tor left feeling it was a step forward but not the success he had hoped for. It was clear that all the Akassa were still struggling with the loss of the Mothoc.

CHAPTER 15

Neither Iria nor Vaha seemed to be having any trouble with their pregnancies. They were not very far apart in timing. Never far from Useaves' thoughts was Laborn's theory that if Dak'Tor cared for Iria, he would not be able to mount Vaha. And so, Useaves made a point of watching Iria and Dak'Tor even more closely.

She had seen the distance that divided them the moment Laborn announced Dak'Tor must seed Vaha. They no longer laughed together, and Iria was not as solicitous of Dak'Tor as she had been. It was difficult to tell what Dak'Tor felt, as he was always guarded in his actions and reactions.

However, not long after Vaha announced she was seeded, Useaves saw an immediate shift in Iria toward Dak'Tor. She was back to being kind and thoughtful, and it did not add up. It went against everything Useaves understood about males and females, and one night at the evening fire, she brought it up with Laborn.

"Perhaps she just came to her senses," he said. "Nothing good will come of it if she rejects Dak'Tor. Being paired to him brings her status, and having his offling will bring even more."

"You yourself said that a male would struggle to mate with a different female once he had developed feelings for the first," Useaves argued. "We all know females are very emotional. If you are saying it would be hard for a male to do, you cannot believe it would be easier for the female to accept her mate mounting another female?"

Laborn threw another large log on the fire, sending sparks flying. Useaves instinctively leaned back from the dangerous embers.

"Perhaps you are right. I will ponder what you are saying. There is a possibility that Dak'Tor has somehow outsmarted me. If so, I have underestimated him."

Laborn did as he had said and spent a great deal of time thinking about Dak'Tor and Iria. He now started watching them with different eyes. Seeing not only what Useaves had said, but for the first time noticing the close relationship between Dak'Tor and his friend Dazal. In a flash of insight, it hit Laborn what Dak'Tor's solution might have been to the situation he had been put in.

The next night, Laborn called the group of friends together. Dazal, Dara, Iria, Zisa, and Dak'Tor all stood before him. As usual, Useaves was right there with Laborn.

"I wanted to congratulate you again on seeding Iria and Vaha," he said to Dak'Tor. Iria threw a quick glance up to her mate, who instinctively reached for her and took her hand.

"I have been talking this over with Useaves," he lied, "And we agreed that my first plan was a mistake. My second idea for you to seed Vaha was the better one. And so, if a second female being seeded by you was a good idea, a third is even better."

Iria's mouth fell open. Dak'Tor shot a nervous glance over to his friend Dazal who had simultaneously done the same. Laborn caught it all.

"Zisa," Laborn said, calling to Iria's best friend. Zisa looked at Iria, then Useaves, and finally Laborn.

"You cannot be serious," she said, in a spontaneous act of defiance.

Laborn laughed. "I see our females are becoming rebellious. There was a time when you would not have dared to talk to me like that. But I am not unreasonable. Make your case, and I will listen," Laborn said in a rare moment of what appeared to be consideration of another's feelings.

"You know what I am going to say. Iria and I are

best friends; we have been close since we were little offling, and she is like a sister to me. It is not right. Dak'Tor is her mate, and it would feel like an abomination to be forced to be mounted by him. Surely, even as dead as you are inside, you can understand that!"

Useaves visibly stiffened at the blatant defiance.

Laborn had briefly enjoyed Zisa's rebellion, only because publicly crushing her spirit later would be so enjoyable. But she had just crossed that line, so her punishment would be even that more severe. He was not sure what, but he knew he would look forward to it. However, it would not be today. He had a flash of inspiration.

"Despite your dim view of me, as I said, I am not without consideration for others. Since it seems you are saying that you feel like Iria's sister due to your close upbringing, then I will pick another. Someone else's sister, perhaps."

Laborn stood up and walked over to them, circling them with his hands behind his back. "Now, let us see. Who does that leave us in our little group of pals? Ah yes. Dazal's sister." He stopped in front of Dara. "You."

Dazal's eyes went wide. His sister. His own sister. No way he could mount his sister. Not even to save his friend. They did not have many taboos, but incest was one of the strongest. Had Laborn seen through what they had done? Or was this just an unfortunate choice?

"I do not want to!" Dara objected. "We are all

friends here. You are only picking me to drive a wedge between us all!"

Now fed up with the females' insolence, Laborn stepped forward until his face was almost touching hers. "You will, whether you want to or not. And if you do not submit to Dak'Tor and allow yourself to become seeded, you will be sent away forever. Banished. So think carefully now. Which is the worse fate? Bearing the seed of the Guardian's brother, or a life lived in exile, never again seeing your family or any of your friends; sent out alone to die?"

"But what if I am barren? Not every female becomes seeded."

"Pffff. Oh, it happens, but it is rare. You wish to play games. Alright. I will give you until the fifth new moon. If you are not seeded by then, until you are, I will stand over you while Dak'Tor mounts you to make sure you are submitting."

Dara nearly lost her balance. Her brother put a protective arm around his sister's shoulder and steadied her.

"Our father will not allow it!" Dazal could think of nothing else to say.

"What part? Dak'Tor and Dara or my watching them mate? What does your father care? It is not like you will be mating your sister; Dak'Tor will."

Both Dazal and Dak'Tor were suddenly convinced that Laborn suspected what they had done. How, they did not know. Dak'Tor trusted Dazal and did not for a moment think that he would have betrayed them. The only other person who knew was Iria, and it did not even occur to Dak'Tor that she could have given them away.

"And you. From all I know, you have not ever been with a female!" Laborn shouted at Dazal.

"You control who we can mate with. So you only have yourself to blame!" Dazal shouted back.

"This is turning into a fine evening to settle problems. So I will take care of that right now." Laborn pointed at Zisa and glared at Dazal. "You will mount this female.

"It works out perfectly. Eventually, your offling can pair with Dak'Tor and Vaha's. I am sure they will produce strong and robust second offling."

Pairing Zisa's offling with Dazal's and Vaha's would result in half-siblings mating. Was Laborn trying to force a confession from the two males? Would he risk the offling being born with deformities, as important as the future and health of the community was to him? It was a dangerous game being played. Not to mention a terrible penalty for an innocent offling to be born handicapped, or worse.

This time Dak'Tor stepped forward, "Enough, Laborn. You seem to enjoy hurting others because what is to be gained by this? It is enough that you say I have to seed Dara. But to force Zisa on Dazal is not necessary. You have made your point; *you are in charge.*"

"Am I? I am not sure," Laborn retorted. "If I were

in charge, all of you would do as I said and not try outright to thwart me." Then he glared at Dak'Tor. "—Or try to outsmart me."

"I want to leave," said Iria, taking Dak'Tor's hand. She tugged at him, and slowly he went with her, the others following. Since they were all in this together, they went back to Dazal's quarters to commiserate with each other over what Laborn had just done.

Useaves had sat quietly watching the entire episode unfold before her. She had no love for Laborn, but she had to marvel at his craftiness. He had put them all in an untenable situation. There was little to do but for them to continue with the ruse, or to confess, in which case Laborn would be justified in whatever punishment he inflicted on them. It was not possible that Dazal could switch places with Dak'Tor this time. There was no way Dazal would mate with his own sister. Useaves had an idea that she now knew the true source of the problem. And it was not about Dak'Tor's feelings for Iria—at least not entirely. What she was unsure of was whether Laborn had figured out that part or not.

In the privacy and safety of Dazal's living space, located far down one of the less used tunnels, the five sat quietly as first, stunned at what had just transpired.

Dak'Tor desperately wanted to talk to Dazal alone. This time, they could not switch places, and Dak'Tor ran the risk of his performance problem being revealed. He was trying to think of a way out, one that did not include confessing to Zisa or Dara what he and Dazal had done. In addition, Dazal did not know that Dak'Tor had broken their Rah'hora by telling Iria about it. It was looking as if there was no way for Dak'Tor to come out of the situation with any relationships intact, except his with Iria.

But what was Laborn's goal? If he had just wanted Dak'Tor to leave, why try to destroy him? Laborn could simply banish him or have Gard dispense with him. Why play this twisted game?

"Why is Laborn doing this?" he asked. "You know him better than I do."

"Control?" offered Zisa. "Laborn rules with an angry heart, and others' happiness is never a consideration. In fact, I think he enjoys upheaval. The more upset his people are, the less opportunity they have to plot against him—perhaps?"

"That makes sense to me," said Dazal. "But why would he fear an uprising against him?"

"I am not sure he ever did, until—" Iria looked at Dak'Tor.

"Me?" he exclaimed. "Until I came, is that what you are saying?"

Dazal thought a moment, cocking his head. "It

does make sense. You are the brother of the Guardian. Despite his embittering everyone against the Akassa and the Sassen, loyalty to and reverence for the Guardian is far more strongly and more deeply embedded than Laborn realizes."

"Perhaps he never truly accepted that you were sent by the Guardian," said Zisa. "She did come here once. Remember, he does not trust anyone except perhaps Useaves. I have never been able to figure that relationship out. I do not think anyone has."

"Lots of speculation, but I agree about Laborn and Useaves," said Dazal. "No one really understands what that is about. Whatever secrets bind them, no one knows. Or at least, no one who is talking."

"Do you think he fears I will bring an uprising against him? Is that it? Why go to all this trouble? Why not just have me killed?" Dak'Tor's mind was still spinning. The tenuous relationships he had established there were all at risk of being irreparably shattered.

"He still needs you," said Zisa. "One, he needs your seed so he can continue with his master plan to build an army to annihilate the Akassa and Sassen. Two, you are the Guardian's brother. You say you are estranged, but even if so, you are still family, and family ties are strong."

"Or," said Dazal, "perhaps he is keeping you as leverage. Something with which to bargain if the

Guardian ever finds out where you are and decides she wants you back for whatever reason."

"Laborn does not fear the Guardian," Iria said. "I heard him and Useaves arguing after the Guardian's visit. Useaves was warning him that no one truly knew the extent of a Guardian's powers. But Laborn said he had seen Moc'Tor in physical battle, and he fought just as any other male would. He said that if Moc'Tor had supernatural powers, he would have used them."

Iria swallowed hard. "There is only one way out of this. And I hate to say it."

Everyone's heads turned in her direction. The chamber was quiet.

"We have to go through with it. The only other choice is to bring about some type of uprising. And I do not know that we have the numbers to do that."

Dak'Tor's heart sank. This meant he would have to mate Dara. He was trapped. If Dara did not become pregnant, Laborn might well accuse her of being barren or refusing to mate. The Leader's threat of standing over watching while Dak'Tor mounted her had horrified him. If it came to that, his performance issue would be discovered, and Dak'Tor had no doubt that Laborn would make it public. And whether or not it would feel like the end of the world to another male, it did to Dak'Tor. Not only because of his pride but because he knew his value to Laborn was based on his seeding a new line of offling who would be able to breed safely with the other future offling in the community. Once Laborn was satisfied he had enough offling from Dak'Tor, he would no doubt lift his restrictions on the younger ones mating.

"We do not have to decide this tonight," Dak'Tor said. "Let us sleep on it. Give it a few days, then we can meet again. Surely between all of us, we can figure a way out of this." Then he looked at Dara. "I do not mean any offense to you."

"No offense taken. I have no desire to have you, or any other male, mount me," she said coldly. "Or to bear your offling."

Later, alone together in their living space, Iria said to her mate, "I truly do not see any way out of this. Your solution of having Dazal mate Vaha is not going to work."

Dak'Tor sighed. "I know that. So does Dazal. Dazal cannot take my place with his own sister."

He sat down. "What is Laborn's goal? To make me confess? Or to publicly humiliate me by disclosing that I cannot always perform as a male? To ridicule me? Does he think by doing so to nullify any influence I might have over the others? By stripping away my malehood, he seeks to make me impotent in all areas."

"I believe the only thing Laborn fears," Iria said, "is the loss of his position as Leader. Without that power, he has no way to bring about his supreme goal; the annihilation of the Akassa and the Sassen. I do not believe there is anyone else who could stand in the way of that. You are the only threat. Because of who you are, you alone might be the one who could change the minds of his followers—those who wish to destroy the Akassa and Sassen."

"So it comes down to destroying any influence I might have, either personally or because I am the brother of the Guardian," Dak'Tor said absentmindedly. "There is nothing to be gained by confessing that Dazal seeded Vaha. That would only give Laborn an excuse to make an example of us both, and it would devastate Vaha. So you are right. The only way out is straight through. Somehow I have to seed Dara."

"But what about Dazal and Zisa?" asked Iria.

"Why does Zisa not want offling? Dazal is a good choice. He is strong, a good provider. He is not selfish like many of the other males. I do not understand her objection."

"Zisa has never cared for males, and she has never wanted offling. She prefers her independence; she does not want to give up her freedom."

"There has to be more to it," said Dak'Tor. In the back of his mind, he felt a pang of conscience at his own negative reaction to Ei'Tol's seeding. He realized now how selfish he had been, not wanting to share any of his mate's attention with an offling. It was he who had driven her away, and then he had blamed her when she asked for their pairing to be set aside. He assumed that Ei'Tol and Jhotin were officially together by now. Saddened, he pulled his thoughts back to the present.

"No," countered Iria. "There does not have to be more to it than that. You do not know what it is like to be a female. To have no control over your own body and what happens to you. The only thing preventing the males from using us at will is Laborn's directive that they may not. That we are too close to inbreeding and producing deformed offling. He has forbidden the younger of us to mate. Too many of our group that left Kayerm were already related. When that problem is worked out, if it is, we will go back to being used at will by any male at his whim. Or Laborn may do as he did with you and me and decide who and who cannot mate. But I assure you, we females will have no say in who it is."

"How ironic. So now Laborn is in the same position Moc'Tor was. Prohibiting indiscriminate pairing for the sake of the community. I suppose that fact is lost on him?"

"If it is not, he is keeping it to himself. Given how much he berates Moc'Tor's decisions, he would certainly not want a parallel drawn with himself!"

Anyone listening to the exchange would realize how quickly the thoughts were turning over in Dak'-Tor's mind. Though the idea of an uprising against Laborn had not been at the forefront, he now started to think of just how he could bring that about.

Perhaps it is time for a change in leadership. There was no place else for Dak'Tor to go, and the vision of a life lived under Laborn's scrutiny and persecution was unacceptable.

Dak'Tor did not know what he would do with it if he did manage to usurp Laborn's position. He no longer let himself think about Pan and where she and the rest of the Mothoc were. This was his situation, and he had to make the best of it or change it. He had at least grown in that much wisdom. Not only had he no idea where Lulnomia was, but he knew that he was not welcome there or at any other Mothoc community but this one.

Dak'Tor knew Laborn was watching their comings and goings. And so did everyone else as they had presumably by now heard the story of what Laborn had ordered. Dak'Tor could only stall so long. Though Dara had made it clear she was in no hurry to be mounted, he would have to do something soon.

One morning, Dak'Tor was down by the shoals trying to lose himself in the mundane responsibilities of daily life by spearfishing to provide for Iria and their offling. He heard someone approaching and turned to see who it was, his spear still in his hand. He was surprised to see Useaves. She seemed unsteady on the slope that led down to where he was, and instinctively he dropped the spear and stepped out of the water to help her. She waved him off.

When she had reached him, she spoke. "I am sure I am the last person you expected to seek you out."

"You are right. Why did you not just send for me?

"Because I need to have a private conversation with you. One no one must know took place," she said, steadying herself as she sat down on the bank. "Now. You have a problem."

"You mean other than those I already know about? Great." The edge to his voice escaped before he could control it.

"No, I am confident that you know about this problem."

Dak'Tor frowned.

"If you are wondering if Laborn has figured out your clever solution with Dazal, you are right. And he has outwitted you by commanding you to seed Dazal's sister, and we both know why that puts you in a tremendous bind."

Dak'Tor held his peace, fearing she might know what the real problem was but not wanting to give it away if she did not.

"Dazal can not take your place and seed his sister," she said. "So that leaves it to you to seed her. And pressure is not your friend, is it?"

Dak'Tor looked away. Finally, he conceded, "I am

sure others have experienced it," he added, trying to be vague.

"It is true. Other males do experience this problem. But for one in your position? Your only value to Laborn lies in your seeding a future generation that can mate with nearly any of the other future offling."

Pushed to the edge of his composure, Dak'Tor snapped. "Have you come here just to taunt me? Do you take the same perverse pleasure in the difficulties of others, just like Laborn? Are you going to expose me, humiliate me in front of everyone, as no doubt Laborn intends to? Then go ahead. Why wait? *Get it over with*."

"I have come here to help you," and she offered up a small hide bag.

"What is this?" he asked as he reached to take it from her.

"It is most likely the solution to your problem."

Dak'Tor untied the top and peered in. "Does it work?"

"Usually. It will take a while to have an effect, though." She reached to take the bag back, then dug out and held up a small portion of dried root. "A small piece. Once a day. Chew slowly. Follow with water; do not choke." She closed it and handed it back to him. "This should last you a while."

"Why are you helping me? And why, if this works, is it a secret?"

"I am helping you because I do not yet know which side I want to have win. Yours or Laborn's. The answer to your second question is that it is a secret that only the female Healers have known about."

Dak'Tor wanted to ask how she knew about it because Useaves was not a real Healer, but he did not. Instead, he asked, "If it is as you said, that my problem is not that uncommon, and there is a treatment, why would the Healers not make this treatment known?"

"Why? Ha!" she scoffed. "We females suffer enough from you males. Always mounting us. Having no concerns for what we want or how many offling we carry. Or how many we lose. Your problem is a relief to us. We welcome it, except in the rare case where a male truly cares for a female and is kind to her. Protects her, helps provide for her offling. But that is by far the exception."

Useaves then struggled to her feet and brushed herself off. "I have entrusted you with a deep secret and helped you out of your very serious dilemma. I suggest you do not betray my kindness." She eyed him harshly.

Dak'Tor took the bag and hid it in his fist. "I will not. And thank you."

"Do not thank me yet," she said as she turned to climb up the slope. "I have still not decided if you or Laborn is to be the victor in this power struggle. It is too early to have you taken out of the game, and there are many moves yet to be played. But to figure that out, I need time, which is all I have given you."

Dak'Tor watched as Useaves slowly made her way back up the incline.

In the background of all the drama, Vaha was struggling. She felt alone. Discarded. With Laborn now giving Dara to Dak'Tor and with Dak'Tor already being paired to Iria, Vaha had fulfilled her purpose. She continued to live with her parents, as she had expected to, but the light was going out of her spirit. Whatever companionship or protection she had secretly and unrealistically hoped for from Dak'Tor was never going to materialize.

Her mother watched all this, brokenhearted and with no idea of how to help her daughter. Finally, in an act of desperation, she sought out Iria.

"Vaha is suffering," she said.

"Is she in pain? Is there something wrong with the offling?" Iria asked, concerned.

"Not physically. I know this has been hard on you emotionally, and probably still is," Vaha's mother said. "But you still have Dak'Tor, and though it was not evident for some time, he cares for you. And Vaha has no one."

So many thoughts came to Iria, all of them logical and probably even fair, as the situation was no fault of hers. But it was also no fault of Vaha's.

"What would help her?" Iria asked.

"Can you not include her somehow? Yours is the

only group her age who would accept her now. Her father thought that bearing Dak'Tor's offling would raise her status. It seems to have done the opposite. Even the other females are avoiding her, perhaps out of loyalty to you?"

As much as she hated it, Iria could see that happening. She felt ashamed that she had not considered how things were for Vaha. "I will talk to her," she said.

"Your mother asked me to speak with you."

With lackluster eyes, Vaha looked up from her task of cleaning roots.

"This is not your fault, Iria. Least of all yours."

"It has been hard on all of us," said Iria. "I do not have a solution, but I promise you I will try to come up with something."

When it had started, Iria was happy. She had cared for Dak'Tor and hoped that, in time, he would care for her. And now he did. But it had become so complicated, and Vaha was suffering. Soon, no doubt, Dara would be too. How could she help them when she could not even help herself?

Iria did what had always worked best for her. She went for a long walk and prayed to the Great Spirit for a solution.

Dazal was standing looking up at the weather when Iria came around the corner.

"Why are you so sad? Or need I even ask?" He had become close to Iria and the others. The whole group had. But now, the twisted mind of Laborn was ruining it for all of them, and the secret between him and Dak'Tor was tormenting Dazal.

Iria told him about Vaha, and Dazal's heart sank. It was because of him that she was in this position. Perhaps if it had been his offling growing in Vaha, Dak'Tor might have found a way to include her in their circle. Then it hit him. *It was his offling.* Even if no one else but Dak'Tor knew it. If anyone's, it was his responsibility to help ease her pain.

"It is probably too much to ask of you," he said, "but is there any way we can bring her into our circle? If the other females are rejecting her, then she is truly alone."

"Dazal. I— I—"

"I should not have asked; it is too much."

"No. That is not it. There was something I wanted to— No. Never mind. We are all being targeted by Laborn. And the only reason I can think of is that it has to do with what we talked about. Laborn trying to destroy Dak'Tor—or at least any influence he might have on others. And now Vaha is, in a way, also being punished. I will talk to her and Zisa if you will talk to your sister. But if you are asking Dak'Tor to—"

. . .

"No. I will look after her," said Dazal. "I will make sure she feels included. As long as you and Dak'Tor are happy to consider it."

As Iria went to find Zisa and then Vaha, she was glad she had stopped herself. She had almost told Dazal she knew what he and Dak'Tor did. She had briefly been tempted to shame him into taking responsibility for Vaha, but that would have betrayed Dak'-Tor, and in the end, Dazal had stepped up on his own. Had the Great Spirit heard and answered her prayer?

CHAPTER 16

The same period that had caused so much trouble in the rebel community had brought good things to Lulnomia. Other than a few disagreements here and there, the community was coming together—with the exception of the group from Kayerm.

Norland met with his people. Despite efforts to fit into the larger community, they still felt uncomfortable. It was not that there were actual acts of aggression or hostility against them—not even spiteful looks. It was more their own discomfort that was causing their isolation.

"You could speak with Pan. Ask her to talk to the other Leaders," Pagara suggested.

"What would she say? Ask them to be nice to us because we are feeling like outsiders?" Norland did not mean it to come off as gruff as it did. "The problem is not them. It is us."

"How can you say that? We have done nothing!" objected someone.

"Exactly. We have done nothing," Norland answered. "I see it now. We came here feeling like outsiders, and that is how we have behaved. They have not ostracized us; we have done it to ourselves. Be honest, how many of us have been in touch with relatives from other communities? Even old friends of our parents?"

They looked around at each other but said nothing.

"We are waiting for them to reach out to us as if it is their burden," pointed out the Leader. "But have we reached out to them? No. If it is going to change, we have to make the change. So, no matter how hard it is, try to join in. The High Protectors have created many individual groups. Pick one and get involved. Instead of waiting for others to make a way for you, make it yourself."

Despite some sideways looks, the community had needed to hear Norland's rebuke. He was right. In anticipating rejection, they had unintentionally rejected the others first.

"Pagara, you are in the Healer's group. Have they been unkind to you? The other Healers?"

"No. They have been welcoming."

"So we must do this. We must create the future of our own making. I am urging you. Go and mingle. Find a way to strike up a conversation. Be helpful to the others. I believe Pan was right when she said we are different people now. Even our Elders who went through the division with Straf'Tor and his brother —time has brought wisdom and humility to us all."

Wosot and Kyana listened but said nothing. They had made some excursions into the greater community, but the last had been some time ago when Lavke had confronted them. It was not that they were intentionally isolating, but with the layout of Lulnomia, the different communities had enough of their own activities and responsibilities that interaction with the others was not really necessary.

When the assembly disbanded, Norland watched the crowd walk away and prayed that each member had taken his words to heart. There was no other place for them on Etera. And this was where they belonged. Compared to their original numbers, there were relatively few of the Mothoc left to serve Etera. Story had it that at one point, their numbers had been so plentiful that all the communities were filled uncomfortably to capacity. And though they had solved the problem of continuing some concentration of their Mothoc blood still circulating on Etera by breeding with the Others, their numbers still needed to grow. And, given time, the Mothoc would once again face the same in-breeding problem created before by the loss of so many by the contagion. Norland wondered if Pan ever worried about their situation.

Pan did worry about their situation. There were times when she was consumed with it. And she worried about the Akassa and the Sassen, too. She wanted so badly to know how they were faring. Had they adjusted to being left alone? She knew her people had done all they could to prepare them. She knew that Tyria, for one, had spent day after day with Tensil, making sure she was ready to take on the role of sole Healer to the Akassa of Kthama. Though they had spoken of it rarely, Pan also knew Tyria had shared with Tensil the secret passed to her during the Ror'Eckrah—one that was to be passed from Healer to Healer only at the High Rocks. Pan feared it would be a long time before it was apparent if her decision for the Healers to set themselves apart was the right one. And no longer having any contact with any of the Akassa communities, how would she even know that?

While things were going fairly well at the High Rocks, at the other communities, the Akassa were struggling. Even though the signs of the Mothoc had been removed, modified, or taken down, the memories remained. The Akassa still felt frail and puny and longed for the safety and protection they had felt with the Mothoc present. The High Council that Takthan'Tor had envisioned was failing to take root. It was as if the entire Akassa community was suffering from depression—from which they could not free themselves.

E'ranale looked up at the bright essence of The Promised One. Though An'Kru was an Akassa Guardian, and in Etera's realm no doubt would not have been taller than her, the physical form his spirit manifested in the Corridor towered over her.

"I had hoped it would not come to this," she said.

"I know. I wish her path was easier. And in some ways, it has been even harder for you, as her mother, to watch."

"Is there no other way than this?" E'ranale asked wistfully.

"You know that if there is, the Order of Functions will provide it," An'Kru replied softly.

"I know. All the times I dreamed of the Corridor —whatever at the time I thought this was—I imagined it would be free from sorrow and heartache."

"But for that to happen, there would have to be no more bonds of love. And how would life be worth continuing without love?"

"She has had so little time without trial. And now

this. The hardest she will ever have to face." E'ranale sighed.

"It would not have been given to her if she were not strong enough. You know this."

"Alright. I will bring her to me. The sooner it starts, the sooner the rest will be put in motion, and the sooner it will be over."

An'Kru knew what E'ranale was trying to say. Since time did not exist in the Corridor, everything that could happen, ever would happen, and ever did happen existed simultaneously as possibilities. But having had a physical existence on Etera, it was difficult for even the spiritual mind to free itself of the limiting perception that events existed within time.

Pan had just handed her daughter to Ei'Tol and Jhotin. The two had become great friends, and one or the other often looked after Tala.

Rohm'Mok was off with a hunting party, so Pan looked forward to some time alone to rest her mind. The worry was wearing at her, and she had so far been unable to get free of it. But despite her heartbreak over Dak'Tor's stealing of the crystal, despite the drain on her from the needs of many, despite her failing faith, she had never given up. She had fulfilled her responsibilities as the Guardian of Etera and the Leader of the High Rocks.

She stretched out on the over-stuffed, but much

appreciated, thick sleeping mat and closed her eyes, about to relish the deep sleep she was praying would soon wash over her. It was early, only just twilight, but she needed to rest—

"Mother!" She closed the few steps separating her from E'ranale. "Oh, Mother. Do you know what has happened?! The crystal is gone. Dak'Tor took it, and I have no idea where he is or if he is even alive. How is Father ever going to be freed now?"

"Your brother is not dead. He is at the rebel camp."

"Oh, no! I mean— I am glad he is alive, but now the rebels have the power of the crystal at their disposal!"

"Dak'Tor has the crystal hidden. It has not fallen into their hands. After he left the High Rocks, he was led to the rebels by Kweak."

"Why would Kweak come to guide him? I have never known Dak'Tor to think about the Great Spirit, let alone turn to the Great Spirit for help."

"The Great Spirit answers all calls for help, and Dak'Tor did ask. The Great Spirit loves your brother in spite of his flaws, just as each one of us is loved, and we are also flawed." E'ranale then told Pan the story of how Dak'Tor had ended up with the rebels.

Pan was distressed. "The rebels want to destroy the Akassa and the Sassen. How can this be of the Order of Functions?"

"Be grateful that Kweak was sent to him, for without Kweak's intercession and Dak'Tor's willingness to believe that Kweak might have been sent to help him, your brother would have died of exposure. But before he died, he would have cast the crystal into a ravine to the rocks below, where it would have shattered into a thousand pieces. Then it would truly have been lost," explained E'ranale gently.

"And all hope of Father's release would have shattered with it," Pan said, overwhelmed by that terrible thought.

"Each of us has our path, and because we have free will, the future is not set. But in spite of free will, life is rigged in our favor. Life is always trying to bring us back into balance.

"Your brother attempts to manipulate life with his intellect, which is considerable. But no intellect alone, no matter how powerful, can bring anyone into alignment with the divine order for their life. And though he tries to control them, Dak'Tor is often overcome by his emotions and driven to act rashly. He must be willing to look within for help from his heart and his soul, which is how we connect with divine guidance for our lives. Your brother's path will now lead him into experiences that allow him to learn this lesson. Already, life is changing him."

"Like a reflection of The Great Mind, The Great Heart, and The Great Will," Pan echoed her mother's statement.

"The same three aspects of the One-Who-Is-Three also exist in us. They must, as we are part of creation. Imbalance is when one of the three rules over the other. Listen carefully to what I am saying. The mind and heart were designed to work in alignment with each other. And when there is alignment, then the will, which is our soul's movement to take action, can most easily move us forward. Without this agreement, we are torn and make decisions influenced by only one aspect. That is why it is not wise to make life-changing decisions when our emotions are drowning out our reason or when our reason is dismissing the voice of our hearts. Or when we are determined to force something to happen against what our reasoning or our hearts are telling us is right."

"Oh, Mama, I have so much to learn about faith and faithfulness, so why did you wait until now to bring me to you?"

"I had to give you the chance to persevere on your own. I know that when you discovered the crystal was missing, you were brought to one of the lowest points in your life so far. But you did not give up. Your heart was not in it, but you did not abandon your responsibilities as Guardian. You were faithful even when you thought all hope of achieving your personal goal was lost."

"Freeing Father from the Order of Functions."

"You had a choice, Pan, just as your brother did. You could have allowed yourself to become bitter and angry. With your feelings of abandonment and betrayal, you could have struck out, turning your back on the Great Spirit. But you did not. In the same way, Dak'Tor had choices as well. He could have accepted responsibility for what he did and asked for mercy, promised to change his ways, and asked for a chance to prove himself. He could have done nothing and cowered in the corner and awaited his fate at the discretion of the High Council. Or he could have done what he did. Remember, we all have our paths. I will say it again; the future is not set."

"There is always hope."

"There is. Hope is not an empty promise made to encourage small offling," E'ranale pointed out. "Hope is real power. When we connect with the creative force of hope, we attract all positive outcomes. The choices we then make of our own free will determine which path opens. But that is the incomprehensible love of creation, that the Order of Functions is always in play, working to bring us to what we most need next. So we may grow to experience the best life possible while deepening our connection with the One who loves us beyond our ability to fathom."

"Is hope the same as faith, then?"

"They are similar. Hope is faith in the promise that love is the strongest and only real power in existence. But we are trying to use words to explain what words cannot describe—energy streams and the soul's movement that connects with them."

"I am trying to understand, I am. But all outcomes are not positive," Pan said.

"At the moment, no, your brother's life is not easy. But it never has been. And when for the first time, he called out for help and followed Kweak, he placed his faith in something bigger than his own attempts at manipulating life. The current consequences of his actions may not feel positive, but what he is going through is only a small period of time on Etera. If you had focused only on the time just before giving birth, you would see only pain and struggle, so the consequence of your pairing with Rohm'Mok would appear to be disastrous. But much more than that followed, did it not?"

"Yes. Great joy when Tala was born."

E'ranale knew their visit was almost up. She could not allow too much time to pass on Etera while Pan was here in the Corridor.

"You must go, but you will know what to do when the time comes. Trust yourself. You criticize yourself because you think your worry is unfounded. But is it? Perhaps it is trying to tell you something. You need someone to turn to, someone besides Rohm'Mok, so look for help, and it will be given to you."

"Thank you. I love you, Mother." But before Pan could reach out to embrace E'ranale, she was back in her own quarters.

Sunlight was breaking through the overhead ventilation shafts. It had been twilight when Pan lay down, and now the dark had passed. She hoped it had only been one night. Not knowing, she got up and padded down the hallway to find out.

She stepped into the first open room she came to. The Healers were meeting there, and they looked up. Joy lit their faces when they saw who it was.

Pagara and Tyria were closest to the door and stood to welcome her in.

"Guardian! What a delightful surprise and great honor!" Pagara exclaimed.

They were so happy to see her that Pan felt she had no choice but to join them, though she really wanted to find Ei'Tol and see her daughter.

It was a group of about twenty, and she walked in and sat among them. Pagara took a moment to have everyone introduce themselves. There was a mixture of Healers, Helpers, and those apprenticing to become Healers. Pan recognized Oragur and his daughter, Krin, from the Deep Valley and was pleased to see Tyria had joined them despite her concern that someone might ask who had seeded her offling.

Sitting among them, Pan thought she recognized Irisa, the female who had been working with Oragur when his mate Lor Onida died. Why had she not seen Irisa since? As their eyes met, some kind of affinity passed through Pan.

When Irisa introduced herself, she did not call herself a Healer, a Helper, or an apprentice, so Pan made a mental note to ask Krin about her at the first opportunity.

"Is there anything I can help you with?" Pan then asked the group.

"Guardian, what can we help *you* with?" someone asked.

"By coming together in unity, you are already helping me—and everyone else here. Your collective intention for the good of this community and all of Etera is very powerful," Pan answered. However, her mind was still foggy. "This may sound peculiar, but I have been asleep. What time of day is it?"

"It is just past dawn, Guardian," Pagara answered.

Pan could not ask the next question as there was no way for the members of the group to answer it. She wanted to know how many days had passed, but with no frame of reference to give them, she could not even formulate it.

"It is the day after yesterday," Irisa said. The others looked at her quizzically, as this was no answer to anything the Guardian had asked. But it meant something to Pan. Was Irisa answering her question, understanding her problem? How could that be?

Tyria tried to pull attention away from Irisa's confusing comment. "Being at Lulnomia is allowing us to learn from each other and support each other in a way that was never before possible. We are all enriched by it. But I do have a request."

Pan waited for her to continue.

"At the High Rocks, there was a special place just for servants such as we are." Tyria started to explain, knowing that most in the group had never been there. "It was one spot set aside for us, where we could privately seek the counsel of the Great Mother. It was a sacred place. It was called the Healer's Cove. I was thinking we might consider finding such a spot for us here, near Lulnomia," she finished.

"That is an excellent idea and an honorable one," Pan said. "I will bring it before the High Council with every confidence that all will agree. In the meantime, perhaps, in your travels about Lulnomia, you can each look for such a place."

"Before we end," Oragur said, "We do have some great news; my daughter, Krin, is seeded again!"

"Congratulations!" Pan said. Even as she spoke, she could feel Irisa's presence stronger than that of any of the others.

When Pan found her, Ei'Tol acted as if nothing was wrong. There were no concerned or curious questions from either her or Jhontin, which reinforced Irisa's answer that only one night had passed since Pan and her mother had met in the Corridor.

After the last High Council meeting at the High Rocks when Ei'Tol had asked for her pairing to Dak'Tor to be dissolved, the community had expected her and Jhotin to come forward and ask to be paired. But it had not yet happened, which led everyone to believe that Dak'Tor had been wrong;

there was no romantic involvement playing a factor in Ei'Tol's request for Bak'tah-Awhidi. Or, if there was, they were being very discrete about acting on it. In the end, Pan had decided they were simply friends.

It was, therefore, doubly sad that Dak'Tor had self-destructed over the matter. She had never thought that his feelings for Ei'Tol were very deep. She felt rather that it was his pride which had driven him into such a frenzied state to confess what he had about the Leader's Staff and making her Leader of the High Rocks.

Their mother had said he was alive and that things were already changing. Would Pan ever see him again? And how would she get the crystal back? She prayed that he would not tell the rebels about it in case they could harness its power. Or destroy it in an attempt to thwart the Promised One.

Pan caught up with Krin later that day. "In your Healers' group, I thought I recognized the female named Irisa." She did not want to bring up Krin's mother's death by saying she had seen Irisa at that time.

"She was a friend of my mother's."

"Is she a Healer? She did not identify herself as either a Healer, Helper, or apprentice."

Krin chuckled a little. "That is because she is not

any of those. We are not sure what she is. And I do not mean that in any negative sense. She seems to know a great deal about healing, but she will not claim the role. I have always thought of her as very old, and how she is still here, I am not sure. It is said she talks to the others."

"As in, the Brothers?"

"No, as in *Shissu*. Those from another realm. The vibration? I am not sure what the word is. She never says much, but when she does, it often has a meaning we do not understand. Like when she said to you that it is the day after yesterday. Every day is the day after yesterday. Strange things like that."

Krin then shrugged. "She may be crazy; we do not know. But she has a powerful essence, and it is always a loving and healing one. When she does offer help, its timing sometimes seems miraculous, but she mostly keeps to herself."

Pan held her tongue. *Shissu*. That was a word seldom spoken.

"Why do I not remember her from the High Rocks except that she was there when Liru was born."

"It is said she never stays long in any one community. I do not remember when she came to the High Rocks; it might only have been to help with Liru's birth, but she did go to the Deep Valley with us when we left Kthama. However, even there, she has come and gone at will. We never know when she will reappear, but we always celebrate her return."

Mysterious and more mysterious. Though she wanted to ask about Liru, she still could not bring herself to. Pan had consciously avoided meeting her, though she had seen her from a distance. She was avoiding having to face the fact that Liru would have no memory of her and her place in the offling's life.

Krin added, "Now that we are talking about Irisa, I am not sure what will happen now that we are all at Lulnomia. I wonder if she will always be here now since there are no other Mothoc communities to go to. Hmmm."

CHAPTER 17

Dak'Tor could not let go of the idea of overthrowing Laborn and taking charge of the rebel community. He had no doubt, though, that if Laborn caught wind of his intentions, he would be ended then and there, future offling regardless. He was glad now that he had never said anything about Lulnomia, the Mothoc leaving the Akassa and Sassen communities, or the sacred crystal he had so expertly hidden. It served no purpose for him to reveal any of this to Laborn, and though he did not know how, the information might somehow be of use to him in the future.

Iria was ready to deliver. Useaves, the closest the group had to a Healer, was in attendance, as well as Iria's friend Zisa. The birthing stone was in place, with soft grasses prepared and an absorbent hide to clean the offling with. It was just a matter of waiting.

Dak'Tor did not know what to hope for. Would it be more advantageous for it to be a male or a female? Males had more status, but a female was more valuable when it came to producing offling. However, a male could seed many, many females in the time it took a female to produce one offling. While he was weighing the pros and cons of each, Zisa came out to tell him he had a son.

In contrast to his indifference and even resentment when Ei'Tol had given birth to his daughter, Dak'Tor could not get in fast enough to see Iria and his new offling. He hurried to Iria's side and knelt down near her. He immediately noticed the tears in her eyes and hoped they were tears of joy.

She held up their son. It was already apparent that the offling had inherited his father's markings. They were not as extensive, but there was a silver-white crest through his hair and down around his shoulders. The rest of his coloring favored his mother's dark coat.

Zisa had brought in Iria's parents, as well as Dara, Dazal, and Vaha. After everyone had seen the offling and offered their congratulations, Useaves shooed them out to give the family some privacy.

Dak'Tor took one of his son's little fingers in his own. "Are you crying because it hurt? Or because you are relieved? Happy?"

"All of that and more," Iria answered. "Oh, what will become of him? How are we to protect him from Laborn? Now he has one more weapon to use against us. Our son's safety and wellbeing."

At that moment, Dak'Tor knew what he had to do. No matter what, Laborn had to be overthrown. Removed. How he was going to accomplish that, and how long it would take, he had no idea. There was always the possibility that they would all outlive Laborn, but that could mean centuries of outsmarting him, trying to stay ahead of the Leader's cruel manipulations. And that would do nothing to lift the dark pall hanging over the community.

Dak'Tor had to find out how many of Iria's generation would stand with him if it came to eliminating Laborn. And to do that was a great risk in itself. But for the first time, Dak'Tor knew what it truly meant to love. And he would do everything in his power to protect his mate and his offling. And his friends.

Outside, their friends and family regrouped.

"No doubt it is his offling," said Dazal.

Vaha raised her eyebrows? "Was there ever any doubt?" She was shocked at such a suggestion.

"Yes, Dazal," Zisa said in defense of her friend.

"What are you implying? How could it be anyone but Dak'Tor's?"

Dazal back-peddled as fast as he could. "I meant no insult, I promise. I only meant that as vindictive as Laborn is, I could see him casting aspersions about the offling's seeding to further try to belittle Dak'Tor."

The others calmed down immediately now that they understood Dazal was not insulting or questioning Iria's character.

"Thank you for explaining," said Zisa. "I have known Iria all my life, and there is no finer female than her. She loves Dak'Tor, and there will never be any other male for her but him. I can assure you all of that."

As Dazal walked away, he was deep in thought. Saying that had been a huge mistake. Secrets were very hard to keep, and he must watch himself more closely. Of course, Iria's offling was fathered by Dak'-Tor, and no one but he and Dak'Tor knew anything otherwise about Vaha's offling.

But Dazal was wrong. Dak'Tor had confided in his mate, and Iria's thoughts had already turned to Vaha's impending delivery. She knew there was no chance that Vaha's offling would have Dak'Tor's markings, and she prayed that, as clearly as her offling's markings would seal any question about his paternity, the lack of those markings or any similar on Vaha's offling would not raise any question about its parentage.

In all the ways that Dak'Tor had failed Ei'Tol and his daughter, he came through for his mate and his son. He was caring and attentive. He doted on Iria and made sure the other females were looking in on her. He brought her presents of special foodstuffs he knew she preferred and made sure she was warm and comfortable.

Had Ei'Tol been able to see his transformation, it would have broken her heart, as everything that Dak'Tor now did was all Ei'Tol had longed for. Dak'Tor realized this too, and for the second time in his life, he reached out to the Great Spirit. Not for help this time, but forgiveness for how he had lived his life so far, for his betrayal of Pan, and for how he had wronged Ei'Tol and their offling.

Dazal had been true to his word in looking after Vaha and always made a point of including her in their get-togethers. At first, despite her loneliness, she was reluctant, but his reassurances wore down her barriers, and she became part of the little group.

Meanwhile, Zisa had no interest in anything

other than friendship with Dazal, and now she had been promised to him by Laborn, she became distant. She made it clear that it would take an ultimatum from Laborn before she would let Dazal mount her, that she had no desire to produce any offling, no matter whose it was, and that she would put it off as long as she could.

The vacuum created by Zisa's rejection of Dazal and her subsequent coldness toward him was filled by Vaha. He found her to be a kind and gentle soul with a subtle sense of humor, and in time, his protective feelings for her turned to something else. Dazal had fallen in love with Vaha.

Before long, it was Vaha's turn to deliver. The birthing was successful, and of course, the offling had no silver markings. It was a female, and now confident in Dak'Tor's love and her place in his heart, and the knowledge that Dak'Tor had never mounted Vaha, Iria's heart opened fully to include Vaha and her daughter. And so she asked Dak'Tor to accept Vaha and her offling into their pod.

Though Dak'Tor knew that Vaha's offling was not his, he also knew it was as much his fault as Dazal's that she had been deceived. So with that in mind, he agreed to Iria's request. Little did he expect that what seemed like an obvious step would cause such problems.

Dazal stared blankly at Dak'Tor, who had just announced they were bringing Vaha into their pod. Vaha's parents were overjoyed at the news as it meant their daughter and granddaughter would have Dak'-Tor's protection and provision. And since both females seemed to be at peace with the arrangement, Vaha's parents gladly supported it. Of course, Vaha would have her own living quarters.

Dazal turned to Vaha, "Is this what you want?" Vaha looked confused, not aware there was any other option.

"He is the father of my offling, and I cannot live with my parents forever. I do not see any better option," she answered. "I am grateful for the offer."

Short of revealing that the offling was his and not Dak'Tor's, Dazal had no reasonable argument to make against the arrangement. He had no standing from which to say he could provide better for her. His feelings were unspoken; they had no romantic relationship with each other. It was Dak'Tor's offling, and that was how it had to be. Dazal pulled himself together, accepting that this indeed was the best for Vaha and his daughter. Besides, Laborn already had suspicions about the offling's parentage, and an offer to provide for them would only reinforce these.

So many words unsaid, so many feelings pushed down. Iria, Dak'Tor, and Dazal all had to live with the choices they had made. And none of them wanted to see Vaha or her offling suffer because of the deception.

Over the next few days, Vaha and her daughter moved into quarters right next to Dak'Tor, Iria, and their son.

Vaha's daughter would have to be presented to Laborn and Useaves before long. Believing everything to be above board, Vaha had no qualms about the necessity.

When Dak'Tor and Iria had presented their son, Isan'Tor, everyone could clearly see that the offling was Dak'Tor's. As a result, the Leader had nothing to say other than to congratulate them.

However, Laborn had already heard that Vaha's offling had no such markings, and he was waiting anxiously for the time when it would be presented to him.

Laborn walked over to Vaha as she held her daughter, Altka. He peered at her as Vaha pulled back the piece of the protective hide covering the offling's face.

He looked at the offling, then, still bending over, looked over at Dak'Tor and smirked. Then he looked at Dazal.

"Congratulations," he said, still staring at Dazal.

Then he looked back at Vaha, stood up, and walked away.

It was enough. In one motion, Laborn had unequivocally told Dak'Tor and Dazal that he knew Dak'Tor had not sired this offling, which gave him tremendous leverage over them both.

Vaha had not noticed Laborn's behavior because she was occupied with adoring the infant in her arms. Her heart was full, and she no longer cared that Dak'Tor was in love with Iria and not her. From the start, she had not expected Dak'Tor to care for her because she had simply been there as a vessel for his seed. She was appreciative of his gentleness and consideration when trying to seed her; it could have been very different, as she knew well from stories told by other females.

So, as it turned out, she had more than she could have hoped for. She felt safe and protected even though she was not in her parent's quarters, and in addition, was one of the few females to have any offling. Vaha was grateful she had a daughter to love and to raise and was deeply at peace with the journey that had brought her to this moment.

Dazal took a long walk. Perhaps there was a way he could still win Vaha's heart. Though he could never say that her daughter was his, he could still play a role in the offling's life. If he could get Vaha to fall in love with him, she might leave Dak'Tor's protection for his. Dazal prayed that there might be some hope for him.

Rohm'Mok had returned, and the family was overjoyed to be reunited. Pan and Tala listened with rapt attention as Rohm'Mok told them stories of his hunting trip, embellished with appropriate animal sounds and some acting. His mate roared with laughter, and Tala clapped with delight at his antics. For a little while, Pan escaped from the weight of her concerns and worries.

That evening, after Tala was sound asleep and their lovemating complete, Pan lay contentedly in Rohm'Mok's arms and had her most peaceful night's sleep in a long time.

E'ranale and An'Kru watched them from the Corridor.

"It brings me joy to see her so happy and relaxed," said E'ranale.

"She is strong. She has weathered all that life has thrown at her so far. Let us pray that this time of peace will last long enough for her to grow even stronger and wiser."

"I know," said E'ranale wistfully. "Because the challenges to come are severe and have the power to break her. So much is yet ahead for my beloved daughter and how I wish I could take it from her."

"It is her path. She is strong enough. We must have faith in her and believe that, in time, the Order of Functions will bring her everything she needs to be prepared."

Meanwhile, in the dark recess of a hastily carved cavity high in one of the walls of Dak'Tor and Iria's chambers, lay the sacred crystal from the 'Tor Leader's Staff. Waiting. It's unimaginable power protected, it's existence concealed— for the time being.

PLEASE READ

So, you made it through Book Three. I am sure you have some unanswered questions. Please feel free to email me at contact@leighrobertsauthor.com and let me know what they are. I certainly do not want to leave you frustrated and as I am close to the story, I may be leaving a loose end that needs to be wrapped up, such as Nimida's story in Series One. And yes, I will get back to that in future books.

At this point I am pretty sure there will be five books in this series; then on to Series Three Wrak-Ashwea: The Age of Light. I may write some short stories in between about specific characters if you are interested. I hope you see this as an ongoing journey we are on together. Of course, the full Etera Chronicles series will conclude at the end of Series Three. Then, on to something else!

The next book will be Book Four: The End of The Age. I have not completely settled on a name for Book Five, but I think it will be "Out of The Dust of Etera"—or some derivative thereof.

At this point if you have not read Series One, I want to encourage you to still go back and read it. Series One, Wrak-Ayya: The Age of Shadows, covers the journey of the People thousands and thousands of years following what takes place in this series. There are some elements from Series One that are fleshed out in Series Two. Aren't you curious what you are missing lol?

Once again—ways to stay engaged with me:

If you enjoyed this book, please leave a positive review or at least a positive rating. Of course, five stars are the best.

But, if you found fault with it, please email me directly and tell me your viewpoint. I do want to know. But a negative rating truly hurts an author.

You can find the link to leave a product review on the book link on Amazon, where you purchased or downloaded the book.

Positive reviews on Goodreads are also greatly appreciated.

I hope you will pick up Book Four and continue the journey with me.

Blessings—

Leigh

ACKNOWLEDGMENTS

My husband, brother, and circle of friends.
You, the readers who have followed this journey
with me.
My editor Joy—always!
The SPS Publishing group and my publishing coach
Ramy Vance.
My Pomeranian pack.
My friend and master craftsman Ken Couden who is
building me a writer's retreat!
And underpinning it all–The One-Who-Is- Three.